ONE & ONLY YOU

CINDY KIRK

WAVERLY
HOUSE

ISBN: 978-1-7329601-7-6

CHAPTER ONE

Rachel Grabinski stood outside the Chicago hotel room and wiped sweaty palms against the skirt of her summer dress. She wasn't an impulsive person, and taking the train into the city to surprise her boyfriend at a conference was out of character for her.

Not to mention, Marc Koenig, her boyfriend of the past year, didn't like surprises. He'd made that clear when she'd popped by his apartment one evening. She felt her heart pound an erratic rhythm just remembering the look on his face.

Yet, he'd also told her many times this past week how disappointed he was that she couldn't get off work to meet him for an early dinner tonight. It had felt to her like their relationship was stumbling, but she wasn't sure how to right it.

She wondered if he'd have been more understanding if she had a different job. Marc didn't approve of her position as the volunteer coordinator at the Hazel Green Food Bank. According to him, working for a nonprofit meant she'd decided to toss aside any hope of a decent career.

Rachel pushed that discussion from her head. Not the time, she reminded herself. A gas leak down the street from the food bank had had everyone leaving early. This was her chance to enjoy a beautiful summer evening with her boyfriend.

This time, she let her knuckles fall against the door. She considered calling out to Marc, but wanted—really wanted—to see the surprised pleasure on his face when he saw her.

On the fourth knock, she heard him yell, "I'm coming. Just wait a damn minute."

Rachel dropped her hand to her side and touched her tongue to her lips, tasting the cherry flavor of the lip balm that she had applied during the ride up in the elevator. She resisted the urge to reach up to straighten her glasses.

The tortoiseshell frames sat just fine on her nose. Adjusting them was a nervous habit she was determined to break.

She widened her eyes as the door flung open.

Her smile turned tentative when she saw the towel he held around his waist. His hair and skin were dry, so obviously she'd caught him just as he was about to step into the shower.

"Rachel." Surprise had him nearly releasing the towel. "I thought you were room service. What are you doing here?"

She'd started to step forward, but he blocked her.

"There was a gas leak just down the block from the food bank. They evacuated everyone, so I got off early." She lifted her hands. "Surprise."

"It was about time they brought up the champagne and strawberries." The sultry voice came from inside the room before Marc could respond.

Rachel shoved him aside and stepped into the suite.

The brunette wasn't a supermodel, but she was pretty, with a mass of tousled dark hair. She'd carelessly tossed on one of the hotel robes, letting the front gap to show an impressive amount of cleavage. Her feet were bare, and her toenails were candy-apple red.

The woman's dark brows slammed together. "You're not room service."

Rachel shifted her gaze from the woman to Marc. "You explain it to her."

He grabbed her arm in a firm grip as she pushed past him out of the room. "It isn't like it looks."

"Tell your lies to someone who'll believe them." She jerked her arm free. "Don't call me ever again. We're done."

"Rachel," he called out, but she strode down the hall without looking back.

Just as she reached the elevator, the ornate silver doors slid open, and a couple holding hands exited. She watched the man lean over and brush his companion's lips with his.

Rachel pressed her cherry-red lips together and punched the button that would take her to the lobby.

Dixon Carlyle considered himself a social creature, one with a talent for reading clients and responding in a way that made them trust him. The talent had come in handy when he was growing up. Only then, he'd needed to read marks. He'd quickly learned that saying one wrong thing could have disastrous consequences.

Those games were in the past. Now, he was a respected financial consultant with a growing list of clients, whom he did right by. The fact that most were pleased with his investment advice and the returns they'd been enjoying guaranteed his business would only continue to grow.

He'd attended the seminar at Palmer House in Chicago this morning on "Understanding the impact of erosion through inflation and taxation." While he listened to the experts, Dixon had been in text communication with a potential client. The twentysomething entrepreneur had hit it big last year and was searching for someone he trusted.

They'd met several times, and Dixon liked the kid's sharp eyes and quick wit. Various strategies for investing the young man's millions had been explored. Now, they were in final negotiations.

Like many Millennials, Raj Agarwal preferred texting over phone calls or face-to-face meetings. Today, while Dixon listened to the presentation at the front of the large ballroom, Raj had confirmed his desire to chart a certain course.

It was the course Dixon had recommended early on…but the boy had wanted to explore all options. Dixon was aware Raj had been consulting with other financial planners, but he hadn't worried. The kid was smart. He would realize Dixon was the best.

Dixon texted his sister. *Finalized deal.*

There was no need to say more.

Congratulations! We need to celebrate.

He added a thumbs-up to the comment, knowing any celebration would wait until all the papers were signed. Their mother had impressed upon both her children that you didn't count on anything, especially not when something seemed like a done deal.

As memories of Gloria threatened to dim his sunny mood, Dixon shoved the thoughts of her aside. The presentations had wrapped for the day, and the gala didn't start until eight.

More than enough time to stroll down Michigan Avenue and enjoy the beautiful day. Many conference attendees must have had the same idea, as hordes of smartly dressed men and women headed for the exits in the main lobby.

Shoved against someone, Dixon turned with an apology already on his lips. The woman, wearing a flirty summer dress covered in large poppies, stood out like a breath of fresh air.

"I'm sorry—" he began, then he realized he knew her. "Rachel?"

She shifted her gaze for a second, just long enough for him to see her reddened eyes. The determined set to her jaw and shoulders was at odds with the evidence of tears. "I need to get out of here."

Dixon, never at a loss for words, hesitated. Rachel was a good friend of his sister. They'd been at many parties together since he'd moved to Hazel Green. Every contact he'd had with her had been brief.

Not only was she dating Marc Koenig, but she was just so… good. Not a single ounce of sass or snark in her.

Still, he narrowed his gaze as he followed her out the front doors of the hotel. The woman had backbone, and something had happened to bring it out in full force.

Even as he told himself to keep to his original plan, Dixon fell into step beside her. She continued to be a good friend to Nell, which meant he needed to at least try to see if he could help.

He was still trying to figure out how to broach the subject of the tears when she stopped in the middle of the glittery sidewalk and whirled. "I don't need you. I don't need any man."

Now they were getting somewhere. Rachel and Marc had obviously had a fight. Something he knew Nell would firmly applaud. Dixon shared his sister's low opinion of Rachel's boyfriend.

"We are mostly scum," he agreed. "You look hungry. I was going to grab something to eat. Will you join me?"

Confusion furrowed her brow. "Why would you want to have dinner with me? We barely know each other."

"You're one of my sister's closest friends." He flashed a smile. "That makes you practically family."

It was lame. Surely he could have thought of something better to address her concerns.

"I am hungry." She expelled a shuddering breath, then appeared to notice his dark suit, crisp white shirt and perfectly knotted red tie. "I'm not really dressed for anyplace fancy."

Since it was barely five, he hadn't planned on going anywhere *fancy*. "What kind of food do you like?"

"Wherever you want to go is fine."

Dixon didn't have any trouble taking the lead, and from

Rachel's response, she would go along with whatever he suggested. He swallowed the words on his lips when he recalled Nell telling him of her frustration that Rachel let Marc run the show. Instead of standing up for what she wanted, she let him decide.

Was that what had happened today? Had Marc broken it off?

Dixon stopped himself from making assumptions. Hadn't he been taught from a young age to gather information before drawing conclusions?

"Tell me what kind of food you like." He placed his hand on her elbow when the mass of people around them threatened to push them apart.

"I like Italian," she said after a long moment. "And Thai. But I really like anything, so—"

He cut her off before she could offer once again to go wherever he wanted. "Both sound good to me. Maggiano's isn't far."

When she hesitated, he added, "Italian is a favorite of mine."

"Okay."

Once they were seated at a table and their orders taken, Dixon could almost see Rachel relax. It wasn't hard. The atmosphere at Maggiano's practically begged patrons to breathe in the scent of fresh bread, garlic and cheese and enjoy.

Dixon had finalized many business deals at the tables covered in red-and-white-checkered oilcloths. The restaurant was a popular place for families, couples and tourists to enjoy a good Italian meal.

When he caught Rachel eyeing the Italian sangria at a neighboring table, he ordered them a pitcher as well as a plate of antipasti.

She picked up a piece of salami and nibbled. Her small, almost delicate hands had nails painted a pale pink.

Dixon ate a roasted pepper, then lifted his glass for a toast.

Tentatively, Rachel lifted her own. "What are we toasting?"

"You."

She flushed, her cheeks turning a bright pink. "Me?"

"Nell mentioned the idea for the field-to-food-bank initiative was yours." Dixon clinked his glass against hers. "To Rachel, for improving the nutrition of struggling families through fresh produce."

"I was just doing my job," she protested, but he saw that the haunted look had left her eyes.

"Now," he set his glass on the table and leaned forward, giving her his full attention, "tell me what brought you to Palmer House."

Instead of answering right away, Rachel let the smooth taste of the sangria slide down her throat. Ignoring Dixon's expectant smile, she dipped a focaccia crisp into the burrata before setting down her glass.

Dixon didn't press for an answer. He simply studied her with those inscrutable gray eyes. When Rachel had first seen Nell's brother, he'd taken her breath away. The truth was, she'd never seen a more beautiful man. His hair was dark, his body lean and muscular. When he moved, he reminded her of a panther.

Her contact with him had been limited to short, impersonal conversations at parties. She knew Marc detested the man, which right now was a check mark in Dixon's favor. Though Marc had said to anyone who would listen that he didn't trust the man, Rachel suspected it was because they were both in the same industry and Marc was jealous.

"You-you don't have to tell me if you don't want to." Dixon stumbled over the words, then pressed his lips together when the server, a pretty redhead, appeared with their salads.

"Can I get either of you anything else? Anything at all?" The comment might have been directed at both of them, but the young woman's gaze remained firmly fixed on Dixon.

"I'm good." Dixon slanted a questioning look at Rachel.

"I'm good, too."

The smile Dixon offered the server was polite, but clearly dismissive.

Rachel swore she heard a sigh as the young woman moved to another table.

Dipping her fork into the house dressing she'd ordered on the side, Rachel considered how much to tell Dixon. Though she didn't know him well, something about him said he could be trusted.

The chuckle that slipped past her lips held a harsh edge. She'd thought she could trust Marc. Obviously, she was not a good judge of character.

Dixon paused his fork midway to his mouth at the sound. "Problem?"

"I was thinking that I trust you. I don't even know you, and yet I trust you. But, you see, that's my problem. I trust too easily, have this fairy-tale outlook on the world." Rachel set down her fork. "You'd think with everything that's happened in my life, I'd be a cynic. But no, I just go along believing the best in people. That's going to change."

His hand closed over hers, and she sucked in a breath.

"Don't let whatever happened today change you." The eyes he fixed on her never wavered. "It's a gift, being able to see the good in people."

"I came to Chicago to surprise Marc. I didn't expect to find him with another woman." She'd blurted the words before she'd even known they were forming on her tongue.

Still, it felt good to put them out there.

Dixon's face displayed no shock, or really any emotion, although his eyes turned as cloudy as the sky before a downpour. "I'm sorry."

"Nell told me he'd propositioned her, you know, when he was married. She warned me."

Dixon laid down his fork and took another sip of sangria, his gaze still riveted to her.

The laughter and chatter that surrounded them faded until it was only her and him.

"Marc had already come to me," she went on, "because he was concerned that Nell had misunderstood his question. It seemed plausible." She paused, waiting for Dixon to say she should have known. That Nell wouldn't have told her if she hadn't been certain of what had occurred. "I chose to believe him. I guess I wanted to believe him."

Dixon nodded. "Did you date much before him?"

"He was my first real boyfriend. Who makes it to their late twenties without one?" Rachel gave a little laugh and lifted one hand. "Me. That's who."

The sympathy shining in his eyes, now gone dove-soft, had her feeling even more like a fool.

"You were busy raising a family." His voice, as soft and soothing as melted butter, wrapped gently around her. "Nell told me how you did it all while working on your degree. I'm impressed."

Rachel wasn't sure what confused her more, that Dixon appeared to think what she'd done was special, or the way she felt when his eyes met hers.

"You'd have done the same." She shoved her glasses up, then took a gulp of sangria. "If it had been you and Nell."

His eyes turned cloudy, and Rachel couldn't read the look that stole over them.

Dixon cleared his throat. "Nell and I are a united front now."

Rachel folded her hands in her lap, resisting the urge to adjust her glasses again. Too late, she recalled that until recently Dixon and Nell had been estranged. She didn't know the details, only that everything was good between them now. "I'm glad."

He smiled suddenly, and she went warm all over.

She didn't have a chance to say more, because the server

arrived with veal Marsala for him and spaghetti with two meat-balls for her.

When the woman started to remove her salad, Rachel touched her arm. "I'm not quite finished." She offered the woman a smile. "I think I'll keep it a little while longer."

Marc would have chided her for the gesture. Dixon only indicated he'd keep his also.

"This looks wonderful." She stabbed a meatball with her fork.

"I agree."

She'd expected the conversation to continue nonstop, but Dixon seemed content to eat, at least for the first few minutes. They ate in a surprisingly comfortable silence until their plates were nearly empty.

Rachel let the sights and sounds of the busy restaurant wash over her—the clank of dishes, the smell of spicy meat and roasted garlic and the sound of laughter. As she did, the tension eased from her shoulders, and she found she could breathe easy once again.

She took a sip of water—Dixon had already refilled her glass of sangria once—and relaxed against the back of her chair. "I can't believe I've lived in the area all these years and had never eaten here before."

"I'm glad I could be the one to introduce it to you." He lifted his sangria, still only his first, and smiled.

"You're easy to be with," she blurted.

He lowered the glass, lifted a brow.

Rachel felt the heat in her cheeks. "I just mean it's like being out with a friend, not with a guy."

"Thank you." He paused. "I think."

Suddenly, their gazes locked, and they were both smiling. Despite the lame comment, he hadn't made her feel uncomfortable. She thought about explaining that's what she'd meant, but feared she'd dig an even bigger hole for herself.

"What was on your list for the evening?" She gazed down at

the rest of the meatball on her plate, told herself to leave it alone. But it was too good to resist. She stabbed it.

"The only thing on my agenda for the evening was a walk down Michigan Avenue." He gestured to the light streaming through the windows. "It's too beautiful a day to be stuck inside."

Rachel nodded. "Have you ever noticed how everyone seems happier on bright, sunny days?"

"I feel that way."

They were discussing the weather, Rachel realized with some degree of astonishment. Even more surprising, it felt natural, comfortable. She'd never have believed someone as smooth and self-assured as Dixon Carlyle could be so down to earth.

"I like seeing you smile."

His words had Rachel blinking. While he'd been talking, she'd been daydreaming.

"I was just wondering," she glanced at the menus the waitress had left, "since you don't have any pressing plans…if you'd be interested in sharing a piece of dessert with me. I'm not ready for the evening to end."

CHAPTER TWO

The next morning, Rachel rolled out of her comfortable bed, the weight of Marc's betrayal heavy on her chest. Normally, they had plans for Saturdays, but since his conference didn't end until this evening, they'd kept things loose.

After everything that had happened yesterday, Rachel was glad she'd be busy today with Pets on Parade. Marc had called the parade, designed to bring attention to animals available for adoption, silly. And he'd complained about wasting community resources on the Putting Your Best Paw Forward party on the Green once the parade concluded.

Rachel was in charge of the float sponsored by food bank employees. Tom, her boss, had allowed her and fellow employees and volunteers to transform his golf cart into the Adoption Express, with names of available animals written in fancy script on both sides.

She would drive the vehicle, while several employees held dogs from the shelter on their laps.

She'd decided earlier in the week, once she'd seen the forecast, to walk the three miles to the parade starting point. That decision provided an extra bonus—working off the heavy Italian meal and dessert she'd consumed the previous evening.

Rachel's progress slowed when she reached the Green, a park-like area in the center of town. The number of people already gathered at this early hour awaiting the start of the parade reinforced that she'd made the right decision to leave her car at home.

Many of those in the park and already lining both sides of the main street had brought along their children and their pets. The parade would start at one end of Hazel Green, so once she wound her way through the crowd, Rachel picked up her pace.

She had a lot of ground to cover, as the floats were being stored in a large, empty warehouse at the far edge of town.

"Where are you headed in such a hurry?" Abby Rollins, one of her closest friends, fell into step beside her just as she cleared the crowds.

"Same place as you." Rachel slanted a sideways glance. "You look adorable. Love the shirt."

Today, the hotel owner wore a lime-green shirt with paw prints on the front and the logo for her business, The Inn at Hazel Green, on the back.

"I wanted something bright that would pop." Abby grinned. "Wait until you see Eva Grace's neon orange. And Jonah's atomic blue could make eyes bleed."

Abby's tone radiated warmth and affection for her husband and daughter. "They went early to work out some final touches."

That answered one of Rachel's questions. She'd been surprised to see Abby alone.

"I didn't realize Jonah was riding with you."

It hadn't been a question of available space. Abby's float, There's Always Room at This Inn, featuring animals behind makeshift hotel room doors, was big enough to hold several animals and humans. "I thought he'd be on duty."

"The chief doesn't have to work all the events," Abby assured her. "Jonah has a great group of officers. They can handle whatever comes up. If there's trouble and they need his input, he's just a phone call away."

"I'm glad you can spend the day as a family." Rachel fought to keep the hint of envy from her voice. She, like the rest of their close circle of friends, knew that family life hadn't come to Abby tied with a perfect bow.

Rachel lifted her face to the sun. She reminded herself she had much to be thankful for—good friends, brothers and sisters she loved and a job that fulfilled her. Even finding out about Marc's duplicity was a blessing.

I could have married him. Rachel inwardly shuddered at the thought.

"You haven't said how last night went." Abby's words had the sun disappearing behind clouds. "Was Marc surprised?"

Rachel had forgotten she'd run into Abby last night as she was leaving the food bank.

"More than surprised." Rachel offered her friend a sardonic smile. "Stunned."

Rachel was spared the need to say more when Cornelia "Nell" Ambrose intersected with them. "What's up with the speed-walking?"

"We can drop it down a notch." Rachel automatically slowed her steps.

"We can't." Abby kept the fast pace. "We'll be late. Besides, Nell beat my time in last year's 5K by almost three minutes."

Rachel heard Nell chuckle, which told her Abby had nailed it.

"I wasn't saying I couldn't keep up," Nell clarified. "I just wondered why the rush."

"I don't know about Abby, but I'm kind of the coordinator for the food bank float, so I didn't want to keep the other employees waiting."

"That makes sense." Nell settled into an easy stride. Scheduled to be on the animal rescue float, she was dressed casually in capris and a shirt with a picture of Rosco, a mixed-breed dog, on the front and Violet, a blue-eyed Siamese, on the back.

"Love the shirt, Nell," Abby said with an impudent smile.

"At least I don't have paw prints all over my chest," Nell shot back.

"How many are on your float?" Rachel asked Nell.

"Do you want to know animals or people?" Nell asked.

"Both."

"Ten adults with two animals each. Other than me, they're all volunteers for Hazel Green Animal Rescue."

"Can the circus truck hold that many?" Abby looked doubtful.

"It could hold twice that number, but then you wouldn't be able to see everyone. This way, the volunteers and animals can be all around the perimeter."

The safari-type vehicle had been decorated with colorful decals of animals and a big sign that proclaimed "Hazel Green Animal Rescue—A History of Caring."

"Has anybody seen Liz?" Rachel asked, determined to keep Abby's mind off of her and Marc.

"She's reporting on the event for the *Chronicle*, and the pictures she takes will be used on the town's social media accounts."

When Abby slanted a glance in her direction, Rachel could almost see the questions forming on her lips.

Rachel turned to Nell. "I can't believe you fit this in. You've got to have a million things on your plate. The wedding is just around the corner."

Abby shot Nell a smile. "Eva Grace is counting down the days."

Eva Grace, Abby's six-year-old daughter, was to be a flower girl. Ever since Nell and Leo had asked her to be in the wedding, it was all the child could talk about.

"She says it's the best gift Nell and Leo could give her," Abby added.

"It's not her gift," Nell insisted. "Leo and I already have something wrapped and ready."

Confused, Rachel cocked her head.

"Eva Grace somehow got it in her head that being Nell and Leo's flower girl is her birthday gift," Abby explained. "Which reminds me, we've finally settled on a date for her party."

Abby offered the particulars regarding date and time, then added, "Be sure and save the date. We had to move it up a little because of all the wedding activities."

"Leo and I will definitely be there," Nell said.

"You can count on me." Rachel had planned to take Marc with her. Now she'd go alone. None of her friends liked her ex-boyfriend. He definitely wouldn't be missed.

Nell smiled. "Did I tell you Marty is flying in this week to help me with the final arrangements?"

Abby frowned. "I thought you had everything in place."

As matron of honor and BFF of the bride, Abby took her duties seriously.

"We do, but it's important to Marty to feel she's done her part." Nell's lips curved in a soft smile. "I couldn't have picked a better mother-in-law."

"You'll be a beautiful bride." Rachel's words came out on a breath that was nearly a sigh.

"When it's your turn, you'll be just as beautiful."

An awkward silence descended over the threesome.

None of her friends wanted her to end up with Marc. She knew they'd been pleasant and tolerated his presence at various events because she was their friend.

Might as well rip off the Band-Aid, Rachel thought. "Marc and I are no longer together."

"What?" Nell's eyes went razor-sharp. "When did this happen?"

Before Rachel could answer, Abby reached over and took her hand. "Are you okay?"

"I'm fine." Rachel gave Abby's hand a squeeze, then released it. She forced a smile as she focused on Nell. "In answer to your question, this all went down yesterday. I got off early at the food bank—"

"Because of the gas leak," Abby explained before the others could ask. With her husband being chief of police, Abby knew everything that went on in Hazel Green.

"Yes," Rachel confirmed. "Because of the leak."

"How does that play into you and Marc calling it quits?" Nell asked. She might push, but concern filled her blue eyes.

"Marc had pressed me to meet him in the city for an early dinner. When I said I couldn't get off work, we had words. Once he calmed down, he appeared to understand."

Abby opened her mouth as if to speak, then shut it, seeming to think better of it.

"Then you were able to get off," Nell prompted.

"That's right. As soon as I left the food bank, I headed to the train station."

That mode of transportation had been better than driving into the madness of what was downtown Chicago. Hazel Green might be at the end of Chicago's Metra rail line, but in less than thirty minutes, she'd been in the city.

"What was Marc doing downtown?" Nell asked.

"Attending a wealth management conference at Palmer House," Rachel explained.

"I love that hotel." Abby's lips curved, as if she was envisioning the nineteenth-century luxury hotel.

"William Jennings Bryan and Mark Twain once stayed there," Nell tossed in.

Nell would know. In her role as Hazel Green, town matriarch and former Chautauqua platform performer, Nell had performed speeches by both Bryan and Twain.

"Marc had mentioned his room number when we talked the previous night. I remembered it and went straight up. The sessions were just getting out for the day, and I hoped he'd gone to his room to change and I could catch him there." Rachel realized she was rambling and clamped her lips shut for a couple of seconds as her heart began to race. "I caught him, all right. With his clothes half off and a busty brunette in his room."

"Oh no." Abby's eyes filled with sympathy. "I'm so sorry, Rachel."

Rachel fixed her gaze on Nell. "You warned me. I didn't listen."

"I hoped, for your sake, he'd changed," Nell said simply. "I didn't want you hurt."

"It's over between us." It felt important that her friends knew where she stood.

"He'll try to get you back." Nell spoke in a matter-of-fact tone. "Men like him have a million excuses, and sometimes the reasons actually make sense."

"I won't trust him again." Rachel shook her head vigorously. "I'm not stupid."

"Nell wasn't saying that—" Abby began.

"These types of people can be very convincing. My mother could steal a car from one of her boyfriends, then convince him he was in the wrong because something he'd done or said had made her take it." Nell's laugh held no humor. "Marc reminds me of her. He won't like losing. He'll see you walking away as a loss."

"We'll support you, Rach." Abby kept her voice low in deference to the increased number of people on the sidewalk. "Last night had to be rough. I wish you'd called. I hate it that you were alone."

"Actually, I wasn't. Alone, I mean." Rachel paused and took a deep breath. "I ran into someone in the lobby, and we had dinner together."

Surprise flickered across Abby's face. "Someone you knew?"

Rachel nodded.

Nell cocked her head. Her gaze turned speculative. "Who was it?"

Before Rachel could reply, the man in question appeared, along with Leo Pomeroy.

"Well, this is my lucky day." Dixon grinned at Leo, but the mayor's focus was on his fiancée. "A trio of beautiful women."

Leo moved to Nell, kissing her gently on the mouth. "Good morning again."

Nell's red lips curved. "I thought we were meeting by the truck."

Leo jerked his head in Dixon's direction. "This guy and I finalized details for my bachelor party early. It's going to be amazing."

Nell shot her brother a glinting glance. "Keep it clean."

Dixon lifted his hands, palms out. "Innocent until proven guilty."

"Your wedding plans are moving at lightning speed." Rachel couldn't believe one of the biggest weddings in the town's history had been planned so quickly.

"Like I said, when you find the one you want to spend the rest of your life with and you put a ring on her finger, why wait?" Leo swung Nell's hand, his fingers locked with hers, as he spoke.

"The minister was already on tap for that night, so when the other wedding canceled on short notice, we slid into the other couple's spot. Not only at the church, but at the Pavilion for the reception." Nell's husky voice softened. "Everything came together perfectly, including having Matilda cater."

"When it's right, it's right." Before Nell could respond, Dixon's gaze shifted to Rachel. "When it's not, it's best to walk away."

Rachel told herself to look away, but she couldn't. She just… couldn't.

"Well, it's definitely right." Leo brushed his free hand across Nell's hair, as if he couldn't stop himself from touching her. "We didn't mean to interrupt your conversation."

"You didn't interrupt," Nell demurred, then clarified, "Actually, you did. Rachel was telling us how she ran into a friend unexpectedly last night at Palmer House. They had dinner together."

"I hope your friend was female." Leo's tone was only half joking. "Marc doesn't seem the understanding sort."

"I don't care what he thinks. We aren't together anymore." Rachel tried for matter-of-fact, but her voice sounded tinny and an octave too high.

Leo glanced at Nell. "I'm sorry to hear that."

"I'm not," Rachel insisted. "The man is a liar and a cheat."

"You deserve better," Dixon said.

"What I'd like to know," Nell spoke quickly as their destination came into sight, "is who was this friend who consoled you last night?"

Rachel slanted a glance at Dixon. "Your brother."

CHAPTER THREE

It really had turned out to be a perfect day, Rachel thought as she drove the golf cart and smiled to the crowd. Clowns walking the route on both sides of the floats tossed candy to the spectators.

The two senior dogs, both Lab mixes—one black, one yellow — sat complacently beside their food bank "handler." The constant petting and treats, as well as a short leash, kept them from jumping from the cart.

Rachel hoped they would find their forever home today. Her family had had a plethora of cats while she was growing up, but had had only one dog. Carl, a basset mix, had died of old age the year before her parents' accident.

Before today, Rachel hadn't given a thought to adopting a pet. Then Rachel had caught Violet, the Siamese on Nell's float, giving her the once-over. Rachel knew the breed's personality and liked that they were affectionate and loyal, yet bold.

She'd returned the cat's stare, but had been the first to glance away. The thought of getting caught up in a cat stare-down made her smile.

"We're nearly at the end of the parade route." Fisher Campbell, a college student who volunteered at the food bank during the summer, gestured with his free hand toward the Green. "Bands are already setting up for the festival."

"I hope the boys find a home." Lenox Wills gave the yellow Lab a pat and glanced at Fisher. "Don't forget you and I have the dogs until two."

Bright orange vests emblazoned with Adopt Me on both sides would be placed on the two Labs and other dogs available for adoption once the parade ended. Fisher and Lenox would spend several hours strolling around the Green with the dogs, giving them face time with the crowd.

If someone was interested, they would be given an adoption application to fill out. While volunteers with dogs roamed the festival area, cats would be shown off in an enclosed area staffed by volunteers. Because the rescue center had reached capacity on felines, today was a name-your-price event for cats.

Which meant, if Rachel wanted Violet, she needed to let someone know before another person snatched her up. But Rachel had to return Tom's golf cart to the food bank after dropping off the two volunteers.

After helping Lenox and Fisher put the orange vests on the dogs, she took a second to text Nell.

I want to adopt Violet. Rachel hesitated, considered, then added the dollar amount she was willing to pay, followed by, *Could you put her on hold for me? TIA.*

The confirmation from Nell came two long minutes later. *The director says she's yours.*

Rachel let out the breath she hadn't realized she'd been holding and reached for the golf cart's key. Once Tom's cart was safely stowed, she'd find out what steps needed to be taken to take Violet home.

"Rachel."

She tightened her fingers on the key and turned toward the familiar voice.

Marc sat down on the other end of the front seat.

"I don't recall inviting you to sit."

He dismissed the terse words with a flick of his hand. If you ignored the absent suit coat and tie, Marc appeared ready for a day at the office in dark gray pants and a crisp white shirt. But this wasn't an office, and he looked out of place at the outdoor summer event.

The scent of the expensive cologne she'd given him for Christmas brought a fresh stab of pain. Had he been cheating on her back then? The brunette couldn't have been the first time he'd strayed.

As if he was reading her thoughts, his pale blue eyes turned calculating. "We need to talk."

"I don't think so." She dug in her proverbial heels. She would not cede control of this conversation to him as she had so many times before. "I don't have anything more to say to you."

She paused, and when she spoke again, her voice held an edge of steel. "I meant what I said. It's over."

"You don't understand."

When Marc started to scoot closer, Rachel held up a staying hand. "Stay where you are."

Out of the corner of her eye, she spotted Dixon approaching. He stopped when he saw who was with her. The tilt of his head held a question.

Rachel gave her head a tiny shake. She had this. She'd gotten herself into this relationship with a cheat and a liar. It was up to her to get herself out of it.

She thought she had, had assumed telling him it was over was clear. There'd been nothing more to say.

Marc appeared to think otherwise. Recalling Nell's words, she prepared herself for the excuses. She'd let him speak until she was tired of listening, then she'd tell him to go.

Hopefully, he'd get the message this time.

"Say what you want to say and then go." Rachel forced a bored tone into her voice, surprised at how easily it came.

"Honey." He reached for her hand, but she pulled it out of reach.

His lips tightened for just a moment, then a sorrowful expression covered his face. "Rachel, sweetheart. Please, I beg you not to give up on us. The love we share is special. How I feel about you, well, I've never felt this way about any woman."

Though her heart twisted, she said nothing.

"I realize how it must have looked—"

"It looked like it was. You and the brunette were about to have sex in your hotel room."

"We didn't." Marc expelled a shuddering breath. For a second, he covered his eyes with his hands, as if hiding tears. "I was feeling low because you couldn't meet me. I was really looking forward to seeing you last night. You put your job—and your friends—before me, and it hurts."

"I do not—" she sputtered.

"You do. Everything has to be your way." He lifted a hand. "You may have allowed me to pick a few movies and restaurants, but last night when I really needed you, you weren't going to be there for me."

"I had to work."

"Exactly my point."

Rachel felt control of the conversation slipping though her fingers. She shook her head. "You're saying it was my fault you had sex with that woman."

"I didn't sleep with her, Rachel. I couldn't. When I saw you in the doorway, everything snapped into focus. If you'd stayed, you would have seen that I sent her away." He expelled a heavy breath. "You're the only one I want to be with. You know that."

Rachel opened her mouth, but he continued, sliding an inch or two closer in the process. "She knocked on my door, invited herself in. Told me she'd noticed how sad I seemed at one of the seminars, asked if she could help. I was vulnerable. I admit it. I love you so much, and I was feeling as if you didn't really care."

"I had to work. I—"

"I realize your job is important to you. But I need attention, too, Rachel. I need to feel important." He shook his head. "You're good at many things, but not so good at making a man feel important. Everything else, everyone else, in your life comes before me. I've tried to understand, God knows I've tried, but it isn't easy."

Rachel had heard this from him before. Last December, her sister Rebecca, who lived in Minneapolis, had fallen on the ice and broken her foot. Rachel had left town to be with Becca for the surgery. Marc had been livid that she'd missed his company Christmas party.

"I had to be with my sister. She—" Rachel clamped her mouth shut. That was not what this conversation was about, and she did not, had not, put Marc last.

"What I'm trying to say is I didn't sleep with that woman."

"I don't believe you."

His eyes widened briefly, then a look of hurt crossed his face. "Everything is black and white with you, isn't it, Rachel? You can't even open your heart to the possibility that you played a role in my being susceptible to this woman's charms."

When she opened her mouth, he waved her silent. "I knew when we started seeing each other that you didn't have much experience in the dating arena. I've dated a lot, and I can honestly say I've never had a woman put me last. If I didn't love you so much, if I didn't believe that what we share is special and could go the distance, I wouldn't have hung around for so long hoping things would change."

Rachel swallowed past the lump forming in her throat. Was she partially to blame for what happened? *Had* she put Marc last?

But she reminded herself she had a job. With that position came responsibilities. While her boss understood emergencies, meeting her boyfriend for dinner in Chicago didn't qualify.

He reached out then and laid his hand on her arm. "I forgive you. We can—"

"Forgive me?" Something inside Rachel exploded, and she batted away his hand. "Get out of this cart and get away from me."

Her voice rose with each word, along with her temper. Too many times, too many blasted times, she'd let that silken voice and his carefully spun words wrap around her. Ignoring her own common sense, she'd gotten drawn into his web of lies.

Well, that was done. It ended today.

Shock blanketed his face, then that supercilious smile returned to his face. "Rachel, honey, calm down."

She shot him the look that would have had any of her siblings quaking in their shoes. "I said, get out of the cart."

The disapproval in his eyes and the tightening of his lips had no effect on her.

Rachel made a shooing motion with her hand.

With obvious reluctance, Marc slid over and stepped from the vehicle. His anger pulsed in the air. "You're making a mistake."

"The only mistake I ever made was trusting you."

Dixon leaned against the massive trunk of a leafy oak and watched Rachel and Marc. He'd never been a voyeur, but he didn't trust Marc Koenig. If Rachel needed assistance, he wanted to be close.

He narrowed his gaze when Marc slid closer to her. Dixon clenched his jaw when the man put his hand on Rachel's shoulder. A cheer rose from deep inside him when she slapped it away.

It didn't take long after that. Raised voices and Marc stomping off, his shoulders tight and a grim look on his face, said the interaction had ended. At least for now.

Dixon pushed upright and waited. For what, he wasn't sure. Maybe for Rachel to drive off in the cart. Or for her to get out.

She did neither. Instead, she simply sat there, hands now on the wheel, staring straight ahead.

He waited. One minute. Then another.

Finally, unable to wait a second longer, he casually strode over to the cart, stopping a couple of feet away.

"It appears the event is a success."

She turned slowly in his direction. Her face might be pale, but her eyes were dry. "What?"

"From the number of people in the crowd, it seems the rescue event is a success."

Rachel gave a jerky nod, but kept her focus over his shoulder. "I adopted a cat."

An interesting transition, but he'd go with it. He shoved his hands into his pockets, rocked back. "Did you?"

Another nod. "A Siamese named Violet."

Dixon didn't know anything about cats. Or dogs, for that matter. His mother had never allowed pets, and once he'd been on his own, he'd never considered getting any.

He could see Rachel's chest moving as she breathed in and out. He realized she was trying to steady herself. The interaction with Marc had left her shaken, but she was holding on to control.

His respect for her inched up a notch. Though he was normally at ease with women, Rachel had him off-balance. Not because of anything she did or said. She was just so sweet. And, he hesitated to apply the word to her, *pure*.

He had plenty of experience with *conniving* and *scheming*, but none with *pure*. "Ah. Where is she?"

Rachel blinked and focused on him rather than on the tree to his left.

"The cat," he prompted.

The ghost of a smile lifted her lips. "She was one of the cats featured today in the cat house. The director has marked her as mine."

What did he say to that? Good for you? Congratulations?

Rachel's brows pulled together. "Do you think I'm stupid?"

Anger spurted like a fountain inside him. "Is that what Marc called you?"

Confusion skittered across her face. "No. Why would you—"

He saw when understanding swept away the confusion.

"No," she said. "I mean about getting the cat."

"Why would adopting an animal that you obviously want be stupid?"

Before she could answer, the town's newspaper editor offered a hearty hello, startling them both.

"Beautiful day," Hank Beaumont called out.

"Absolutely perfect." Rachel beamed.

Dixon only smiled, relieved that the man continued on without slowing his steps.

"What were we talking about?"

Dixon thought about saying it was nothing important, but pulled back the words. She wouldn't have brought up the deal with the cat if it was nothing.

"You were wondering if it was smart to adopt a cat."

"I'm away from home all day." She paused and gazed at him expectantly.

"I'm not a cat expert, but I've heard they like their own company."

That made her smile, though he wasn't sure why.

"You're right. And now I'll be home most evenings since Marc and I aren't…" Her voice trailed off.

"I saw the two of you talking."

She nodded. "Actually, he was doing most of the talking."

Despite his curiosity, Dixon wouldn't ask what the guy had said. Not only wasn't it his business, but the sad look in Rachel's eyes had disappeared and Dixon didn't want to take the chance the question might bring it back.

"He said I bore the blame for the woman being in his room." She huffed out a breath. "Marc claimed he didn't sleep with her."

A coldness that started from deep inside Dixon flooded every inch of his body. He'd pegged Marc correctly, right from the start. The man was a narcissist, just like Gloria. While he didn't have Gloria's charisma, Marc was just as ballsy.

"Really?" It was the best Dixon could manage. The men—and women—his mother had deceived couldn't be convinced with logic. Once Gloria spun her web, they believed what she wanted them to believe.

If Rachel had fallen under Marc's spell, Dixon would be wasting his breath.

The snorting sound Rachel made had his head jerking up. "He had me going for, say, one or two seconds, until my brain kicked in."

Dixon's lips curved, and he couldn't stop the chuckle.

"I think he really expected me to take him back." Her normally sweet tone held an edge of derision. "As if."

"You two were together for a…" Dixon realized he didn't really know how long. Only that she'd been dating Marc when Dixon had arrived in Hazel Green.

"Too long," Rachel supplied in a matter-of-fact tone. "I made too many excuses for him, let too many things slide. That ended yesterday. My dad used to say, 'Trust once lost cannot be regained.'"

She heaved out a breath when Dixon remained silent.

"I've never been big on absolutes," she continued, "but one thing I can tell you with absolute certainty is that Marc is out of my life for good."

CHAPTER FOUR

"I wish I could have convinced Rachel to join us this evening." Nell, seated on the outdoor settee beside her fiancé, took a sip of wine and cast a speculative glance at Dixon.

He took a pull from his beer and ignored the questioning look. Dixon saw no point in saying that when he'd agreed to attend this private patio party at Leo and Nell's home, he'd thought Rachel might be there.

It wasn't as if he was interested in her as, well, a woman. Certainly not. The bookish librarian kind wasn't his type at all. Dixon simply understood what she'd gone through with Marc, and if he could lend his support, he was happy to be there for her.

"She was able to bring her new cat home early this evening," Abby advised. "She didn't want to leave Violet home alone her first night."

Jonah chuckled. "Violet would probably have enjoyed prowling the house, making a mental list of all the places she can hide from Rachel."

When all eyes turned to him, he only shrugged. "My sister loved cats, and we had several growing up. I'm more of a dog person, but I have to say I can see a cat in the future."

"Far in the future," Abby said, the intensity of her words making her husband laugh.

"Far in the future," he agreed.

The talk turned to the wedding, and Dixon considered excusing himself when the conversation made a sudden switch to the wickets in the lawn.

"Leo and I thought it might be fun to play croquet." The hint of pink on his sister's cheeks amused Dixon. "Everyone seemed to enjoy it at Liz's barbecue."

The light in his sister's eyes dimmed briefly. Dixon knew she was remembering the revelation that had come that night, news that had nearly ended Nell and Leo's relationship. But they'd survived. Now they would soon be married.

"I can only imagine what Gloria would think if she saw her two children playing such a game," Dixon drawled. The only way their mother would excuse such pedestrian behavior was if some kind of con was involved.

In their mother's mind, a con excused any and all behavior, even the most egregious.

"Gloria isn't a part of our lives," Nell snapped, then caught herself. "Leo put up the wickets this afternoon. All that's left is choosing our mallets."

Abby pushed to her feet. "Rachel will be so sad to have missed this. She loves croquet."

And kitties and rainbows, Dixon thought. He immediately cast aside the comment as unfair. The woman had a sunny disposition and a glass-half-full philosophy. There was absolutely nothing wrong with that, except, of course, when the real world came calling.

He stood and meandered his way over to Nell, leaning close and lowering his voice for her ears only. "Sorry for bringing up dear old Gloria."

Nell's blue eyes met his gray ones. "She's in jail. We don't have to concern ourselves with her anymore."

Dixon only nodded. Now was not the time to bring up the information he'd received from his source in Bakersfield.

"We've got a variety of colors to choose from." Leo gestured to a stand holding numerous mallets. "Once you've picked, we'll toss a coin to start the game."

The melodious tone of the doorbell echoed through the house and spilled out onto the patio.

Leo lifted a mallet and handed it to Abby. "I wonder who that could be."

"I'll get it." Dixon offered.

"Thanks." Nell pointed to the mallets. "Any favorite color?"

"Anything works." He flashed his sister a smile as he headed into the house.

The art deco house, built in the 1920s by Jasper Pomeroy, had a pleasant, soothing vibe. Good energy, Dixon thought as he pulled open the door.

"Rachel. Nell said you weren't coming."

Wearing a summer dress the color of a ripe peach, Rachel looked summer fresh. Her hair hung loose to her shoulders, and the gloss on her lips matched her dress.

For a second, Dixon found himself staring at those full, luscious lips. If he kissed her, would she taste like ripe peaches?

The thought had him taking a step back, a move that had Rachel moving past him into the house.

She glanced around. "Where is everyone?"

Dixon gestured with one hand. "We're just about to be forced into a game of croquet. There's still time to run."

Puzzlement furrowed her brow. "I like croquet."

Obviously, his attempt at a little light humor had fallen very, very flat. Dixon rubbed his hands together. "I thought you were at home with your new cat."

A smile lifted her lips, and she chuckled. "She's enjoying some quiet time and getting to know my spare room."

He lifted a brow. "Not roaming the house?"

She shook her head, remaining where she was, obviously in no apparent hurry to join the croquet group. "Coming into a new home can be stressful. I did some reading, and it seems keeping them confined to one room for the first couple of days helps them settle."

"They don't go stir crazy?"

She smiled, and he felt the warmth of it. "Before I took her out of the carrier, I set out her water dish and food on one side of the room and litter box on the other. I also placed some treats around the room as a way of encouraging her to check out the area."

"Sounds like you thought of everything." He liked listening to her talk and seeing her dark eyes shine behind her glasses.

"Oh, I also put in a scratching post and a box."

"A box of what?"

She laughed. "An empty box. Cats love empty boxes."

The extent of his knowledge regarding felines could be summed up by an encounter with a neighbor cat when he'd been ten. He'd reached out to pet it, and it had swiped him with its claws. He saw no need to bring up that episode.

"Shouldn't you be home supervising?" Too late, Dixon realized the question made it sound as if he didn't want her there. Nothing could be further from the truth.

"That's what I planned to do." She lifted her partially bared shoulders in a slight shrug. "I sat in the room with her and read my emails. Went out. Came back in. Petted her a little. The next time I left and came back in, she hissed and growled at me. I decided she needed some alone time, and I, well—"

When she didn't continue, Dixon knew what had brought her here tonight. Knew it as surely as if she'd said the words aloud.

"I didn't want to be alone tonight either." The words slipped from his lips, surprising them both.

It might be the reason she'd come here tonight, but Dixon realized it was why he'd come as well. The information from his contact had shaken him. He didn't want to sit at home and think about what would happen if they tracked him down.

He tried to push his thoughts back to the here and now—no use thinking about what might be—when he was jolted back to the present by Rachel's hand on his arm.

When Dixon looked up, his gaze locked with hers.

"You know what I think, Dixon?" she said, her gaze firm and intense.

"What?"

"I think we both need a game of croquet."

Whenever Rachel had bested Marc at anything, he had turned petulant. For a whole ten seconds tonight, she'd considered holding back on her croquet ability. Then she'd realized that none of those in the group playing croquet this evening would hold a win against her.

The expectation of each man for himself—and that this was all-out good-natured warfare—was clear from the first crack of a mallet on a ball.

"May the best man—or woman—win," Leo had declared when he'd tossed the coin that determined who started the game.

Rachel had learned that watching out for a moving ball was essential. But while she was noticing how amazing Dixon looked tonight, Abby's ball brushed her foot.

"Rachel loses her next turn," Leo called out.

She jerked her attention from Dixon to Leo. "What did I do?"

For one horrible second, Rachel was convinced she was being punished for making googly eyes at Dixon. Nell must have thought the same thing, because she elbowed Leo and shot him a warning glance.

"Abby's ball hit you," Leo explained.

"My fault," Abby said immediately.

"Doesn't matter whose fault." Leo turned to Abby. "You have the choice of leaving the ball where it ended up, or put it back where it was before."

Abby shrugged. "It's fine where it's at."

"Sorry, Abs." Rachel gave her friend a hug.

"No worries. Next time, it'll be me."

Next time, it was Abby. Then Dixon picked up several balls and began to juggle.

"What are you doing?" Leo turned to Jonah and pointed. "Arrest that man."

If Rachel hadn't been watching Dixon, she wouldn't have noticed the falter. He quickly rallied, then set the balls back where they'd been with exaggerated precision.

By the time the game ended with Abby declared the winner, everyone was laughing and in high spirits.

As Rachel joined in on the laughter, she realized it had never been like this with Marc. He had either tried too hard to show off or he'd fawned all over Leo and the rest of the Pomeroys.

Not because he particularly liked Leo or his brothers, but because they were sons of a US senator. Tonight, there had been none of that kind of stuff. Just six friends hanging out, having fun.

"I'm so happy you came, Rachel," Abby said for what felt like the zillionth time.

"It's been fun." Rachel glanced at her watch when the lights flicked on, bathing the backyard in soft light. "But I should get home. See what kind of damage Violet has inflicted on her new bedroom."

"What do you think she'll do?" Nell asked.

"No idea. I'm hoping she's been a good girl, but I don't know. Thanks for inviting me. I had a really nice time."

"How did you get here?" Leo slipped his arm around his fiancée's waist. "I didn't hear a car drive up."

"I walked." Rachel smiled. "It's a beautiful evening."

No need, she thought, to add that she'd had some thinking to do. She did some of her best work while in motion.

Dixon stepped forward. "I'll walk you home."

"My house is a good three miles from here," Rachel protested.

"All the more reason for you to not walk that distance alone."

Rachel knew the argument was lost when she saw the others nod their agreement. But Dixon hadn't thought this through. "How will you get back?"

"Don't worry about me." He slung an arm around her shoulders. "Ask Nell. I'm very resourceful."

Accustomed to Marc's incessant chatter, Rachel stepped off the porch and waited for Dixon to begin talking. They'd made it nearly a block in the warm night air before she broke the silence between them.

"You really didn't need to do this."

"I was ready to leave." He slanted a mischievous smile at her. "There's only so much croquet and conversation one man can take."

She chuckled. "I was surprised by how much fun I had. I could have stayed home with Violet, but I was feeling sort of low. Tonight, well, it was just the change of scenery I needed."

"Was it?" he asked as they turned onto the street that would lead them—eventually—to her home.

"Yes." She nodded for extra emphasis. "I may live alone, and my family might be scattered across the country, but tonight reminded me that I have friends, good friends, to turn to if I need them. I imagine you feel the same way."

Rachel paused to take a breath and realized she'd been babbling. But if Dixon minded, he didn't show it.

"I'm not sure I follow."

A man of few words, she decided. It wasn't how she'd had him pegged. When she thought back to the times they'd been at the same events, he always seemed to be talking or joking.

"I was referring to you being close to your sister." She smiled. "When you moved to Hazel Green, you didn't just reconnect with Nell, you found a whole group of friends."

"They're her friends, not mine."

"Not true." She was surprised that she felt comfortable enough with him to say exactly what was on her mind. When she'd been with Marc, she had carefully considered her words before speaking. "They like you. Leo asked you to be his best man."

"He's marrying my sister," Dixon said dryly. "And by choosing me, he didn't have to pick between his brothers."

Rachel considered. "Maybe, but if he didn't like you, I think you'd be an usher or something like that."

Dixon laughed, a deep, husky sound that wrapped around her spine and sent warmth skidding through her veins. "Good point."

"What can I say? I'm a smart girl."

Her teasing tone had his lips quirking upward. "No argument from me."

They strolled side by side for several blocks, close but not touching. The scent of flowers from pots on porches and strategically positioned in perfectly manicured yards filled the air.

With each step, Rachel felt herself relax even more. The moon, extra bright this evening, bathed the quiet residential neighborhood in a golden light. Other than their breathing, only an occasional barking dog or the chirp of crickets broke the silence.

Rachel inhaled deeply, and the last of the tension gripping her shoulders slipped away. She glanced up at the star-filled sky. "I remember when Becca—she's one of my sisters—was a little girl and we were in the backyard looking up at the sky. She said to me, 'Doesn't that remind you of God's promise to Abraham?'" Rachel chuckled. "I didn't have a clue what she was talking about.

Thankfully, she went on to explain that she was referring to 'your children will number as many as the stars in the sky.'"

"I'd have been lost, too." He grinned. "Our mother would more likely have set fire to a church than set foot in one."

Though Rachel laughed, she remembered Nell telling her about her mom being an arsonist. One of those fire-setting incidents had brought a man to Hazel Green who had nearly derailed Nell and Leo's relationship.

Thankfully, they'd survived, and the man—she believed his name was Stanley—had gone back to where he'd come from, and they hadn't heard from him since.

"Did you admit your cluelessness?" Dixon asked, sounding genuinely interested.

"I believe I said something like, 'Hmmmm.'" Rachel smiled and expelled a soft breath, the memory sweet. "When people act as if raising my brothers and sisters was some big sacrifice, it's times like that with Becca I remember. It wasn't a sacrifice, but a privilege."

Dixon only nodded.

She fell silent once again. He'd generously offered to walk her home. He hadn't agreed to listen to her blather on about her family. "Marc hated it, too, when I talked about my family."

The comment appeared to bring Dixon out of his stupor. "I don't hate hearing about your family."

"It's okay. I think it's like cute things your baby or your pets do. No one is as interested as you are in their antics."

"Seriously." He put his hand on her arm, touching her for the first time since they'd left Leo and Nell's home. "I like listening to your stories. It's just that your life was so different from mine that I'm not quite sure how to respond."

Rachel found it difficult to believe that this man was ever at a loss for words. She nodded, accepting the reasoning. "Nell is older than you."

He nodded. "Four years."

"I bet she was protective of you." Rachel smiled.

He inclined his head. "What makes you think that?"

"She's fierce."

Dixon's brows shot upward. "Fierce."

"Strong. Determined." Rachel sighed. "I wish I could be more like her."

"You're just fine the way you are." A little smile tipped his lips. "I'm betting you can be fierce, too. Anyone messes with you or yours, watch out."

She laughed, liking the image of herself as a warrior, but not sure it was accurate. "This is my block."

The homes in the area were two-story boxes with covered porches across the front. As this had been their parents' home, Rachel had planned to buy out her brothers and sisters so she could own it outright.

Her siblings had stood strong and signed over their interest to her, insisting she deserved the house. Just thinking of all the nice things they'd said then had a lump forming in her throat as she started down the block.

She slanted a glance at Dixon. "You really don't have to walk me all the way to the door."

"I promised to make sure you got home safely." He offered a teasing smile. "The end is in sight. You won't have to put up with me for much longer."

"It's been nice—" Rachel didn't have a chance to say more. Her breath caught at the sudden movement to her right.

A second later, a dark figure stepped from behind a neighbor's tall hedge to stand directly in front of her.

CHAPTER FIVE

In one smooth movement, Dixon grabbed Rachel's arm and put his body between her and the potential assailant. It took only that amount of time for him to realize this wasn't some hopped-up kid or mugger, but Marc.

The man's eyes shifted from Dixon to Rachel, who'd stepped around him.

"Marc." Her voice was filled with more puzzlement than anger. "What are you doing skulking around in the bushes?"

"What do you think? I was waiting for you." His gaze shifted dismissively toward Dixon, then refocused on her. "We need to talk."

"No," she said quite primly. "We don't."

Dixon barely kept a smile from his face. Though this woman and his sister couldn't be more different, the firmness in Rachel's tone reminded him of Nell.

"You can leave." Marc made a dismissive gesture with one hand at Dixon. "This doesn't concern you."

This time, Dixon did smile. While this might not be his battle, he wasn't going anywhere. He'd be here for Rachel as long as she wanted—or needed—him here.

"Now that you've had more time," Marc's voice turned persuasive, "I hope you're able to see the truth in what I told you."

Rachel cocked her head. "Are you by any chance referring to your comment about it being my fault that you had sex with that woman in your hotel room?"

"We didn't have sex." A muscle in Marc's jaw jumped. "While having her there wasn't exactly your fault, it—"

Dixon burst into laughter, even as part of him felt sick inside. "Give it up, man. That excuse blows."

Marc shot Dixon a dark look. "I told you to go."

"I don't take orders from you." Dixon's tone might be easy and conversational, but everything in him went as sharp as a finely tuned blade. "Neither does Rachel."

"Is that how it is?" Marc blustered. "You're accusing me of fooling around when you've been doing it with him? Playing the shy virgin with me all the while you're screwing him?"

Dixon's fist shot out. He pulled the punch, but the man still went down.

"Dixon. No." Rachel grabbed his arm. "He's not worth it."

Marc rose to his feet, rubbing his jaw, anger flaring in his pale blue eyes. "You assaulted me. I can put you in jail."

"You can try." Dixon's voice remained cool and utterly devoid of emotion. "I wonder what Lilian would think when she hears how you disrespected Rachel."

Lilian de Burgh was a wealthy widow whose business Marc had been courting for the past year. Marc knew as well as Dixon that if word of this got out to Lilian, he could kiss her investments goodbye.

"You could tell her anyway."

"We won't say anything." Rachel's fingers remained wrapped around Dixon's biceps. "Just go. And don't come back."

Marc stared at her for a long moment, his gaze turning sharp and assessing. "We were good together. We can be again."

Rachel shook her head. "It's over."

He turned on his heel, but not before Dixon heard him mutter, "For now," as he strode down the sidewalk.

"Wow." Rachel expelled a shaky breath. "I didn't expect that."

"Let me get you inside."

She'd appeared in control, but when Dixon put his hand on her shoulder, he felt her entire body trembling. Without thinking, he drew her to him.

Wrapping his arms around her, he held her close until she stopped shaking.

She was the one who finally took a step back, her breath coming in ragged puffs and two bright swaths of pink coloring her cheeks. "Thank you. I do-don't know why I was so off-balanced. I guess I didn't expect to see him jump out of the bushes."

Dixon chuckled. "Surprised the heck out of me, too."

She glanced around. "I wonder where he parked his car."

"If you don't recognize his vehicle as one of those parked on the street, it means he planned this out."

Rachel climbed the steps to her porch, and he followed. But she made no move to go inside. "What do you mean?"

"He likely parked around the corner on another street. Then he positioned himself in the shadows so he could watch and wait."

She visibly shivered despite the warmth of the evening. "That's creepy."

Dixon nodded in agreement. He didn't want to scare her, but she needed to be aware. "Marc shares many of my mother's characteristics. He doesn't like hearing the word no."

Rachel emitted a nervous laugh. "Who does?"

"Some won't take no for an answer." Dixon gazed out into the darkness. "This won't be the last you see of him."

"I made it clear it was over. You heard me. He heard me."

"I'm betting you also made it clear the previous time you spoke with him."

Rachel paused, then slowly nodded. "You're scaring me."

"I don't mean to, but I want you to be safe." Dixon forced reassurance into his voice. "That means for the next couple of weeks, until you know for sure he's moved on, you need to pay particular attention to your surroundings. Keep your house and your car doors locked. When you leave work, walk out with a friend."

"Do you really think he'd hurt me?"

"I think it pays to be safe." Dixon glanced at the door. "I'll wait until you're inside and locked up."

He watched her unlock the door with unsteady hands, then push it open. Dixon expected her to step inside. Instead, she covered the short distance to him and brushed her lips across his cheek.

"Thank you." Her large dark eyes, beautiful and luminous behind her glasses, met his. "For everything."

"What do you think of the old place?" Dixon gestured with one hand toward the spacious living room of the condominium he now called home.

Nell's lips quirked upward as she set her bag on the floor and dropped into one of the overstuffed leather chairs. "Since the place comes furnished, it looks the same."

When Nell had decided to move in with Leo, she'd sublet the high-end unit in Greenbriar Place to him. The twenty-unit brick-and-stone condominium building not only boasted a rooftop garden and underground parking, but it also had exceptional security.

"Except that wasn't on the wall when you lived here." He pointed to a particularly ugly painting of a cat with fairy wings and a mermaid tail sitting on a pear in the ocean above the fireplace.

"No," she said slowly. "There was a lovely picture there. Why that one, Ky?"

She didn't often use his childhood name. The only thing Dixon could figure was that the hideous picture had rattled her.

"It's a conversation piece."

She rolled her eyes and lifted her hands. "I get it. Your place, your pictures on the wall."

Her exaggerated sigh had him smiling.

"You said you had something to tell me." She leaned slightly forward in her seat, her gaze sharp on his face. "You said it was important."

"It is important." Dixon sat in the chair opposite her. "Before we get to that, I need to tell you what happened when I walked Rachel home last night."

She straightened.

"Marc was lurking in the shadows of a neighbor's bushes." Just thinking about how he'd stepped out onto the sidewalk in front of them had Dixon surging to his feet. "He tried to make nice with her. When that didn't work, he turned into Gloria."

Dixon didn't need to explain what that meant. Nell was well-schooled in the tricks of a narcissist or, in Gloria's case, a psychopath.

"How did Rachel handle him?" Nell's tone, quiet and controlled, didn't fool him. His sister was a mama bear when it came to her friends.

"She kept her cool and didn't back down." Dixon leaned against the granite countertop. "I was the one who lost it."

Nell only lifted a brow.

"He accused Rachel of screwing me while playing the shy virgin with him." Dixon pressed his lips together, just remembering the venom in the man's eyes and the hurt on Rachel's face, a hurt she'd tried to hide. "I hit him."

"Oh, Dixon, you didn't." Despite the words, a snort of laughter escaped his sister's lips.

"Dropped him to the sidewalk." Dixon couldn't keep the pride from his voice. "Piece of sh—"

Dixon stopped himself. That wasn't the point. "I don't believe he'll give up on her, not right away anyway."

"I agree." Nell's blue eyes turned to ice. "It's pride and it's control."

Dixon returned to sit. "Keep a close watch on her."

"I will." Nell paused. "If that's not what you wanted to discuss with me, I hesitate to ask what else is going on."

"I realize you're busy, but since this may concern you as well as me, you need the information."

The tiny smile that had been hovering on her lips disappeared. "What is it?"

"Rumor is Gloria has decided to throw me under the bus in exchange for leniency in the Bakersfield incident."

Again, no need to go into detail. Earlier in the summer, Dixon had told his sister what had occurred in California shortly before he quit "working" with their mother. Though the crime had taken place years ago, it remained relevant.

She'd nearly groaned aloud as he'd recounted how their mother had gotten close to a city manager whose responsibilities included overseeing city funds, embezzled money from one of the accounts he oversaw and framed him for it.

"There is no statute of limitations in California on embezzlement of public funds."

"Don't you think I know that?" Dixon snapped out the words. Raking a hand through his hair, he stood and began to pace.

Nell closed her eyes briefly, then opened them and met his. "How do you know she's trying to blame it on you?"

"I've got sources who keep their ears to the ground for me."

"What's the plan?"

She'd expect him to have a plan. He always thought ahead. "I'm going after her."

"How?" Nell asked, obviously not content with generalities.

"I've started making a list of crimes in which she's been suspected but never charged, crimes that law enforcement might be interested in looking at again should the right information come their way."

"I can help with the list."

"You've got a wedding to plan."

"When you make out the list, let me look it over to see if there's anything I recall that can be added." Nell's blue eyes hardened again. "I want Gloria put away for good."

"That's the dream." Dixon lightened his tone. "I'll keep you in the loop."

"Why does that sound as if you're showing me to the door?"

He slid an arm around her shoulders. "Maybe because I am."

"You have something going on this afternoon?"

"Nothing that would interest you."

"Will you be seeing Rachel again?"

Dixon didn't have to feign surprise. "If you're referring to seeing as dating, the answer is no. Why would you think that's even a possibility?"

"I saw the way you looked at her last night." Nell expelled a breath. "And the way she looked at you."

Dixon forced a chuckle. "I never thought I'd say this, but you're seeing things through some seriously defective rose-colored glasses."

"It's okay for you to have a life, Ky." A soft look filled her eyes. Then she frowned. "But be careful with Rachel. She's, well, she's not like us."

Easier, Dixon thought, to respond to the last part rather than deny his interest. "How is she not like us?"

"I'm not saying she isn't strong. Because, hey, it takes some chutzpah to take on the raising of all those kids when you're barely more than a child yourself."

"What are you saying?"

"Her heart is tender and easily bruised."

"You need to be giving this lecture to Marc," he said pointedly. "He's the one stomping all over it."

"He's like Gloria. Speaking with him would be a waste of breath."

On that, they were in total agreement.

"Rachel likes you," she said. "I see that."

"Well, I'm a likable guy." Dixon wanted this conversation over. While he appreciated his sister's concern, this was much ado about nothing. "Trust me. Rachel and I are simply friends, actually probably more like acquaintances than friends."

Nell shot him a skeptical glance. "You punched Marc."

"Seriously," he said, ushering her toward the door, "if you'd been there, you would have hit him, too."

After Nell left, Dixon opened a beer and got busy writing out the details of every crime that he knew his mother had committed. He started first by being general, listing a month, year and brief description. Once he got the general outline down, he figured he could fill in the details.

Details that would result in Gloria's conviction. His hope was, even if the police could charge her with only half of everything she'd done, it would be enough to keep her in prison for the rest of her life.

If the police could arrest her for murder, that would be the maraschino cherry on top of the sundae. The problem was, his memory of the details of the crime that had led to Robert John Owen's death was sketchy. This was where he hoped Nell could provide details.

He'd been twelve and, well, for years he'd tried to erase that night in the desert from his memory.

Until that night he'd believed his mother, a woman with the face of an angel and a soul of darkness, was capable of many things. He hadn't thought she'd kill—and especially wouldn't pull the trigger herself.

Bobby John had made his money in oil. He'd been a handsome man with coal-black hair and a bushy mustache. The man had gotten on Gloria's radar during one of their times in Palm Desert.

If Dixon recalled correctly, Bobby John had started flashing hundred-dollar bills around at one of the country clubs, and Gloria had been instantly smitten.

She'd underestimated him. But then, he'd underestimated her. Bobby John had liked the sex, but Gloria's mood swings had exhausted him to the point that he'd broken up with her. That hadn't gone over well.

Dixon paused, his thoughts drifting to Marc. Rachel might think the man would move on, but the part of Marc who was like Gloria told Dixon that was just wishful thinking.

He tightened his fingers around the beer bottle and took a pull before refocusing. Gloria had been unwilling to give up on Bobby John until she'd bled him dry.

The man's mistake had been in threatening her.

She'd drugged him, driven him out to the desert in the trunk of his Lincoln Continental, with Nell and Dixon in the back seat. Dixon still remembered the gunshot. With the sound ringing in his ears, he and Nell had watched Gloria put the gun in Bobby John's hand to make it look like a suicide.

Then her friend—what was the woman's name?—had picked them up.

It hadn't mattered that their fingerprints were all over the back seat. They'd ridden in Bobby John's car plenty of times.

Dixon set down his beer and jerked to his feet.

The fear of what Gloria would do when she found him or

Nell had dogged them since they'd left her. The only way to stop her from one day doing to them what she'd done to Bobby John was to see her dead or in jail.

Dixon dropped back into the chair and, pressing his lips together, returned to the list.

CHAPTER SIX

Rachel didn't have a day off until Wednesday. While her days were busy with food bank duties, her evenings were equally full. Months ago, she'd agreed to supervise volunteers at two drives for canned goods—one that took place in the Green, the other at one of the Pomeroy properties on the edge of town.

Being busy kept her mind off Marc and the cold look in his eyes when he'd strode off Saturday night. Despite his words, love for her hadn't been shining in those pale blue depths, but anger.

When she arose on Wednesday morning, her day off, she realized there was another benefit to no longer being with Marc. She hadn't had to listen to him go on and on about her not being available every evening.

He'd had plenty of meetings of his own in the evening, and she'd been understanding. When it was her turn to be busy—and unavailable to him—she'd had to listen to his complaints.

Offers to have him assist her in these activities had been rebuffed.

Yes, it was pleasant not having to deal with him. If she'd had more time to ponder how sad that was after so many months of dating, she might have wondered why she put up with him for so long.

But she didn't have time. Last night, Abby had called and asked if she could watch Eva Grace today. Jonah normally watched her on Wednesdays, but one of his officers had called in with the stomach flu.

The drive to Abby and Jonah's Victorian home was quick, and when Abby opened the door, Eva Grace flew into Rachel's arms.

"Mommy said we get to spend the whole day together." Eva Grace released her hold on Rachel to twirl around, the skirt of her hot-pink dress covered in cat faces spreading out around her. "I'm so excited."

Eva Grace punctuated the words with a fist pump.

Rachel could only laugh. She adored Abby's daughter. Despite the trials she'd gone through to walk normally, the almost-first-grader had a perpetually sunny disposition.

"I lost another tooth." Eva Grace opened her mouth just as a golden retriever bounded into the room to nuzzle at Rachel's leg.

Rachel dropped a hand to the dog's head while she peered into Eva Grace's mouth. "Wow. That is so cool. Now you've lost both of your front teeth."

Eva Grace nodded, setting her curly ponytail bobbing. "The tooth fairy comes tonight."

"That's exciting," Rachel said, quite seriously. "What will she bring you? Do you know?"

"A silver dollar." Eva Grace looked up at her mother for confirmation.

Abby nodded.

"I haven't seen one of those in a long time," Rachel told her.

"I'll show you mine." Eva Grace took off, the dog at her feet. "I got it for my first tooth."

"She's super excited to spend the day with you." Abby placed a hand on Rachel's arm. "Thank you so much."

"I love spending time with her." Rachel smiled, hoping her

friend heard the sincerity in her voice. "Being with Eva Grace will help keep my mind—"

Rachel clamped her lips shut when the child raced back into the room, the silver coin clasped in her small fingers.

Eva Grace thrust out the silver dollar. "It's really cool. Matilda had never seen one either, so I showed mine to her."

There was not a single doubt in Rachel's mind that Matilda Lovejoy had seen many silver dollars. But it was such fun to watch the joy in the little girl's eyes as she showed off the gift from the tooth fairy.

"Eva Grace, I'm very excited to spend the day with you." Rachel paused, making sure she had the child's complete attention. "It's a beautiful day. I thought we could go to the park and then maybe grab some lunch at Lily Belle's."

Abby's eyes lit up. "I didn't know Lily Belle's served food."

Walking into the ice cream shop, located in the historic district, was like taking a step back in time. The onyx soda fountain from the 1893 World's Fair was a big hit with tourists, as well as the tin ceiling with richly patterned tiles.

"They just started serving sandwiches last week." Rachel tried to recall what had been on the chalkboard. "I had a rainbow veggie. It was basically a pita pocket with roasted veggies and hummus."

Abby cast a doubtful glance at Eva Grace. "She likes her veggies, but—"

"One of the volunteers had a sandwich made with Wowbutter and homemade grape jam. She said it was amazing."

"I like Wowbutter," Eva Grace said, apparently feeling left out of the conversation. "At school, we're peanut-free 'cause some kids have allergies. Sandwiches with Wowbutter are okay because it has no nuts."

Rachel nodded. "Plus, it tastes yummy?"

"Super yummy." Eva Grace's smile turned sly. "If we go to Lily Belle's, we could get ice cream for dessert."

Rachel slanted a glanced at Abby, who appeared to be hiding a smile. Her friend gave a slight nod.

"I suppose we could." Rachel held out a hand to the child. "Ready for the park?"

Eva Grace squealed, taking both Abby and Rachel by surprise. Then the girl flung out her arms and twirled again. "This is going to be the bestest day ever."

For the next hour, Rachel played with Eva Grace at the small park enclosed by an ornate black wrought-iron fence with a gilt-edged gate. The bushes inside the park had been sculpted into the shapes of various animals, including mythical ones.

Right now, Rachel sat on a wooden bench painted a deep forest green, watching Eva Grace swing beside a girl she knew from school. The girl's mother stood beside a tree, on her phone.

Rachel considered pulling out her own phone. Then, recalling something she'd read recently about living in the moment, she let herself relax. She reveled in the feel of the sun on her face and the light breeze against her cheek. The sound of Eva Grace's giggles and the shouts of laughter from the merry-go-round wrapped around her.

"I thought that was you."

Rachel looked up.

Lilian de Burgh stood beside the bench. Considered one of the movers and shakers of Hazel Green, Lilian exuded confidence. Though she had to be in her early seventies, the woman's white hair, cut in a stylish bob, and porcelain complexion made her look years younger.

"Lilian, it's so nice to see you." Rachel gestured to the empty spot beside her on the bench. "Do you have time to sit?"

Dressed casually in capris and a cotton shirt with a nautical theme, the businesswoman didn't appear headed to a meeting.

Still, Hazel Green tended to be much more laid-back than Chicago in terms of what passed for business attire.

"If you don't mind."

"I'd love to catch up." Seeing the question in Lilian's eyes, Rachel gestured to Eva Grace. "I'm watching the munchkin today. Abby and Jonah ran into a babysitting snafu and—"

"You stepped up to help," Lilian finished the sentence.

"It's a pleasure." Rachel smiled, watching Eva Grace pump her legs and go flying high on the u-shaped swing. "I adore her."

"Did you take a day off work?" Lilian asked.

"Today's my day off," Rachel said, chuckling when Eva Grace and her friend on the next swing howled like coyotes.

"You're a good friend."

Rachel shook her head at the praise. "I'm glad Abby asked."

"I hear Marty is coming into town this weekend." Lilian's eyes held a speculative gleam. "Wells will be hosting a small cocktail party at his house for the wedding party and close friends. I assume you and Marc will be there."

Lilian was well acquainted with Marc. After her husband died, Lilian had divested herself of several commercial real estate holdings and had netted a tidy sum. In the past few months, both Dixon and Marc had been discussing various investment strategies with her.

Marc had believed Lilian was close to making a decision on whom to work with and felt he had the inside track over Dixon. Rachel wasn't as certain.

When Rachel saw Lilian was staring at her with an expectant expression, she realized the woman was waiting for a response.

"I'll definitely be there," Rachel informed her. "But Marc won't be with me."

"Does he have a conflict?"

"No conflict." Rachel twisted her hands together, trying to decide how much to divulge.

Lilian's brows pulled together. "Surely Wells made it clear

you're welcome to bring a plus-one to the event. If not, I could speak—"

"Marc and I are no longer together." Rachel was glad to get the words out. The more people who knew, the more the word would spread and she wouldn't have to explain herself.

"Oh, my dear." Lilian reached over and covered her hand with her own. She gave it a squeeze before pulling back. "I'm so sorry."

"I'm not. It's for the best." Rachel kept her tone matter-of-fact. "He's not the man I thought him to be."

The older woman's gaze turned thoughtful. "That had to be disappointing."

Rachel was tempted to say nothing more, knowing her lack of response could torpedo any chance Marc had of gaining Lilian's business. Did the fact that he could cheat and lie in his personal life mean he'd have no qualms about doing it in his business?

She didn't know the answer to the question. All she could do was be honest with Lilian and let the woman make her own decision.

"Marc cheated on me. I know that for a fact. I don't know if it was only that one time, or if there were others."

Lilian pressed her lips together, shook her head. "What was he thinking?"

Rachel shrugged. "I don't know. Frankly, I don't care why he did it."

She couldn't quite quell the defensiveness in her voice. He'd tried to turn the tables and make her feel responsible. Worse, she'd nearly fallen for it.

"Oh, honey, I only meant that for him to ruin a relationship with a wonderful woman like yourself shows that he doesn't have much good sense."

Rachel shrugged, then plastered a smile on her face as Eva Grace ran full speed toward them.

The child skidded to a stop in front of her and Lilian, her sneakers flashing hot-pink sparks.

"I met a friend from school, and we swung so high we touched the clouds," Eva Grace announced proudly.

Rachel resisted the urge to gather the child in her arms and hug her tight. "I saw you swinging super-duper high."

"Did you hear us when we howled at the sky? There was no moon."

"The sound made me shiver." Lilian pretended to shudder. "I thought the wolves were coming for me."

Eva Grace laughed. "It was just me and Divinity."

"That's good to know," Lilian said in all seriousness.

Eva Grace's eyes darted from Rachel to Lilian. "Are you coming to lunch with us?"

Since Lilian was practically a member of the Pomeroy family and Abby and Nell were besties, Eva Grace was well acquainted with the woman.

Lilian glanced at Rachel. "I don't want to intrude."

"I'd love for you to join us," Rachel told Lilian.

Eva Grace clapped her hands and howled, making them all laugh.

"We thought we'd go to Lily Belle's," Rachel said, fully prepared to explain about the new lunch menu.

"I had the most marvelous peanut butter and jelly sandwich there last week," Lilian said, surprising Rachel and delighting Eva Grace. "Only, it wasn't made with peanut butter, but with—"

"Wowbutter," Eva Grace said. "It's my favorite."

"Have you tried the kale chips?" Lilian asked the girl.

"No, but Mommy makes them at home sometimes," Eva Grace said.

"You'll have to see if these measure up to your mother's."

Thirty minutes later, the three of them basked in the sunlight in the outdoor eating area of Lily Belle's, only a few chips left on their plates.

"Well," Lilian wiped the edges of her mouth with a paper napkin, "how do they compare?"

Though she'd already eaten a handful of the chips, Eva Grace picked one up and bit into it. She chewed for several seconds, like a critic on one of those food shows Rachel loved to watch. "Crunchy. A tie with Mommy's."

"Good to know." Lilian paused as Nevaeh approached the table.

Today, the high school girl was waiting tables at Lily Belle's. Yesterday, she'd been cleaning rooms for Abby at the inn. When they'd first been seated, Rachel had told Nev that they'd be wanting dessert.

"What sounds good to you?" Nev asked Eva Grace.

Eva Grace tapped a finger against her lips. "What do you recommend?"

Precocious should be the girl's middle name, Rachel thought. She glanced at Lilian, and they exchanged a smile.

After some consideration, Eva Grace picked a trail mix ice cream, while Lilian and Rachel went with a dip of a new flavor— caramel balsamic swirl.

Nev brought out Eva Grace's selection in a cone, while Rachel's and Lilian's came in pretty little cups garnished with raspberries, blackberries and blueberries.

"This is amazing." Rachel dipped her spoon into the sweet but savory ice cream, eager for a second taste.

"I love it, too," Lilian agreed. "It—"

"Well, what do we have here?" Marc stopped beside the small fence that separated the outdoor eating area from the sidewalk. "Three of my favorite girls."

Eva Grace giggled.

Rachel forgave her, as the child was too young to recognize a snake in a hand-tailored suit. She kept her gaze cool as it flickered over him, then she returned it to her ice cream.

"Mind if I join you?"

Before Rachel could respond, he'd slipped through the opening in the fence and waved Nev over.

"A cup of coffee and whatever they're having." With a bright smile, he pulled out a chair and sat down.

"You look as if you're headed to a meeting," Lilian said politely when silence settled over the table.

"Just finished one." He shifted in his chair toward Rachel. "You remember me speaking about the Thompson manufacturing group out of Gurnee? I'm going to be overseeing their 401(k) retirement funds."

Next to Lilian's money, the Thompson group had been a focus of Marc's efforts for months. He'd often talked about how, once he got the account, they'd go to Goose Island Grog for dinner and drinks. *Do it up big* had been his words.

"Congratulations," Lilian said when the silence lengthened.

Marc's gaze narrowed at the woman's polite response. Clearly, he'd expected more.

More from Lilian.

More from Rachel.

Rachel took another bite of her ice cream, but the caramelized balsamic vinegar now tasted like sawdust against her tongue.

Nev brought his coffee and ice cream. He said nothing, just pulled a large bill from a money clip. "My treat."

Rachel opened her mouth to protest, then shut it with a snap, remembering the times he'd left his credit card at home and she'd had to pick up the tab.

If he wanted to pay, he could knock himself out. It wouldn't change her feelings about him.

"Why, thank you, Marc." Lilian shifted her gaze to Eva Grace. "How's the ice cream?"

Eva Grace flashed a smile and howled.

Marc scowled. "What kind of response is that?"

The child cocked her head. "Wolves do it when they're happy. Everyone knows that."

"Wolves don't howl because they're happy," he shot back.

"Yes, they do." Eva Grace lifted her chin. "My teacher told us."

"You misunderstood." He took a sip of coffee, his expression turning petulant.

Rachel exchanged a pointed glance with Lilian. The man was really arguing with a six-year-old?

"Look it up on your phone," Eva Grace said to Rachel. "That's what Mommy and Daddy do." The child offered her an enticing smile. "I'm sorry. I forgot to add 'please.'"

"Sure." As Rachel picked up her phone, she prayed the child was correct. She quickly found an article about wolf howls and skimmed it. Lifting her gaze from the screen, she smiled and read, "'Researchers also believe wolves howl for fun. Because it makes them happy, and it's something they enjoy doing.'"

Casting Marc a smile that on an older child would have been a smirk, Eva Grace took another lick of her cone.

"Let me see." Marc held out his hand. "I want to read it myself."

Rachel dropped the phone in her bag, her gaze never leaving his face. "Look it up yourself."

"You made it up," he blustered.

"Who made what up?" Dixon said, before leaning over and giving Eva Grace's ponytail a tug. "Hey, munchkin."

"Uncle Dixon." Pleasure spread across the child's face.

Marc lifted a brow. "Uncle?"

"Nell is Aunt Nell, so…" Dixon smiled, his eyes sharpening as they rested on Marc.

"Lilian and I brought Eva Grace to have lunch," Rachel told him.

"He," Eva Grace pointed to Marc, "doesn't believe that wolves howl because they're happy."

The exaggerated look of startled surprise on Dixon's face had a choked laugh escaping Rachel's throat.

"Doesn't everyone know that?" Dixon asked, sounding truly shocked.

Eva Grace giggled. "I like you."

"I like you, too, munchkin." Dixon turned to Lilian. "It's nice to see you again, Mrs. de Burgh."

Lilian only shook her head and laughed. "If you insist on such formality, I'll be forced to call you Mr. Carlyle."

Marc took a bite of ice cream, made a face and pushed it aside.

"Well, we can't have that." Now, Dixon settled his gaze on Rachel. "I heard you were spending the day with Eva Grace."

Heard, Rachel wondered, from who? His sister, more than likely.

"Rachel took me to the park," Eva Grace answered. "Then we came here."

"Fun." Dixon cocked his head. "What's next?"

"Well, I don't know about these two, but I'm headed to a meeting at the town hall." Lilian pushed back her chair and rose. After a glance at Rachel and Dixon, she fixed her gaze on Marc. "Perhaps you can walk with me there."

Marc hesitated for only a second before rising to his feet and flashing a smile. It was obvious, at least to Rachel, that he'd been torn between wanting some time with her versus having some one-on-one time with Lilian.

She knew his ambition would always win out. Rachel had the feeling Lilian knew that, too. Which was undoubtedly why she'd made the offer.

As the town hall wasn't far, Rachel had only a brief window of time for her and Eva Grace to make their escape.

Dixon cocked his head. "Mind if I sit?"

Gesturing to the empty chair, Rachel smiled. "Please do."

Unlike Marc, Dixon actually waited for permission before joining them. He slanted a brief glance at Eva Grace, who was now intent on finishing up her cone. "I assume you have a plan."

While somewhat cryptic, Rachel understood exactly what he'd meant with the comment. "I believe Abby and Jonah have a tent. I thought it might be fun to set it up in the backyard and bring out the dollies to play."

"Yay." The child leaned back her head and howled, proving she wasn't totally focused on her cone.

The added advantage would be that she wouldn't run into Marc once he finished with Lilian.

"Are you going to come help us, Uncle Dixon?" The child took a lick of ice cream and offered him an imploring look.

Dixon hesitated, shooting Rachel a questioning look.

"Do you have time?" She didn't take the fact that he wasn't wearing a suit as a reason to assume he wasn't working today.

"I do."

"Good." Rachel rose to her feet. "C'mon, Eva Grace. Let's put this man to work."

CHAPTER SEVEN

Dixon had never put up a tent, but the way he saw it, he was a smart guy and he could figure it out. He stood on Abby's porch, surrounded by hanging baskets of brightly blooming flowers. If that weren't enough, planters on the porch were also filled with an abundance of bright foliage.

Eva Grace, who'd been hanging out with him, had run inside to do, well, something.

Rachel had decided she best call Abby just to make sure she had no objection to turning the backyard into a campground. Dixon had told her he'd just wait while she stepped inside to make the call.

He'd never been the kind to horn in on private conversations, not like Marc.

Dixon had to admit that when he'd spotted the man sitting at the table with Rachel, a cold knot had formed in the pit of his stomach.

For one horrible second, he'd feared the smooth-talking snake had somehow managed to convince Rachel to give him one more chance.

As he'd drawn closer, the tight set to Rachel's shoulders and the way she'd ignored Marc had told him that nothing had changed.

The screen door opening had him turning.

"Abby said that's fine." Rachel pushed a strand of hair back from her face. "In fact, she says she and Jonah might sleep out there with Eva Grace."

Dixon chuckled.

"Kids love that kind of stuff." Rachel moved to stand beside him. "I remember when we were little, we did our share of backyard camping."

Dixon, thinking of his own childhood, had no response.

"This is a peaceful neighborhood," he said, changing the subject.

"I know." Rachel smiled. "I used to love to walk this neighborhood and gawk at all the lovely Victorian homes, especially around the holidays."

"Why the holidays?"

"You were here during the Christmas season."

He shook his head. "I wasn't living here. I was still in Chicago."

"Well, you'll have to check it out this year. Of course, because it'll be December, you'll drive by the homes, not walk." Her lips curved. "Seriously, it's worth the time. Everyone in this area goes overboard on lights. It's amazing."

He wondered if she knew how her eyes lit up when she was excited. She was so, well, so sweet. Definitely unlike most women he'd dated.

Dixon pulled himself up short. He and Rachel weren't dating. Dinner wasn't dating. Walking her home after a party with mutual friends wasn't dating. Neither was putting up a tent in a friend's backyard.

Reassured by the logic, he smiled. "Where's Eva Grace?"

"In the bathroom. I think the ice cream upset her stomach."

Rachel sighed. "She'll be fine and down in a minute. The tent is in the basement."

"Do you want me to get it now?"

"Let's wait until she comes out. That way, it can be a team effort. Even if Eva Grace is simply holding open the door, she'll feel more ownership in the effort."

"How'd you get so smart?"

She flushed and made a brushing motion with one hand.

"I'm serious," he said. "I wouldn't have thought of it that way."

"You haven't had as much experience around children as I have."

"True, but there are lots of parents out there without your wisdom." Thoughts of his mother washed over him, but Dixon shoved the memories aside. Gloria had ruined so many years of his life, he wasn't about to let her ruin any more.

"Do you," she gestured vaguely in the direction of the porch swing, "want to sit?"

He was fine standing, but something in the way she looked at the white-lacquered wood swing had him changing his response. "I'd like that."

She took a seat, and he sat beside her, but left enough distance between them so she wouldn't feel as if he was crowding her.

"There's something about porch swings." Rachel pushed off with her feet, and a delighted look crossed her face at the motion. "They're so relaxing."

"You have a swing on your porch." He remembered it from when he'd walked her home. "Not the kind that hangs, though."

She nodded. "Sometimes, after work, I'll just sit out there with a glass of iced tea and breathe in the sweet summer air. Sometimes, I'll take a book and read for a while before making dinner."

Dixon found it difficult to imagine such a life. "Simple pleasures."

Her laugh held an embarrassed edge. "I'm sure it sounds very pedestrian to you."

He surprised them both by reaching over and squeezing her hand. "It sounds nice."

Dixon pulled back his hand. There was something about Rachel that called to him, that made him wish he wasn't different, that wanted him to be the kind of man she deserved.

"Marc just came and sat down at the table. He didn't even ask if he could join us."

"People like him don't think they need to ask. He wanted to do it, so he did."

"I don't want him to come around me."

He slanted a glance in her direction and found her gaze focused straight ahead. "You'll need to be firm and consistent. Waver at all, give him an inch and—"

"—he'll take a mile."

Dixon smiled. "I was actually going to say that he'll see a little opening as a sign your resolve is weakening."

"Once he's convinced I'm really done with him, he'll leave me alone."

Dixon wished he could reassure her, but he refused to offer false hope.

"He will leave me alone, won't he?" she asked when the silence lengthened.

"If I had to guess, I'd say once he stops trying to convince you that you're making a big mistake, he'll turn his anger on you." A muscle in Dixon's jaw jumped. The anger was better than the worry that would take its place if he let down his guard. "That's when he'll be the most dangerous."

Dixon thought of his mother and Bobby John. Granted, that was an extreme case, but he'd seen the mean in Marc.

"Do-do you think he'd hurt me?" The worry he'd been trying to keep at bay filled Rachel's voice.

He'd frightened her. He didn't want her scared, but he did want her careful.

"During the time you dated, did he ever hurt you?"

"He said some mean things," Rachel admitted. "Or things I took wrong. He hurt my feelings."

He knew she understood what he was asking and had deliberately side-stepped the question.

"Physically hurt you."

Color stained her cheeks, and she let out a ragged breath.

Anger surged, and in that moment, Dixon wanted nothing more than to wrap his hands around Marc's scrawny neck.

"He squeezed my arm one time when he was trying to make a point." Her voice sounded small, as if coming from a thousand miles away. "His fingers left bruises. Later, he said he was sorry, that he didn't realize he was gripping my arm so tightly. But he also said I wasn't listening, so he had to get my attention."

"He turned it back on you," Dixon said in a flat tone. "Made you the one to blame."

"Yes."

"Did he ever hit you? Punch you?"

Dixon felt her swivel to face him. He shifted his body and met her gaze.

"I wouldn't have stayed with him if he'd done that."

There was no need to remind her she'd stayed with Marc even after he'd left marks on her. Dixon knew how persuasive people like Marc and his mother could be. Though he hadn't observed Marc having any charisma, he assumed he must have some to have captured Rachel's interest.

Dixon nodded.

"I'm going to tell Jonah," she said, referring to the police chief, who was also a friend. "I realize there isn't anything he can do now, but at least he'll be aware."

Dixon's admiration for her inched up. Just when he thought he had Rachel pegged, she surprised him. "If there's anything I can ever do—"

"You're sweet, but—"

"Give me your phone."

She shot him a questioning glance, but slipped the phone out of her pocket without comment.

Once she had it unlocked, he took it, and his thumbs flew across the keyboard.

She leaned close, and he caught a whiff of strawberry. Shampoo, he decided, liking the scent.

When she lifted her gaze, her mouth was only inches from his. "You put in your phone number."

"Now you can reach me." He wanted to kiss her. Wanted to put his arms around her and crush his mouth to hers. Taste those sweet lips, feel her soft curves pressed against him. "Day or night."

A tiny pulse fluttered in her neck, and her breathing turned uneven.

He put a hand on her shoulder, leaned in. "Rach—"

The screen door banging open had them jerking apart.

"I'm ready to put up the tent." Eva Grace bounded to the swing and dropped into the space that had just opened up between them. "This is a fantabulous day."

Abby stood beside Rachel on the back porch, staring out over the yard. Rachel sniffed. Smiled.

Her friend smelled like Love's Baby Soft, the sweet baby-powder scent that had been popular in the 1990s. Which totally fit with Abby's appearance today.

As a merchant in the historic district, Abby was expected to don vintage garb when she headed into work. Today, she'd given the nod to the last decade of the twentieth century, wearing a boldly patterned slip dress and platform sandals.

"You smell so good," she told Abby. "And look amazing."

Abby gave a little twirl, reminding Rachel of Eva Grace, then dropped a curtsy. "Thank you."

Rachel grinned. Being around her friends always lifted her spirits.

Her gaze drifted to Dixon. He'd done a pretty good job of that, too.

"Has Dixon been here the entire afternoon?"

Rachel pulled her gaze from him and back to Abby. "Pretty much."

Right now, the man in question sat in a green-and-white-striped lawn chair outside the entrance to the tent, the golden retriever sprawled at his feet. The dog had started to get up when Abby and Rachel had stepped onto the back porch, but Abby made a sharp gesture that had Ginger immediately lowering her head back to the grass.

Dixon, who usually seemed to notice everything, didn't appear aware of their presence on the porch. Or, if he did, he gave no indication.

Right now, he sipped his drink, his gaze firmly focused on Eva Grace as the child read from a book and acted out the characters.

Though there had been both beer and wine in the refrigerator, his frosted glass held only iced tea. They'd decided that drinking alcohol while watching a child had a certain ick factor.

Or, rather, Rachel had made her thoughts known, and Dixon had agreed.

"I really appreciate you watching Eva Grace, Rachel." Determined to not interrupt the girl's performance, Abby kept her voice low.

"It's my pleasure." Rachel smiled. "We've kept busy."

"What's up with you and Dixon?" Though Abby's tone remained conversational, an underlying hint of...something put Rachel on alert.

"I guess you could say we're friends." Yes, Rachel decided, *friends* was the right word.

"Since when?"

Rachel understood Abby's confusion. Until she'd run into

Dixon at Palmer House, Rachel had exchanged only a handful of words with the man.

"Since I broke up with Marc." Rachel let her gaze settle back on Dixon. "He's been very kind."

"Just be careful."

"Of what?" Rachel turned to her friend and frowned. "What are you saying?"

"You're just coming out of one relationship. You're vulnerable." Abby laid a hand on her arm. "I don't want to see you hurt."

Vulnerable. The word stung.

While Rachel knew her friend's heart was in the right space, she wondered if Nell had been standing here, would Abby be warning her? Labeling her *vulnerable*?

"I may not have a lot of experience around men, but I'm not a pushover." Rachel pressed her lips together, feeling irritation surge. "I can take care of myself."

"Of course—"

"The end," Eva Grace announced and took a bow when Dixon applauded.

"Stellar performance." Dixon smiled at the child before shifting his gaze to Rachel.

When his eyes met hers, Rachel realized that no matter how focused he'd appeared, he'd known that she and Abby were there.

"Mommy." Eva Grace ran across the lawn, wrapping her arms around Abby, who was walking toward her.

Ginger rose to her feet and began to bark, not at anyone in particular, but just because she wanted to be part of the action.

Rachel stepped around the mom and daughter to stand by Dixon. "I was going to bring out more tea, but I ran into Abby and realized our shift was coming to a close."

"It's been fun." His gray eyes searched her face, sending a shiver coursing down her spine. "Thank you for allowing me to share your day."

"Thank you for all your help." She glanced at the tent. "That was more difficult to put together than I thought. I don't believe Eva Grace and I would have gotten it together."

"I think you would have." His eyes never left her face. "You're strong and competent. I believe you can do whatever you set your mind to."

In that moment, without warning, Rachel felt her defenses crumble and her heart open. "I appreciate the vote of confidence."

Their gazes remained locked until Abby cleared her throat. "Would you like to stay for dinner? Jonah should be home any minute."

"Thanks," Dixon said. "But I have some work needing my attention."

"It's sweet of you to invite me, but I want to check on Violet." Rachel gave a little chuckle. "See what mischief she's gotten into."

"I understand." Abby gave Rachel a hug and patted Dixon's arm. "Thank you both again."

"See you later, Eva Grace."

Rachel's words had the child wailing, "I don't want you to go."

"We'll be back." Dixon's voice was matter-of-fact. "You can act out the next book in the Humphrey series."

"Humphrey?" Rachel asked.

"He's a hamster," Dixon informed her. "A funny, clever hamster."

"Next time," Eva Grace declared, appearing mollified, "we'll do two books."

"Deal." Dixon lifted a hand, and the two bumped fists.

Rachel strode down the front steps with Dixon at her side, pausing at the bottom to turn and wave before turning toward home.

They'd gone nearly a block when she realized that Greenbriar Place was in the opposite direction.

Rachel stopped abruptly and pointed. "Your home is that way."

Dixon pointed in the direction they'd been traveling. "Your place is that way."

"What does that matter?"

"I'd think it'd be obvious." He smiled. "I'm going home with you."

CHAPTER EIGHT

Dixon whistled under his breath as he left Rachel's house. The look in her eyes when he'd said he was coming home with her had been priceless. Actually, he'd simply wanted to make sure she got safely inside.

It was a beautiful day, and he didn't mind the extra walking. His appointment with Lilian this evening wasn't until seven thirty, so he had plenty of time.

"Can I give you a lift?"

Dixon walked over to Leo's shiny BMW roadster. "Since you're driving this, sure."

He rounded the front of the vehicle and took a seat.

"Where are you headed?" Leo asked.

"Home."

"What are you doing in this neighborhood?"

"I could ask you the same question."

"There's an accident over on Cedar. Traffic is backed up. I thought I'd wind my way through the neighborhood." Leo slanted a glance at Dixon.

"I walked Rachel home from Abby's." Dixon lifted a staying hand at the speculation in Leo's eyes. "Nothing like that. Marc has been giving her a hard time since she broke up with him. We were over at Abby's, and I wanted to make sure she got home without him causing trouble."

Leo's blue eyes hardened. "Do you think he might?"

"He's a lot like Gloria." Dixon shrugged. "Oh, not as charismatic or wily, but same narcissistic personality. Once he realizes he isn't going to get her back, his thoughts will turn to payback."

"Nell isn't going to like hearing this." Leo slammed a hand against the steering wheel. "What am I saying? I don't like hearing that joker might hurt Rachel."

"Not on my watch," Dixon muttered, his gaze focused on the trees whizzing by.

Leo cocked his head. "How are you going to stop it from happening?"

"I'm going to stay close." Dixon had realized that during the short distance he'd covered from Rachel's house, and a solid plan had formed in his head. "She should be safe at the food bank and around friends. Her most vulnerable times are when she's alone at night."

"Too bad she didn't get a dog instead of a cat," Leo mused.

"I reminded her to keep her doors locked."

"Do you think she heard you?"

"I'm not sure she truly believes he could be dangerous." Dixon's lips quirked up. "Just like no one would believe our mother is a psychopath."

Dixon didn't need to convince Leo. He'd seen the scars on Nell's body, most of them on her torso where they would be hidden by her clothing.

"When did Rachel last see Marc?"

"Today. She was having lunch with Lilian and Eva Grace, and he sat himself down at their table." A simmering anger heated Dixon's blood. "He wouldn't have left if Lilian hadn't asked him to walk her to the courthouse."

"Why don't you and Rachel come over for dinner tonight? We can toss some steaks on the grill."

"Rachel's got pride. If Nell pushes too hard—"

"Nell and Rachel have been friends for a long time."

Which Dixon translated as *she knows her better than you do.* Which should be true, was likely true, but Dixon and Rachel had a connection that was impossible to explain.

"I don't think she'll come for dinner. She won't want to leave the cat." Dixon gave him the reason she'd given Abby.

"Then we'll just have to go to her."

Other than her siblings, Rachel had never had anyone invite themselves over for dinner. But that's what Nell had done. Actually, she'd invited herself, her fiancée and Dixon.

When Rachel had stammered a protest, Nell had told her they'd bring the steaks and the sides, so all she needed to provide was the grill.

"I hope you don't mind, Violet." Rachel turned to the cat as she freshened her makeup at the small dressing table in Violet's room.

The cat stared at her for a long moment with those eerie blue eyes, then shot one leg up in the air and began to wash.

Rachel's hands shook slightly as she added more mascara. She wasn't nervous. She knew Leo and Nell too well to be nervous about hosting them in her home. Heck, Nell felt like family.

It was Dixon who had her insides quivering.

For one heart-stopping moment this afternoon, she'd thought he was going to kiss her. And she'd have let him.

There was this strange electricity in the air whenever they were together. Perhaps once she kissed him, the electricity would drop to a dull hum.

The doorbell rang, and Rachel pushed to her feet, glancing at the clock on the wall. "They're early."

The cat looked up, then rose and stretched.

"I'm glad you came to live with me, Violet," she said, shutting the door behind her on the way out of the room.

Her blood surged with anticipation as she crossed to the heavy wooden door. Locked, just as Dixon had instructed, though she really thought that was overkill.

"If you'd come fifteen minutes earlier, you would have caught me in the shower…" Her voice trailed off.

Marc stood in the doorway, a bouquet of wildflowers in his hand. He stepped inside and glanced around the living room before turning back to her.

"Planning a party?" His voice took on a hard edge. "Or do you have a date?"

"Nell and Leo are coming for dinner." Though her heart hammered in her chest, Rachel managed a smile. "What are you doing here?"

"I saw these in the florist's window and thought of you." He handed the bouquet to her. "I know spider mums are your favorite."

"Thank you, Marc." How long had it been since she'd told him her favorite flower? "That's sweet of you."

Some of the tension left his face as he moved around the room, trailing his fingers over the furniture. He paused when Violet cried out in the other room.

His gaze shot to her. "You have a baby?"

"Cat." She couldn't help but smile. "Siamese."

"I've never liked cats."

He made the declaration as if that ended the topic. Though Rachel bristled, she reminded herself that plenty of people didn't like cats.

Marc shoved his hands into his pockets, rocked back on his heels. "You and I were together for a long time. I know you're angry with me, but I believe we can get through this. I want us to get through this. Tell me you're willing to put aside your pride and meet me halfway."

Rachel steeled herself against the nearly overwhelming urge to agree. Standing before her was sweet, conciliatory Marc. This was the side of him that caused her such confusion.

At one time, she'd wanted to be fair, to try to make things work between them. She didn't feel that way anymore.

Rachel casually moved back, placing just a little extra distance between them. Marc likely expected the flowers and the appeal to her soft nature were enough to get back in her good graces.

How many minutes had passed? One? Three? Five?

Her company should be arriving within the next ten minutes. Hopefully, they'd be early. Could she stall that long?

"Let me put these beauties in some water." Though the house was the perfect size for her, at the moment Rachel wished it was larger.

She pulled a vase from one cupboard and was grateful Marc didn't follow her. Unfortunately, due to her home's open-floor plan, he remained only steps away.

His eyes remained fixed on her as she arranged the mixture, which included Peruvian lilies and bicolored carnations as well as lush greenery.

Instead of putting the vase in the living room, she put it in the center of the dining table. She looked up to find him still staring at her.

Something in those pale blue eyes sent a shiver down her spine. Still, she managed a smile. "The lavender color is striking."

It was as if she'd issued an invitation. She saw it in his eyes as he started across the room.

Rachel held up a hand. "Marc. I want to be friends. But nothing more."

He stopped, a little closer than she preferred, but he halted. "Are you saying you're willing to toss everything we've shared out the window over something that was your fault? I said I'm willing to meet you halfway."

"My fault?" Rachel didn't have to close her eyes to see him and that woman in the hotel room.

"You put me last. Over and over. Still, I tried." He blew out a harsh breath. "I already explained about me and Lori."

"Lori." Rachel knew better than to poke a bear, but the hurt and anger of that afternoon returned in spades. "Well, you and *Lori* can have all the hotel room fun you want. I'm not in the picture. I appreciate you wanting to smooth things over, but—"

"Think again."

Rachel gasped as his fingers closed around her biceps, and he gave her a little shake.

"You don't tell me how things will be." The look in his eyes had fear coursing up her spine. "I tell you."

"Marc, let go." She struggled to pull free, but he was stronger. "You're hurting me."

He moved closer, and Rachel smelled the alcohol on his breath.

"You'll do just as I say."

Remain calm, she told herself. Whatever he had planned, she wanted no part of it.

He pulled her to him and licked her ear, causing her stomach to revolt.

Stay calm, she repeated. *Now.*

Quick as a snake, she hit him in the face with an open-handed strike.

Ignoring his howl of outrage and pain, she followed up with a knee to his groin.

He cried out and dropped to the floor.

"Is everything okay?"

Rachel looked up to see Leo, Nell and Dixon gazing down at Marc. She wasn't sure which of them had asked the question, wasn't sure it even mattered.

She met their shocked gazes with a steady one of her own. "I'd appreciate it if you'd get him out of my house."

"Would you like us to call Jonah?" Nell asked as Leo and Dixon jerked Marc to his feet.

"If he comes around again, I'll press charges."

"He'll stay away. Won't you, Marky?" Dixon's voice had a sinister quality unlike anything she'd heard from him before.

Leo gave the arm he held a shake, and Marc stared at her through surprisingly defiant eyes. "I could charge you with assault."

Rachel laughed, the sound loud, robust and full. Why had she put up with this man for as long as she had? "Go ahead. I dare you."

"You're not worth the trouble."

"Get him out of here," Nell said to her fiancé, then moved to Rachel's side. "We'll start the grill."

It was nearly nine. Time for him to head home. Instead, Dixon sat on the sofa, Violet on his lap.

After they'd eaten, Rachel had let the cat out of her room. Well, actually, she'd opened the door to introduce Nell to her new housemate, and Violet had shot past the two women.

When the feline saw Dixon, it stopped and began to purr, weaving her way in and out of his legs. Violet hadn't left his side since.

Nell and Leo had left for home, and Dixon had planned to leave then, too. But Rachel had asked him to "babysit" Violet while she disposed of "something."

"Thanks for keeping her occupied," she said upon her return.

"What was wrong with the flowers?" He'd watched her scoop up the pretty bouquet and take it outside.

"Marc gave them to me."

"That's the first time you've mentioned his name since we arrived."

She paused, considered. "I didn't want this evening to be about him. It was fun, talking about Violet—"

Dixon stopped stroking the cat when Violet turned around and nipped him. He merely shrugged and put his hand on the arm of the sofa.

Rachel frowned.

"I know when to stop." He searched her eyes. "I'm guessing Marc didn't."

"He thought he could bring me flowers, say a few nice things —which really weren't all that nice—and everything would be back to the way it was before." Setting the now-empty vase on the counter, she dropped down on the sofa beside him. She reached for the cat. "Let me take her—"

Violet hissed.

Rachel released her hold and sat back. Hurt filled her dark eyes. "I don't think she likes me."

"She does." Dixon stared down at the feline sprawled on his lap, licking her paw. "If I had to guess, I'd say her good experiences have likely been more with men. Once she knows that you can be trusted, she'll warm up."

"Thank you for tossing Marc outside."

"Trust me when I say it was my profound pleasure." He flashed a smile. "You laid him out pretty good."

"Open-handed strike followed by a knee to the groin." This time, it was her turn to smile. "I never knew a basic self-defense course would come in so handy."

"You kept your head."

For some reason, the admiration in his tone had her straightening. "I don't know why people seem to think I'm this sweet, fragile orchid. When, in fact, I'm a milk thistle."

He arched a brow. "Milk thistle? The noxious weed?"

"I prefer to think of it as the prickly plant with the pretty purple flower." Rachel's lips curved ever so slightly. "At times. I believe Marc saw the prickly side of me today."

"I wish we'd gotten here earlier." Dixon blew out a breath, glanced down at the cat.

Soft fingers on his arm had him returning his focus to her.

"I may look like a school librarian," she pushed her glasses up more firmly on her nose, "but I'm strong. I made a mistake in not checking the peephole before opening the door. I won't make that mistake again. I really can take care of myself."

Though on the way over Dixon had told himself he'd keep his hands to himself tonight, he took her fingers and laced them with his. "We all need friends at one point or another in our lives. I hope you know you can call me anytime, day or night."

"I know." Her voice was soft, a little husky and a whole lot sexy. "You're a good man, Dixon Carlyle."

He had no time to think before she leaned forward and kissed him on the mouth.

CHAPTER NINE

Rachel felt the cat streak across her lap and head out of the room. But she wasn't thinking of the cat right now. As soon as her mouth had touched Dixon's, she realized one little kiss wasn't going to be enough.

Not for her.

And from the way his arms rose around her and his mouth returned to hers, not for him either. He tasted sweet, like…she knew it was like something, but her brain was having difficulty making connections.

She'd never, in her entire time on this earth, been kissed like this. He took it slowly, his arms light around her, giving her the time and space he seemed to think she needed.

Instead, she moved in closer, her fingers sliding into his soft hair as his mouth continued to return to hers. There was something about being in his arms, about feeling those firm lips pressed to hers that felt so right.

She didn't want to pull away. The way she felt right now, she could sit here and kiss him all night. Short, sweet kisses. Long, leisurely ones. And when he angled his head and his tongue swept inside her mouth, his kisses made her want to crawl under his skin.

Her heart pounded against her rib cage. The ache that had formed low in her belly had her pressing her body closer, so close that it seemed practically a necessity for him to haul her up onto his lap.

Still, they continued to kiss. Rachel's breath came short and fast, and her fingers slid from his hair to grasp his shoulders. His lips moved to her neck, and she arched back, giving him access, digging her fingers into his skin.

Dixon scattered kisses across her face, behind her ear and down her neck. As his lips approached the scoop of her top, her breasts strained against the lacy fabric of her bra, yearning for his touch.

In all the months that she and Marc had dated, she'd held firm to the lessons her parents had instilled in her growing up. Lessons more suited to another century, if the media hype about sex was to be believed.

She wanted his hands everywhere, and his mouth, that amazing mouth, too. But when she stiffened, need battling with the line in the sand she'd set as a teenager, his mouth drifted upward.

His hands cupped her face, and he kissed her long and slow and sweet before pulling back.

He seemed equally out of breath and off-kilter.

"I should probably get ready for bed."

She hadn't meant anything salacious by the comment, but the word *bed* felt different on her kiss-swollen lips, and an answering heat flared in his eyes.

"Alone," she said, feeling gauche.

"I knew that." He grinned.

Her world steadied. She hadn't been sure how he'd react. Heck, she hadn't been sure they'd ever get to this point. They were friends, that's all.

She'd just gotten out of one relationship and wasn't in any hurry to jump into another one. Especially with a guy who appeared to have his own share of secrets.

But she wouldn't mind kissing him again.

She liked him.

Violet liked him.

Yes, she would kiss him again.

Just not tonight.

"I appreciate you thinking of me." Dixon kept his tone cordial as he saw disappointment skitter across Leo's face. "I simply don't have time to be on a committee."

This wasn't the first time someone had asked, and Dixon doubted it would be the last. But his contact had gone radio-silent the past few days, and Dixon wanted to be ready to roll, depending on which way the cards fell.

Besides, between his clients and attempting to add new ones —like Lilian—his free time was limited. He certainly didn't want to fill those precious hours with Green Machine committee work.

"I think you need to be on this one," Leo pressed. "You—"

Dixon lifted a hand. "Hey, I get it. Your wedding is approaching, and the last thing you want to do is plan some fall festival. I'm sure there are plenty of others you could ask to take your slot."

"Marc and Rachel are on the committee."

Dixon, who'd already started to push up from the chair in Leo's office, dropped back down. "Since when?"

"Since the beginning."

"Who else?"

Leo inclined his head.

"Who else is on the committee?" Dixon repeated the question.

If it was a large one with a lot of members, there would be plenty of people to act as buffers between Rachel and Marc.

If Marc even showed his face.

"Just Marc, Rachel and Lilian. And me. Or you." Leo's expression turned serious. He leaned forward. "Rachel is convinced she can handle him. She did a pretty good job doing just that the other night. But he's a wild card. I don't trust him."

Dixon blew out a breath. "I don't trust him either."

"So will you do it? Will you take my place on the committee?"

The committee met at Matilda's on Friday at ten a.m. As the restaurant didn't open to the public until eleven, they would have all the privacy they needed.

Rachel left work shortly before ten, knowing she could walk to the restaurant in less than five minutes. Because the committee focused on a community event, her supervisor had told her to take whatever time she needed.

It really shouldn't take longer than her lunch hour, though. The plans for the fall festival were nearly completed, with only a few loose ends to be tied up. As Rachel rounded the corner and the inn came in sight, she wondered—for not the first time that morning—if Marc would show up.

If he did, it would be because he wanted the time with Lilian. Rachel firmly believed her knee to his groin had convinced Marc they were done. He would move on, and—her lips tingled as she recalled Dixon's kisses—she would, too.

The clock in the courthouse bell tower began to chime.

One. Two. Three.

Rachel picked up her pace, head down, speed-walking the last block.

Nine. Ten.

She swerved toward the inn's front door, but when her

fingers reached for the large brass handle, she found another hand already there.

"I'm so sorry." She looked up into Dixon's smiling face.

"I wondered when you'd notice me." He spoke in a lazy tone, his appreciative gaze scanning her face. "You look lovely."

"I curled my hair," she mumbled, then reached for the handle, this time jerking the door open. "I'd love to stay and chat, but I'm late for a meeting."

"It just so happens that I'm also late." He stepped back, holding the door open, and gestured her inside.

Rachel hadn't realized there was another meeting going on, but didn't have the time to ask him about it. It didn't really matter. Her committee wouldn't be discussing anything sensitive.

Though late, she paused to greet Matilda. As far as she was concerned, lateness was no excuse for rudeness.

"Good morning." Rachel let her gaze linger on Matilda and her stylish blue-and-white-checked day dress popular in the 1940s. The lace handkerchief peeking from one breast pocket was a sweet touch. "You're wearing one of my favorite dresses today."

"Each time I put it on, I'm reminded why day dresses were so popular. It's very comfortable." Matilda glanced down and held up one foot, showing off a pair of white heeled oxfords. "And these keep my feet comfortable all day."

"Thank you for letting us meet—"

"It's my pleasure." Matilda cut her off with an apologetic smile. "Lilian is giving me the send-them-over wave. She said something about having another meeting at eleven. I'll give you five minutes, then I'll be over to get your order."

Matilda turned to Dixon. "Always a pleasure to see you, Mr. Carlyle."

Dixon leaned over and brushed her cheeks with his lips. "The pleasure is all mine, Ms. Lovejoy."

Matilda's trill of laughter followed Rachel to the table. She told herself she didn't care who the man kissed. But her bright mood dimmed and she had to force a smile as she reached the table.

"I'm sorry I'm late." Rachel slipped into the seat next to Lilian.

"I'm simply happy the two of you showed up. For a second, I wondered if I'd be a committee of one."

"The two of us?" Before the question left her lips, Dixon took the seat beside her.

"Dixon is replacing Leo on the committee." Lilian offered him a brilliant smile. "Thank you for taking on the challenge."

"Always happy to serve my new community."

To Rachel's ears, he sounded surprisingly sincere.

"What happened to Leo?" Rachel asked.

"Too much work, too little time." Lilian glanced at the diamond-encrusted watch on her wrist. "It appears Marc won't be joining us, though I didn't receive any notification from him."

Rachel said nothing, but the knot in her chest relaxed. And when Matilda arrived to take their order, she actually felt as if she could eat.

"What still needs to be done?" Dixon asked when Matilda left to get their drinks.

"You're eager to jump right in." Lilian nodded her approval. "I like your attitude."

"Apologies," Marc called out as he breezed into the restaurant and wound his way to their table. His hair was windblown, and he wore a suit. He took the chair between Dixon and Lilian at the four-top. "I saw a client in the city this morning, and the train back was running late."

He smiled at Lilian, ignoring Dixon and Rachel. "What have I missed?"

"We've ordered, and was just explaining to Rachel that Dixon has replaced Leo on the committee."

Marc frowned, still keeping his focus on Lilian. "Why?"

"Leo has too much on his plate right now. He approached

Dixon, who agreed to help us tie up the final details." Lilian's tone made it clear that was the end of the subject.

The slight tightening of Matilda's lips when she brought the drinks and took Marc's order told Rachel that Matilda had heard about her altercation with the man.

"Well," Lilian smiled pleasantly, "as we all have places to go and things to do, shall we get down to business?"

The knot in the pit of Rachel's belly returned as she sensed Marc's assessing gaze. She tried her best to keep her eyes on Lilian. It wasn't easy, considering Marc sat directly across from her.

She pushed her food around on her plate while Lilian handed out the list of vendors confirmed for booths in the Green. "I apologize for not getting this emailed out before our meeting. It's been a crazy few days for me."

"In what regard?" Marc's pale eyes gleamed.

Lilian offered him an enigmatic smile. "Since time is short, I think we should stick to committee work."

"I'm impressed." Dixon studied the sheet. "There's a little something here to appeal to everyone."

"That was the goal." Rachel exchanged a smile with Dixon.

"I don't see anything on here about leftover party prizes, Rachel." Marc used her name, apparently figuring it would be the only way to get her attention.

Instead of responding directly to Marc, Rachel turned back to Dixon. "He's referring to the plan to solicit community members for prizes that were left over from their children's parties. The thought was that it would reduce our cost for game prizes."

Rachel shifted her attention to Lilian. "I apologize for not getting this information to you sooner, since I was the one who brought up the possibility. However, after doing more research I discovered it isn't practical. As we're already getting a very good discount on the prizes we're ordering, my recommendation is to order all prizes. The amount of time to oversee donations would make buying the prizes more practical for a large community event."

"Taking that option off the table wasn't your decision to make." Marc's voice stopped just short of rudeness. "This is a committee and—"

"Marc." Lilian's voice held a firmness that reminded Rachel this woman could be a formidable foe. Or ally. "In the past months, we've all been charged with researching different possibilities. Rachel has researched this matter, so I trust her judgment. The figures and report will be in the email. Now, let's move on."

By the time the meeting ended, Rachel was tasked with touching base with the volunteer committee chair. Dixon was to review the social media plan and offer suggestions, while Marc would do one last review of booth placement.

"Marc and Rachel, thank you for your help in making this committee run smoothly." Lilian smiled at Dixon. "It's good to have you on the team." She glanced at her watch and rose. "I'm sorry, but I need to scoot."

Marc pushed back his chair with a clatter. He startled Lilian by stepping in front of her. "I just need a few minutes of your time."

Rachel slowly stood, wishing she could simply walk away. The lunch bill had been paid, and there was really no reason to linger. Other than she refused to leave Lilian alone with this man.

Dixon pushed to his feet and pretended to be reading a text. But Rachel noticed he, too, was watching what was going on between Lilian and Marc.

"I'm sorry, Marc." Lilian's voice carried to where Rachel and Dixon stood. "I've got an appointment, and I don't want to be late."

"It won't take long." His jaw jutted out. "Five minutes is all I need."

"Unfortunately, I don't have even that much time." Though

she was still amiable, ice coated Lilian's words. "Now please step out of my way and let me pass."

Dixon tensed.

Rachel held her breath.

Lilian inclined her head, the polite smile still fixed on her lips.

"Of course," Marc said in a pleasant voice. "Another time."

Once Lilian moved past them, Rachel was ready to leave. She felt Marc's eyes on her as she brushed past him, but she didn't turn back.

She'd already made it clear she wanted nothing more to do with him. Hopefully, today's committee meeting had reinforced that fact.

CHAPTER TEN

Dixon strolled beside Rachel toward the food bank in companionable silence. He hadn't asked if he could walk her back to work. Instead, he simply fell into step beside her as if that's the direction he was headed.

He thought about telling her just how much he admired her composure during the meeting, but swallowed the words at the last minute. For the past few days, it seemed as if far too many of their conversations had involved Marc Koenig.

When the large metal building that housed the food bank came into view, Dixon cleared his throat.

"I assume you'll be at the party Saturday night." Well, that was smooth, he thought with disgust. What was it about this woman that turned him into a teenager?

No, not a teenager. He'd been smooth around girls even back then.

Rachel slanted a sideways glance at him. "Are you referring to the cocktail party at Leo's home?"

"That's the one." And his downward slide continued.

"Of course I'm going." Her dark eyes searched his, and he saw the puzzlement. "You'll be there, right?"

Why had he even asked? It was a given that they'd both be there, since he was the bride's brother and the groom's best man, and Rachel was not only a bridesmaid, she was also Nell's good friend.

"I am." He cleared his throat again as his mouth went dry. "I thought—hoped—we might go together."

A smile lifted the corners of her lips. "That sounds nice."

The weight pressing against Dixon's chest lifted. "Yeah?"

"Yeah." Her dark eyes shone. "Pick me up at eight?"

"I'll be there." He couldn't help it. Dixon gave her a quick hug, surprised and pleased when she hugged him back.

Dixon turned to go, his mind leaping ahead to Saturday night and the fun he and Rachel would have at the party. He whistled under his breath as he started back down the street, not noticing the man with the pale eyes standing against a nearby building, watching him leave.

His long strides covered the distance he and Rachel had just come in half the time. He unlocked his car and opened the door when a ping sounded.

Pulling the phone from his pocket, he scrolled to his texts. His lips tightened as he read the latest.

Slipping into the car, he pulled the door shut and called his sister.

The fact that she answered told him she could talk. At least briefly. "I got another text from my contact in Bakersfield."

"And?" Nell's voice betrayed no emotion.

"Gloria, or rather her attorney—"

"You know she's calling the shots."

"Yes," he agreed. "Well, word is she's been offered a deal, but she's balking. She refuses to admit any guilt."

"Which means she wants it all on you."

Dixon closed his eyes for a second, rubbed the bridge of his nose. "We both knew this is how she'd play it. Taking no responsibility is classic Gloria."

Nell gave a humorless laugh. "The thing is, there's so much of her in that crime and very little of you. Other than they probably guess she needed assistance with the technical part."

"I'm thinking of calling the ADA, offering to make my own deal in exchange for immunity." As he spoke, he slipped out of the car, unable to sit still any longer.

"It's a risk." His sister hesitated for several long moments. "As it stands right now, they don't know where you are. It would take time and resources to find you, especially for this kind of case."

"What do you mean by 'this kind of case'?"

"It isn't exactly high profile, and it occurred a number of years ago."

Dixon, too tense to sit still, exited the car and crossed the street. As the sidewalk grew crowded, he chose a deserted path that wound its way through the Green. Still, when he responded, he kept his voice low. "Remember how you felt when Stanley Britten found you?"

Nell's eyes closed for a brief moment. "I was convinced the life I'd been building here was over."

"Well, yours had a happy ending—"

"I don't know if Stanley will come back and—"

"He's headed for a federal penitentiary." Dixon waved aside her worries. "The reason I bring him up is because I don't want that to be me. Whether it's in two years or ten, I don't want to worry about my past showing up when I least expect it. The only thing from my time with Gloria that could pose a problem is the Bakersfield job."

"They might never find you. You covered your tracks well."

"You did, too. Stanley still found you."

"Yes, he did." Nell expelled a breath. "Think very carefully before acting."

"It's all I've thought of since I heard of her arrest." Dixon paused at a small bridge over a meandering stream. "I'm going to ask my contact in Bakersfield to see if he can get a feel for how much it's worth to those agencies to nail Gloria to the wall."

When Nell said nothing, Dixon added, "The murder of Bobby John is still an open case."

"We were kids when she killed him." Nell lowered her voice, though he knew she was alone. She never would have spoken so freely if there was the slightest chance someone could overhear.

"I remember enough. Details that would help them solve that case. Information that could be used to obtain a conviction." His voice turned taut as steel. "Gloria deserves to pay for everything she did, not only to others, but to us. The beatings and, well, everything."

Dixon didn't like to think about his childhood. The abuse had been both mental and physical. It had scarred him and Nell. But the happiness that Nell had found with Leo gave Dixon hope. That time in their lives didn't have to define them. "I'll keep you updated."

"You'll be at the party on Saturday?"

He didn't like hearing the question in her voice, the wondering if she could count on him. Still, he understood. They'd spent a number of years apart and had only recently found their way back to each other.

"I wouldn't miss it," he told her.

One of these days, he would prove to Nell—and to himself—that Dixon Carlyle was someone who could be counted on.

Rachel gazed down at the red, open-backed, lace dress. She'd picked it up on sale during a Chicago shopping trip last year, but hadn't conjured up the nerve to wear it before tonight. The dress was stylish and totally not her normal vibe.

Still, when she slipped it on, it made her feel young, carefree and…well, sexy. She'd experimented with her hair, pulling the cream-colored strands up and back in a kind of messy bun. When that was done, her makeup had gotten the attention.

She shifted her gaze back to the mirror on her living room wall as she waited for Dixon's knock. A stranger stared back at her, and she found herself smiling at the woman with the shining eyes and red lips.

A knock sounded at the door. Or was that simply the beating of her own heart?

Rachel paused and waited for the second knock before moving to the peephole. She'd made the mistake once of assuming she knew who stood on her porch. She wouldn't do that again.

Once she confirmed who was on the other side, she pulled the door open.

Dixon looked amazing. His classically handsome features and dark suit, gray shirt and burgundy tie were a potent combination.

Rachel swallowed against the sudden dryness in her throat. The man could have easily graced the cover of any men's fashion magazine. Even his dark hair looked freshly cut.

Then again, Dixon's raven-colored hair always looked perfect. She motioned him inside. "You're right on time."

"I aim to please."

Once she shut the door behind him, he studied her.

Rachel shivered even as heat raced through her veins at his slow, head-to-toe perusal.

"You look amazing." Dixon practically breathed the words, his gaze seeming to linger on her cherry-red lips.

"That's exactly what I was about to say about you." She gave a little laugh. "I'd say we clean up good, but you, well, you always look amazing."

She clamped her lips together as humor danced in his gray eyes. Why oh why had she added that last comment? Even as she thought the question, Rachel knew why. Being this close to Dixon had her feeling off-balance.

The way he looked at her, at her mouth, had her remembering how good he tasted.

"Thank you, Rachel."

She blinked.

"For the nice compliment."

"Oh, yeah, that." She fluttered a hand in the air and moistened her tingling lips with the tip of her tongue.

Big mistake.

Or, maybe not.

His eyes went dark. He took a step closer just as her phone began to play *Flight of the Bumblebee.*

Dixon's gaze shot to her beaded clutch.

"I put an alert on my phone so I'd know when it was time to leave." She flushed as she moved to the purse to still the music. Anal to the nth degree, that's how she sounded. Nothing said they had to be there precisely at the time listed on the invitation. This was a cocktail party, not a sit-down dinner.

Marc had constantly told her she needed to chill out, that she was too serious, too intense. More times than she could count, he'd told her that her attitude took the fun out of events.

"We don't have to rush off," she said quickly. Her voice trembled with nerves. Even her laugh spiked too high. "Nothing says we have to walk through the door at eight o'clock."

Dixon studied her for a long moment. "Your attention to detail is only one of the many things I admire about you."

Though his words brought a warm rush of pleasure, Rachel told herself he was likely only being kind. She waved aside the compliment.

He took her hand and closed his over it, his gaze remaining steady on her face. "I'm serious. You realize that seeing us there will ease any of Nell's worries."

When he gave her hand a squeeze, then released it, she nearly sighed. She grabbed her purse, signaling she was ready to leave.

On the short drive over to Leo's house, Rachel turned his

comment over and over in her mind. "Why would your sister be worried we wouldn't show? We both RSVP'd."

"Some people RSVP, then blow off the party."

"Not us," Rachel said.

"No. Not us." Dixon slanted a look in her direction. "I said that about Nell because I think she knows how much I like having you all to myself."

Rachel didn't immediately speak as she fought to process his words. If she hadn't known better, she might think Dixon really liked her. Not just the way friends like each other, but more…

A chuckle escaped his lips, a low, pleasant, rumbling sound. "But as much as that thought appeals to me, I'm not sure it holds the same appeal for you. So, we'll—"

She placed a hand on his coat sleeve, surprised at her boldness. "I wish I could spend the evening with just you."

Those slate-gray eyes searched hers. "But tonight we go to the party."

She nodded. "Tonight we go to the party."

"Which is okay," Dixon said, opening the door for her. "There will be other nights for us."

Rachel smiled. She liked the sound of that. In fact, she liked it very much.

"You and Rachel?" Leo gestured with a glass of champagne to where Rachel was talking with Abby and Nell. "Are you two…?"

As it was just Dixon and his future brother-in-law at the moment, Dixon answered honestly. "We're exploring options."

"I don't see the two of you together." Leo searched the room, and his gaze settled on Jackie Rollins. "You seem more like someone who'd be drawn to Jackie."

Abby's sister-in-law was not only blonde and beautiful, with a mane of curly hair and a killer figure, she had a vibrant personality that drew men to her.

Right now, she was entertaining several with a story that had everyone around her laughing.

"Jackie and I went out a couple of times." At the moment, Dixon couldn't recall what he and the grade-school teacher had even discussed.

Leo arched a brow. "No spark?"

Dixon lifted a tiny cracker topped with paté from his plate. "Not enough to keep seeing her."

"After my previous fiancée and I split, I dated a lot of different women." Once again, Leo's gaze sought out Nell. "Once I met your sister, it was all over."

As if she could feel his eyes on her, Nell turned and shot Leo a blinding smile.

"Well, all over for me," Leo added with a rueful smile. "I still had to convince her to give me a shot."

"Nell and I, we come with a lot of baggage."

"All the more reason to find someone willing to share the load." Leo slapped him on the shoulder.

"I'm not sure I know anyone that strong." Still, Dixon found his gaze shifting to Rachel. "I've left her alone for too long."

At Leo's questioning glance, Dixon shrugged. "We came together. I don't want her to think I dumped her to socialize."

Leo opened his mouth, then appeared to think better of his initial impulse. "Marc used to do that to her, especially if there was someone in attendance he wanted to suck up to. She may be more sensitive because of that."

"Rachel wouldn't complain. She likely doesn't even notice I'm not around. She seems to be enjoying herself." As Dixon watched her lean close to Nell and say something that once again had the group laughing, he wondered if Rachel realized she outshone every woman in this room tonight.

"You want to spend time with her."

"I do," Dixon admitted. "I don't know how much time together we'll have."

Leo waved over a passing waiter and took a spring roll from the tray.

"No, thank you," Dixon said in response to the young waiter's questioning glance.

Leo waited to speak until the waiter was out of earshot. Even then, he kept his voice low. "You're referring to the California incident."

A muscle in Dixon's jaw jumped. While he knew Nell shared practically everything with her fiancé—and he was fine with that —this was a sensitive, legal matter. The less anyone else knew about it, and that included Leo, the better. "She told you."

He heard the accusation in his voice. Which wasn't fair. Nell was the one he needed to be speaking with about this breach of trust.

"Only that you were facing your own Waterloo. I only know that it has to do with your mother's incarceration in California."

Dixon felt his shoulders relax.

"I won't press Nell for details." Leo met Dixon's eyes. "But I want you to know that if you need me, I'll help in any way I can."

Oddly touched, Dixon had to clear his throat. "I appreciate the offer."

"Hey, we're practically brothers." Leo flashed a grin. "If you can't count on family, who can you count on?"

Near the large French doors that opened out to a lovely garden area, Mathis, Leo's middle brother, studied his eldest brother, Wells. Wells, in that pointed way of his, appeared determined to convince Lilian that her plan was stupid and should be abandoned.

Okay, Matt thought, so maybe Wells hadn't used the word

stupid. Like all the Pomeroys, Wells adored Lilian. He would never disparage her by using such a word to describe the renovation plan she was proposing.

But that was clearly the point his arrogant brother was trying to drive home. And Wells was becoming increasingly frustrated. Despite all his practical points, which he recited slowly and in a tone more appropriate for counseling a third-grader, Lilian refused to concede to his wisdom.

Her expression held a bulldog look that would have had Matt holding up his hands and backing away. Wells stood his ground.

When she finally replied, Lilian resorted to grade-schoolese, speaking to Wells as he'd spoken to her. "While it may not make sense to you, this is not purely a financial issue for me. I—"

The sudden tight set to his eldest brother's jaw had Matt hiding a grin.

Suddenly, Wells whirled, fixing his intense gaze on Matt. "Surely you see my point."

"Innocent bystander." Matt lifted his hands as Lilian's gaze settled on him. "This battle is between the two of you."

"It's your development company as well as mine," Wells snapped.

They both knew that was a load of crap. WLM might be a partnership, but Wells ran the show. If the business mattered more to him, Matt would have done more to assert his rights. For now, it was easier to sit back and let Wells call the shots.

When the silence lengthened and Matt realized that Wells expected an answer, he simply shrugged. "I thought this was a party. Why are we even talking business?"

"I'm afraid that's my fault." Lilian shot an apologetic look in Wells's direction

The quick flash of anger in his brother's eyes toward him was no surprise. "That's a cop-out. You never want to commit."

The disparaging comment wasn't anything Matt hadn't heard

before. Still, it stung. He could get along with most people, but he and Wells were like oil and water.

Always had been. Likely always would be.

Unless he made the break. But it would have to be complete, or he'd get sucked back into the family.

Wells took a step toward Matt, a belligerent look on his face. He was in the mood to argue, and it showed.

As much as his brother could irritate the hell out of him, Matt understood what had Wells wound so tightly tonight.

Matt had no doubt that seeing Leo so happy with Nell had thoughts of Dani, Wells's wife and the love of his life, front and center tonight. Dani had perished, along with their sister Kit, in a helicopter crash several years back.

Wells had changed since Dani's death, and now, seeing Leo enjoying a loving relationship only made his own loss more pronounced.

"Tell us your thoughts on this matter, and we'll let the subject drop." Wells's smile looked more like a grimace, but for Lilian's sake he was trying.

Matt glanced at the French doors and cursed himself. If he'd been more proactive, he could have slipped out ten minutes ago and avoided this conversation.

"Let me make sure I've got this right." Matt spread his hands and kept his gaze on Lilian. "You're interested in renovating the dance hall building out on Appley?"

"That's right." A wistful smile lifted Lilian's lips. "When we were young, my husband and I spent many happy Saturday nights there. They used to have dances for teenagers—they called it Keen Time. And the high school held their proms there."

Matt offered her an encouraging smile. "What is it you have in mind in terms of renovation?"

"Weren't you listening?" Wells interjected. "We've already gone over this."

They probably had, but Wells's suspicions were correct. Matt hadn't been listening. But there was no chance he was admitting that to his brother. He kept his gaze focused on Lilian. "You thought maybe it could be transformed into…"

Matt let his voice trail off, and just as he hoped, she jumped in.

"Perhaps a series of shops geared toward small entrepreneurs. Maybe a restaurant. Whatever it is, I'd like it to also house something that would appeal to teenagers." Lilian finally took a sip of the champagne she'd been holding for the past ten minutes. "There are so many possibilities. That's where your firm and an architect could come in. I just don't want the building destroyed or to fall into further ruin. It's nearly there now. If it sits empty for much longer, it'll be too far gone and have to be torn down."

"That seems an accurate assessment," Matt agreed. "While I'm not sure putting money in the place is a good use of your resources—"

"Thank Goodness, you're showing some common sense," Wells said. "I—"

"It is her money." He glanced at Wells. "I say if she wants to do it, we find a way to make it happen."

Lilian's tense expression softened. She reached out a hand and grasped Matt's coat sleeve. "Thank you."

"I'm sorry. I don't agree." To his credit, Wells actually did look sorry.

Was Wells sorry that he'd pushed for his brother's input? Or sorry that he felt compelled to say no to a woman who was like a second mother to him?

"Lilian." Wells stepped close, his voice thick with emotion. "You know I love you. Every single member of the Pomeroy family loves you. Which is why I can't give my blessing to this venture. It would be a costly and time-consuming restoration with very little chance of success."

The smile that had blossomed on Lilian's lips faded. She blinked rapidly and cleared her throat.

Matt opened his mouth, but shut it at the slight shake of her head.

Perfect timing, he thought, when he saw Leo and Nell approach.

"Enjoying the party?" Leo asked, his fingers linked with Nell's, a goofy *I'm so in love* smile on his face.

Wells had looked that way once, Matt recalled, and felt some of his anger toward his brother ebb. Dani's death had hit his brother hard.

In many ways, she'd been the glue that had kept him and Wells together.

"It's a great party," Matt said when the heartbeat of silence lengthened. He gestured toward Lilian and Wells.

"You appeared to be having an intense discussion when we walked up." Nell's voice might be light, but concern filled her eyes.

Leo was right. The woman missed nothing.

Matt was still trying to formulate a suitable reply when Lilian spoke.

"My fault." She offered Leo and Nell an apologetic smile. "I just wanted to pick the brains of these two about a project I'm considering."

Interest sparked in Leo's eyes. "What kind of project?"

"One that—" Wells began before Lilian cut him off.

"We don't need to discuss at a party." Lilian waved an airy hand, then turned to Matt. "I'm in the mood to peruse the dessert table, but I'd like company. Come with me?"

"There is nothing I'd like more."

CHAPTER ELEVEN

Dixon reunited with Rachel, and over the next hour, they made their way around the room. The woman knew everyone, he realized with a sense of awe. Not only knew their names, but was well acquainted with the details of their lives.

The other thing he noticed was that everyone seemed to like her. Of course, what wasn't to like? She was smart, with a keen wit, but she didn't feel the need to be the focus of every conversation. In fact, quite the opposite. He noticed Rachel preferred to listen, rather than talk.

It was easy to feel comfortable in her presence. Even he, who prided himself on blending in, felt more relaxed when he was with her.

"Nell." Rachel's voice pulled him back from his thoughts.

Dixon looked up just in time to see her give his sister a hug. "This is such a lovely party. Thank you so much for inviting me."

For the first time that night, Nell and Leo weren't surrounded by a bunch of friends or family.

"I couldn't imagine having a party without you." Nell shifted her gaze to Dixon. "Or without you."

"Good food. Excellent champagne." Dixon lifted his glass. "Not to mention lots of interesting people."

"It's been fun for us, also." Leo glanced over to where his parents, Tim and Marty, chatted amiably with Hank and his son, Beau. "I've seen Mom and Dad more in the last three months than I have in the last three years."

"You're going to love having Marty for a mother-in-law." Rachel's voice softened as she spoke to Nell. "She's a genuinely nice person."

"I feel blessed." Nell cast a quick glance in Dixon's direction. "Leo's entire family has been welcoming. And to have my brother in town is the icing on the cake."

"Blessed? Icing on the cake?" Dixon stepped forward and laid the back of his hand against Nell's forehead. "No temperature. Who are you? What have you done with my sister?"

Nell laughed, the sound so joyous it arrowed straight to Dixon's heart.

How many times when they were younger had they promised themselves that once they got away from Gloria, they could have the life they wanted, the life they deserved?

Now, it was happening for Nell. In a few weeks, she would marry a man she not only loved, but one she considered her best friend. His family had accepted her and made her one of them.

Which meant if things went south for him and he had to leave Hazel Green, she'd be okay.

The conversation switched back to the wedding, which was all anyone could seem to talk about lately. Nell, he knew, would have been happy getting married by a justice of the peace. It had been Marty who'd wanted her to have the wedding of her dreams.

The past six months had been stressful ones for Marty and the US senator. When Tim's good friend and legislative director, Steve Olssen, had been charged with taking bribes, Tim's entire political future had been put at risk.

The latest polls indicated Tim was weathering the political storm, and the upcoming wedding of her youngest son had given Marty something happy to focus on.

"—you and Rachel?"

Dixon pulled his thoughts back and realized the wedding chatter must have ended. The expectant looks on everyone's faces had Dixon realizing that whatever question he'd missed had been directed at him.

Leo offered a smile, as if understanding the tedium of wedding-plan discussions. "Nell was asking if you and Rachel would like to go out with us on the boat Sunday afternoon."

"I've never water-skied before," Rachel demurred, although the light in her eyes told Dixon she'd be willing to give it a try.

Still, she didn't say more, as if realizing this was a couple's invitation.

Dixon had skied a handful of times. He was athletic, so he'd caught on quickly. He wasn't sure why he hesitated. This should be an easy yes. And yet, he hesitated. Somehow, to plan a happy double date while everything in Bakersfield was hanging over him, seemed wrong.

But, heck, he thought as Rachel's smile dimmed, it was simply an afternoon in the water. And being with her would keep his mind off his tenuous future.

"Sounds like fun to me." He slanted a glance at Rachel. "If you're available, that is."

The smile she offered him before shifting her attention to Nell and Leo to get the details told Dixon one thing.

He could easily lose his heart over this woman.

For his sake, and hers, he had to make sure that didn't happen.

∽

In the water, Rachel pushed a wet strand of hair behind her ear and let the sun warm her face. She tried to recall why she'd ever thought an afternoon of water-skiing would be fun.

Oh, the lake was beautiful and remarkably uncrowded, thanks to a big boat and sports show going on in a nearby town. She'd loved watching from the safety of the boat as Nell, Leo and Dixon got up on skis.

When it came her time, she was willing to try. But according to Leo, she straightened her legs too soon. And she'd held on to the handle, instead of letting go.

"You can do it," Dixon called from the back of the boat. "Arms straight. Knees to chest."

He'd been better than he let on, Rachel thought, or perhaps he simply had more natural talent. She'd never been particularly athletic, although she could hit a ball, shoot a basket and ride a unicycle.

None of these skills helped her now.

"Ready?" Dixon called.

She nodded.

Instead of hitting the throttle as he'd done before, Leo started picking up speed slowly. Nell kept her eyes on Rachel.

"Keep your arms locked straight."

Rachel could barely hear Dixon's shout over the roar of the motor. He was repeating what he'd said seconds before.

As she rose out of the water, Rachel forced herself to keep her knees slightly bent and her shoulders back. Oh, and arms locked straight out.

So many things to remember. Too many things…

Then she was up and gliding over the water. Rachel wanted to cheer, but she had to focus. Why had she thought this was difficult?

Rachel laughed out of sheer joy. On her second turn around the lake, she tapped her head—a sign she was ready to let go— and seconds later, she released the handle.

When the boat circled to pick her up, she couldn't keep a goofy smile from her lips. Even once she was back in the boat, the smile remained.

"Ready for some food?" Nell asked.

"I'm starving," Rachel said. "Skiing is hard work."

"You did great." Dixon surprised them all when he planted a kiss on the top of her head. "I'm proud of you for persevering."

She met his gaze, feeling a rush of pleasure at his words. "Ask anyone. I've never been a quitter."

An odd look filled his eyes, but he grinned. "My kind of gal."

They pulled into a secluded cove and got out of the boat. Nell opened the picnic basket, while Rachel spread the cloth on the ground. Leo uncorked a bottle of wine, while Dixon brought out an assortment of soft drinks from a cooler.

Leo stared at the variety of tiny sandwiches, pieces of fruit and stuffed dates, a frown furrowing his brow.

"Where's the fried chicken?" Leo asked.

"You asked your cook to make up the basket." Nell cocked her head. "Did you specify fried chicken?"

Leo frowned. "Isn't that a given?"

Nell chuckled. "Apparently not."

"I think everything looks amazing." Rachel expelled a breath. "So pretty and such a variety."

"Good sport."

Did she only imagine the words coming from Dixon? When she glanced in his direction, he was holding out two glasses, while Leo poured the wine.

"I can't imagine anything better," Nell said, lifting her glass, "than being here today with all of you."

A strange expression crossed Dixon's face.

Rachel wondered if Dixon sometimes still felt like an outsider. Despite building a circle of friends, he hadn't been in Hazel Green long.

She scooted closer to him, wanting him to know that she was glad to be here with him.

When his arm slipped around her shoulders, Rachel leaned her head against his chest and emitted a happy sigh.

"Are you two going to fix a plate?" Amusement laced Leo's tone. "Or just sit there making puppy-dog eyes at each other?"

"Puppy-dog eyes," Rachel said at the same time as Dixon, and they both laughed.

Reluctantly, she straightened. "I am hungry."

"You've got to try this wine. It's excellent." Nell pressed a glass into her hand.

The four of them ate, drank and talked for nearly an hour. When Nell and Leo went for a walk, Dixon and Rachel stayed behind to clean up.

Rachel hummed to herself. "I can't remember the last time I had so much fun."

Dixon glanced up, a stack of plates in hand. "It's been a good day."

"I'm usually too serious." Though they'd be put in the laundry when the basket was unpacked, Rachel carefully folded the pretty paisley napkins. "Today, for whatever reason, I was able to relax."

"Too serious?" Dixon shook his head. "That's not how I'd ever describe you."

"Plenty of people have told me that." She reached for the silverware.

"Plenty of people?" Dixon asked in a low voice. "Or Marc Koenig?"

There had been others who'd told her that, she was practically sure of it. Most recently, the comment had come from Marc. Rachel shrugged.

Dixon stood, then reached down and pulled her up.

"Hey, I was putting the silverware—"

"It's not going anywhere." With one finger, he pushed aside a wavy strand of hair.

"Wh-what are we, I mean, you doing?"

The look in his eyes had her heart thumping wildly. Or maybe it was that he held her in his arms the way he had the other night when he'd kissed her.

When she'd kissed him.

When they'd kissed each other until she'd felt as if she was drowning in him. Would he kiss her now?

"It's kinda crazy," he said, his gaze never leaving hers.

"What is?" she whispered, barely able to get the words past lips that felt frozen.

"How awkward and unsure I feel around you."

"You're kidding me."

His head shook slowly back and forth. "Scout's honor."

"You were never a scout."

He only smiled, and the palm that rested against her back began to move slowly up and down. The gauzy coverup over her suit was the only barrier between his fingers and her skin.

Heat blossomed beneath his touch. Rachel inched even closer. Like Leo, Dixon had pulled on a T-shirt once they were on dry land, but he still wore only swim trunks. Though clothing separated them, Rachel felt naked and exposed.

"I want to kiss you again." Those beautiful gray eyes never left hers as his hands continued to stroke. "I don't want to push too fast. You just got out of a relationship. You—"

She pressed her fingers against his lips. "You need to stop talking and kiss me."

Smart guy that he was, Dixon took her at his word and covered her mouth with his.

When he did, the perfect day got a whole lot more perfect.

On Tuesday, Rachel sat in her office at the food bank, reviewing the fall schedule. In the summer, high school and college volunteers were plentiful. But once school began in the fall, their availability plummeted.

Even though she could get by with less help in the community garden during the fall, the need for volunteers to sort and pack the food items remained high year-round.

Tapping a pencil against the gray metal desk, Rachel considered various recruitment options. Volunteers had become increasingly harder to find.

With the economy strong, many of the kids who used to volunteer to gain experience and a good reference were now able to secure part-time jobs. Not only that, other agencies in the area were out there recruiting volunteers.

She knew she was going to have to approach Tom—again—and suggest he meet with the high school principal to see if there was any way they could offer students high school credit for volunteering.

Something like that would undoubtedly require more work from her, with lots of documentation and perhaps an end-of-the-semester report. Still, she believed in the mission of the food bank and knew volunteers gained valuable skills in the process.

"Rachel." Fisher stood in the doorway. Today was the college sophomore's last day volunteering before heading back to the University of Illinois in Champaign.

She pushed back her chair and rose. "What can I do for you?"

"You've got a visitor."

"Who is it?" For a second, Rachel wondered if Hank had decided to stop over and speak with her about the newspaper article she'd proposed.

"A guy. Says he needs to speak with you." Fisher lifted one bony shoulder and shrugged. "Says it's important. Sorry I didn't get his name."

"It's okay. Send him back."

Rachel hoped it was Hank. Or maybe Dixon. Perhaps Dixon had been walking by and decided he'd like to take a tour of where she spent her working hours. Or maybe he'd seen that it was getting close to dinnertime and had stopped to see if she was interested in sharing a pizza.

She glanced down at the dress she wore under her food bank smock. The simple brown muslin wouldn't win any style awards, although once she took off the smock, the open crisscross back made it a little more interesting.

Heart hammering, she opened a drawer, pulled out a mirror and tube of lipstick and managed to brighten her lips just before Fisher returned.

Hank wasn't with the boy.

Neither was Dixon.

Marc stood in the doorway to her office, an inscrutable look on his face.

"I'll be out there if you need anything." Fisher jerked his thumb toward the sorting area.

Strangely, Rachel felt no fear. Maybe because she knew that, outside her door, there were a dozen or so people who would rush to her aid in seconds should she need them.

"What are you doing here?" She could have cheered when her tone came out cool and controlled, just as she intended.

When he started to shut the door, she shook her head. "Leave it open."

Not a request, an order.

His hand stilled, then he crossed the small space to her desk. Despite it being the size of a postage stamp, the well-ordered area had a place for everything…and everything was in its place, including a visitor's chair.

Rachel didn't offer him a seat, and she didn't give him the advantage of towering over her by dropping into her own chair.

"You didn't answer my question," she said when he only stared.

"You know exactly why I'm—" Marc stopped and visibly pulled himself under control. When he spoke again, his voice, which had begun to rise, was lower. "I came to apologize for any misunderstanding. I want to move on."

"Then move on." As much as she wanted to shift her gaze from his face, something told her he'd view that as a sign of weakness. "I'm not stopping you."

For a second, confusion blanketed his face. Then a steely hardness returned to his eyes. "I'm sorry for the misunderstanding the other night. I-I'd had too much to drink, but you were being deliberately obtuse. There was no call for you to assault me, but I'm willing to take the high road—"

"Me? Assault you?" Rachel laughed, a harsh sound of disbelief and incredulity. Then her blood turned to ice. "I have nothing more to say to you. I mean it when I say don't come around again."

"You think he's so wonderful." Marc's tone turned mocking. Not surprising, since the man's emotions were as volatile as spring weather. "You think you can't trust me? I'm a Boy Scout compared to Dixon Carlyle."

She would not debate with him. "Get out, Marc."

"You'll find out."

Before she could call out to have someone escort him from the building, he moved to the door, then turned back. "Don't say I didn't warn you."

Rachel waited until she heard his footsteps fade. Only then did she drop down into her chair, her heart pounding.

It's over now, she reassured herself. He'd finally gotten the message. She wouldn't be bothered by him again.

Rachel leaned back in the chair. How had they gotten to this point? Why had it taken her so long to see him for the man he was, instead of the one she wanted him to be? Her mind drifted back to their early days together. Marc had been so nice, so considerate. So…normal. The perfect boyfriend.

She thought of what he'd said about Dixon. A shiver of fear

slid up her spine. Had she missed signs that Dixon couldn't be trusted, the way she had with Marc?

Still early days, she reassured herself. Plenty of time to become better acquainted with Dixon. Plenty of time to determine he was who he appeared to be.

Plenty of time to determine if he could be trusted.

CHAPTER TWELVE

Rachel stared at herself in the beauty salon mirror and blinked rapidly. She would not cry.

"What do you think?" The young stylist with the nose ring and sleeve tattoo on one arm snapped her gum. "Majorly cool, right?"

Rachel leaned closer to the mirror and studied her hair. "It looks…gray. Does it look gray to you?"

The girl's dark bushy brows pulled together. "Platinum. It's what you said you wanted."

"No," Rachel kept her voice steady, "I said I wanted highlights."

"You said a different shade. You wanted to switch things up." Leeza's violet eyes—the vivid color had to be from contacts—turned sharp and assessing. "Platinum is all the rage right now. I think it looks amazing on you."

Rachel cast another doubtful glance at the mirror, feeling as if she'd aged twenty years in two hours.

"Can you get it back to its natural color?" *Please*, Rachel thought, *please say yes.*

The young woman heaved a sigh. "Yes, but not today. I'm

completely booked the rest of the afternoon. If you want it done today, Mandy might be able to help you."

As Mandy had come over to ask for Leeza's help numerous times in the past two hours, Rachel decided she could wait. She might have to attend the couples shower tonight looking like someone's maiden aunt, but it couldn't be helped.

"When is your next appointment?"

"Two thirty on Monday."

Rachel closed her eyes for just a second. She'd have to take vacation time, but it couldn't be helped. "Okay. Put me down."

Leeza rested a hand briefly on Rachel's shoulder. "I see now this isn't what you had in mind. I'm sorry."

"Not your fault." Rachel waved an airy hand, knowing this would be the last time she'd attempt to switch things up and be cool. "Our wires just got crossed."

Rachel sighed at her reflection, looking for the positive. Strands that once hung straight past her shoulders now curled softly, stopping just short of those same shoulders. Yes, the cut was a success. Since Leeza had styled her hair, Rachel wouldn't need to do any more with it before Dixon picked her up.

After paying, and adding a generous tip—after all, it wasn't Leeza's fault their wires got crossed—Rachel left the salon, walking in brisk strides to her car. When Dixon had called to ask if she'd be interested in going with him to the bridal shower, Rachel hadn't been able to think of a reason to say no.

Marc's words of warning still ran through her head, but she stilled the noise as much as she could. She refused to look at Dixon as if he could be a lowlife just because Marc had been an untrustworthy jerk.

By the time she walked through her front door, Rachel had to scramble to get ready. Abby and Jonah were hosting the shower at their home, and her hair appointment had taken longer than she'd anticipated.

After donning a sleeveless dress and freshening her makeup,

Rachel found herself with a few extra minutes, so she played with Violet with the laser pointer.

She caught the cat eyeing her a couple of times. It had to be the hair. By the look on Violet's face, her new friend wasn't impressed.

The doorbell had Rachel grabbing the bottle of maple bacon moonshine she'd dressed up with a series of brightly colored, curled ribbons. After glancing through the peephole, she flung the door open and felt her heart leap.

Even dressed casually in khakis and a black knit shirt, Dixon stole her breath.

"Looks like you're ready." He paused, a tiny smile playing at the corners of his lips as he looked at her—really looked at her. He pointed. "You changed the color of your hair."

Her hand rose self-consciously to the silky strands. "I wanted highlights. I got gray."

"You look lovely." He reached out, fingered one of the curls. "These are nice, too."

"You don't have to be kind." Despite her resolve, tears pushed at the backs of her eyes. "I look like someone's old, dowdy aunt."

"Hey, hey." He lifted the moonshine from her hand. After placing it on the side table, Dixon tugged her to him. "You look incredible no matter what color of hair you have or what you're wearing."

Rachel rested her head against the front of his shirt and let his warmth envelop her. "You're just saying that."

"I'm not." He rested his cheek against the top of her head, and her heart lurched at the tender gesture. "While I adore your regular hair color, there's nothing wrong with punching things up once in a while."

Sniffling, she stepped back, swiping at her eyes. "I worried you wouldn't want to go with me once you got a good look at my hair."

His brows pulled together. "Do you think I'm that shallow?"

Though his expression gave nothing away, she sensed she'd hurt him with her careless comment.

"No." She shook her head. "No. I just, well, I wanted to look extra good this evening. There will be so many pretty women there tonight, and I wanted you to be glad you were with me."

"The muck is getting deeper by the second. If I had hip waders, now would be the time for me to bring them out."

For a second, he lost her. Then Rachel realized what she'd said. She lifted her hands. "I give up. With every word, I'm making things worse. I won't say anything else the entire night."

He grabbed her hand and gave it a swing. "Don't do that. I like listening to you and hearing your views."

She laughed. "Even when I make you sound shallow and judgmental?"

"Even then." He leaned down and kissed her. "We best get going. If we stay here much longer, I'm afraid I'll be tempted to show you just how very attractive I find you."

A receiving line of sorts greeted their arrival at Abby and Jonah's home. Ginger, their golden retriever, and Eva Grace were nowhere in sight.

"I can't believe you banished the munchkin," Rachel said in a teasing tone.

"Jonah's parents have big plans for her this weekend. They spirited her away this morning. I miss her already." Abby glanced up at Jonah. "Having her gone is hard on both of us."

"True statement." Jonah took the bottle from Abby. "Maple bacon moonshine?"

She smiled. "It's from a distillery in Gatlinburg, Tennessee. It's great in almost anything, or you can drink it straight."

Jonah glanced at Abby. "Almost makes me wish we'd had a stock-the-bar wedding shower."

"We had our chance." Abby poked him in the ribs. "All these gifts go to Nell and Leo."

"What gifts?" Nell, who'd been speaking with Leo's parents, strolled over to greet Rachel and Dixon.

"Moonshine," Rachel pointed. "From me."

"Stainless-steel pint glasses from me." Dixon lifted a gift sack from a local store that specialized in lagers and ales.

"Thank you both." Leo, who'd strolled up, stared curiously at the moonshine, then at his fiancée. "We're definitely going to have to try some of this. Maybe later tonight."

"It's great in hot chocolate," Rachel said, her comment drawing their attention back to her.

"You look different." Nell's gaze narrowed. Her head cocked. "You changed your hair."

Dixon stepped forward. "I like it."

Rachel nearly groaned. The way he said it and the look in his eyes dared anyone to disagree.

"Platinum is very trendy right now." Nell smiled. "I agree with Dixon. And I love the cut."

"I'm having it changed back on Monday," Rachel informed her. "The color, I mean."

"A woman's prerogative." Nell lifted a shoulder in a shrug. "I've been known to change my hair color several times in one day, thanks to wigs."

The last of the tension slipped from Rachel's shoulders as she and Dixon made their way around the room. How could she have forgotten? The party tonight was filled with friends. They were kind.

The only wild card was Jackie Rollins. Jonah's sister was a newcomer to Hazel Green. While the schoolteacher was always nice, it was clear—at least to Rachel—that she had her eye on Dixon.

But the smile she directed to Rachel this evening was warm

and friendly. If she gave Dixon an extra-long hug, well, that was Jackie.

"I hear you brought moonshine."

Rachel nodded, and she felt Dixon's hand slip around her back to rest on her waist. "Maple bacon. One of my brothers brought some back from a trip to Gatlinburg. I'm not a big drinker, but I have some butter pecan that's especially good in hot cocoa on cold winter nights." Rachel clamped her mouth shut, realizing she'd been rambling.

"I love moonshine. I never thought to put it in cocoa, but I can see where that would be an excellent combination." With her blonde curly hair pulled back in a high tail, Jackie looked so much like her niece, Eva Grace, that Rachel couldn't help but smile.

"I'd love to come over and check out the butter pecan."

"You're always welcome." Rachel wondered if Jackie was lonely. It would be difficult to relocate to a town where you didn't know anyone except your brother and his wife and child. "I have a new cat. You could meet her."

"School just started, but I've got my lesson plans for these first couple weeks already done." Jackie shrugged. "I'm grateful that Hazel Green has so much going on during the weekends and nights. Otherwise, I'd likely be sitting at home drinking a bottle of wine by myself."

Who was rambling now? Rachel thought. But she understood loneliness and how it felt to be single when everyone else around you was married, most with kids.

She also understood what it was like to feel lonely when you had a boyfriend, because that's how she'd felt with Marc.

Reaching into her bag, Rachel pulled out her phone and handed it to Jackie. "Put in your number, and we can connect."

"I'd like that," Jackie said, her thumbs already flying across the keyboard.

Once she was done, the pretty blonde handed the phone back to Rachel.

"You did something interesting with your hair." There was no judgment in the comment, only curiosity.

"I tried to switch things up a bit, but ended up looking like the old gray mare."

Dixon's arm tensed, but before he could speak, Jackie laughed. "You don't look like an old anything." Jackie's eyes danced. "One day, over some of your butter pecan moonshine, I'll tell you about the time I decided to darken my hair right before the junior-senior prom."

Rachel smiled. "I take it the change didn't go well."

"No, but it makes one heckuva story now." Jackie turned to Dixon. "It's good to see you. I hadn't heard from you in a while. Then I heard you and Rachel are dating."

Was that what they were doing? Rachel wondered. Were she and Dixon *dating*? Or did he see her as simply a friend? Was it smart for her to be jumping back into the dating pond so soon after splitting with Marc?

"Rachel and I are enjoying getting better acquainted." Dixon turned to her and brushed a strand of hair back from her face with a finger. "Everything I see, I like."

"I'm happy." Jackie glanced at Rachel, a genuine smile on her face. "For both of you."

A groan rose up from the other side of the room.

"What's that all about?" Rachel asked.

Jackie tapped a finger against her lips. "If I were to hazard a guess, I'd say my darling sister-in-law just announced that it's time for the games to begin."

"Games?" Shock traveled across Dixon's handsome face. "What kind of games? Are you serious?"

Though Rachel had not been involved in any of the party planning, when he'd asked on the way over to Abby's home what normally occurred at these kinds of events, she hadn't even mentioned the games.

"I'm surprised Nell, or Leo, for that matter, would want to play games." Rachel kept her voice noncommittal. While she knew some people hated playing games at bridal and baby showers, she didn't mind them. In fact, she kind of liked them.

Jackie lowered her voice. "Apparently, Marty thought it would be fun to play one or two."

"Games can be fun." Rachel glanced at Dixon before returning her gaze to Jackie. "Especially when alcohol is involved."

Jackie's eyes brightened. "Which means we just might be tasting Rachel's moonshine before the night is over."

Hyperalertness, a survival mechanism that had been a part of Dixon since he was five and had awakened to a drunk Gloria stabbing him in the side with a cattle prod, had eased in recent years.

He'd made a determined effort to avoid socializing with volatile men and women.

Though they were still in the getting-acquainted stage, Dixon found Rachel to be a soothing presence.

Unlike many women of his acquaintance, she didn't seem to feel the need to constantly chatter. She talked, sure, but not incessantly—unless she was nervous.

Once she'd gotten over worrying how everyone was going to react to the change in her hair, she'd begun to relax and enjoy the evening.

Apparently, Jackie's pronouncement that games were on the way had been a false alarm. No games, at least not at that moment. Only encouragement to eat, drink and mingle.

Dixon stood at Rachel's side as she laughingly told Marty about her misadventures at the salon.

"I think you could have magenta hair and still be beautiful." Leo's mother patted her arm. "But in my opinion, your natural hair color is unique and very lovely."

US Senator Tim Pomeroy stood beside his wife. While the women discussed hair color, his gaze settled on Dixon. "How are things for you?"

It might have been an innocent question, a simple conversation starter, but something in his eyes had Dixon wondering—for just a second—if Nell or Leo had said something to the man.

He immediately put the thought aside. There was no one he trusted more than Nell. "Business is good."

"Glad to hear it."

When Tim directed his gaze at Rachel, a puzzled look in his eyes, Dixon knew what was coming. And he knew just how to avoid the interrogation. "Your latest poll numbers are excellent."

Tim was running for reelection to the US Senate in November. Though he'd been a popular senator from the state of Illinois for four terms, a recent scandal involving a trusted staffer had rocked his campaign and threatened his hopes for a fifth term.

"All I can do is run a clean campaign, focus on the issues and continue to do my best for my constituents."

"Dixon."

Relieved, he turned toward Rachel.

"Marty said all the gifts are arranged on a table over there. Would you like to check them out?" Only then did Rachel appear to notice that Dixon and Tim had also been having a conversation while she and Marty had talked. "I'm sorry. I didn't mean to interrupt."

"You didn't." Dixon smiled at Tim, then at Marty. "Good to see you both again."

He placed a hand against Rachel's back. "Let's check out the loot."

It took them longer to cross to the second parlor than Dixon anticipated. Every few feet, they were stopped by someone wanting to talk. At last, the gift table came into view. It held a chalkboard with Gifts written in a decorative font, a basket for cards and a balloon and floral bouquet.

Beneath the plethora of gifts, a lace tablecloth peeked out.

"When did Leo and Nell unwrap the gifts?" Dixon asked as they covered the last couple of feet to the table, and he noticed all the gifts on full display.

While Abby and Jonah's house was large, the festivities were basically confined to two parlors and the kitchen. There was no way he'd have missed his sister unwrapping gifts.

"They didn't," Rachel responded in a matter-of-fact tone. "That's why they asked everyone to bring the gifts unwrapped. That way, there would be no endless sheets of wrapping paper to deal with…and no time taken to unwrap."

"Makes sense." Dixon lifted a stainless-steel electric corkscrew. "I wouldn't mind having one of these."

Rachel smiled and nodded, but when Dixon looked at her, he saw her eyes were focused on a set of gorgeous uniquely sculpted wineglasses.

"Those, too," he added.

"This stock-the-bar theme was a good idea." Rachel lifted one of the wineglasses, turning it over in hand, feeling its weight. "I mean, both of them have everything in terms of housewares and stuff like that. But these gifts are unique and—"

"We thought so," Abby interrupted. "Are you having fun?"

Dixon looked at Rachel, and they exchanged a smile and nodded.

"Good." Abby gestured with one hand. "I need you to head into the other parlor. We're ready to start the game portion of the evening."

Dixon glanced in the direction of the front door.

Interpreting the look he shot Rachel, Abby shook her head.

"Neither of you are going anywhere. It's one game, and it'll be fun. And informative. I promise."

When Abby moved on to another couple in the room, obviously spreading the good news about the game, Dixon slanted a look at Rachel. "What do you think she meant by 'informative'?"

Rachel inclined her head and thought for a moment before taking his arm and tugging him along. "I guess we're about to find out."

CHAPTER THIRTEEN

Rachel told him the game they were about to play was called The Mr. and Mrs. Quiz. Basically, it would show how well Nell and Leo knew each other, as determined by their answers to three questions each. The shower attendees could win a prize for guessing the number of questions that they would answer correctly.

Rachel's pencil hovered above the small sheet of paper. She chewed on her lip and considered, then wrote down a guess.

"How many did you put?" Dixon peered over her shoulder from the seat beside her.

"Four." She arched a questioning brow. "How many did you say?"

"Six." Scrawling his name at the bottom of the paper, he handed it to Liz Canfield, a former reporter he'd once dated.

"Thanks, Dixon." Liz was a pretty woman with dark hair, brown eyes and a supremely confident manner.

Dixon liked Liz, admired her for the way she'd dealt with the disappointments in her life. When he'd stopped calling her, he'd told himself it was because of her journalism background and the way she questioned everything.

He realized now that he simply hadn't cared enough to continue the relationship.

"Six?" Liz's dark eyes sparkled as she read the number on the paper he handed her. "I'm not surprised. You always were a go-for-broke kind of guy."

Dixon felt Rachel tense beside him on the sofa. Without taking his gaze from Liz, he took Rachel's hand and brought it to his lips. "When it's worth the risk."

Liz's smile widened, and she winked at Rachel. "You've got yourself a good guy. Even if his ego is, as my nine-year-old would say, humongous."

The comment had Dixon remembering the generous nature that had attracted him to Liz in the first place. She and Rachel were a lot alike in many ways. But there was something extraspecial about Rachel.

"Anyone not turned in their vote?" Jonah's gaze shifted around the parlor, where guests sat on sofas and settees and various chairs brought in from the dining room, then gave his wife the thumbs-up.

"Fabulous." Abby flashed a bright smile, the cherry red of her wrap dress perfectly matching her lipstick. "Now, Jonah, my love, please take Leo to the back porch while Nell answers the questions we will soon pose to him."

Leo rose, reluctantly if Dixon was any judge. He took one step, then as if remembering something important, he returned to Nell and kissed her, his hands cupping her face.

The gentleness, the love he saw between his sister and her future husband had Dixon smiling. Even if they didn't get a single question correct, these two would be all right.

Nell's life was on track, and Dixon couldn't be happier for her.

"Okay, Nell." Abby gestured toward a Queen Anne-style chair. "Have a seat."

His sister cocked her head. "Is that the hot seat?"

Abby laughed, gave Nell a hug. "Is it any wonder I adore you?"

Once Nell was seated, Abby turned to Marty. "We're ready."

Dixon realized that Abby was giving Marty a chance to feel like part of the event. His own mother would never have been so generous.

For starters, she'd never hosted any kind of party for someone else. Everything always had to be about Gloria.

"Nell, this is the first question." Marty lifted the pair of cheaters from the side table, slipped them on and read from the card in her hand. "You will answer this the way you believe Leo will answer. Are you ready?"

Nell nodded.

"What is Leo's most-prized possession?"

Dixon saw, for just a second, surprise flicker in Nell's blue eyes. Apparently, she'd expected more lighthearted, tabloid-type questions.

"I'd say it's the political pin collection you and his father gave him on his twelfth birthday." Nell smiled at Tim. "The letter you enclosed in his birthday card made that particular gift extraspecial."

"He'd just won his first election." Tim cleared his throat. "Student council."

What would it have been like, Dixon wondered, to have a parent who encouraged you? One who wanted you to grow and succeed in life?

Marty smiled and flipped to the second card. "If Leo could meet one famous person, who would it be?"

"Hmmm." Nell tapped her lips with two fingers, and her brow furrowed in thought. "I'd have to say Elizabeth Cochran Seaman."

"Who?" Marty blurted, then laughed with embarrassment.

"Don't apologize, Marty." Abby lifted her hands. "I don't know who that is either."

Liz answered before Nell could reply. "Her pen name was Nellie Bly."

"The reporter," Rachel said in a low tone to Dixon. "The one who went undercover in the insane asylum."

"That's right," Nell responded to Liz before refocusing on Marty. "He's fascinated by her investigative reporting."

Perhaps it was only Dixon's imagination, but he could have sworn that his sister's gaze held a spark of humor when it sought his. Neither he, nor his sister, were fans of anyone who pried into personal lives.

Marty nodded. "Here's the last one. If Leo were alone for an evening, what would he make for dinner?"

"Finally." Nell pretended to wipe sweat from her brow with the back of her hand. "This one is easy. Mac and cheese from a box."

"My kind of guy," Mathis called out.

Laughter rippled through the room.

Leo was brought back in, and Nell had nailed two out of three. Instead of Nellie Bly as the one famous person he'd like to meet, he chose Hazel Green.

"Why her?" Nell's eyes filled with confusion.

"You've done such an amazing job of bringing our town matriarch to life that I feel like I know her. But we've only scraped the surface. It'd be great to sit down and talk with her face-to-face."

Could you ever really know someone completely? Dixon wondered as he inhaled the sweet scent of Rachel's perfume.

Nell reached over and took Leo's hand.

"If Nellie Bly could be there," he added, "that'd be even sweeter."

Nell laughed and kissed his cheek.

"Leo, it's your chance to show us how well you know Nell." Tim stepped forward and motioned to his wife. "Marty, if you'll take Nell out to the porch, I'll ask Leo these questions."

Tim glanced around the room. "While the ladies are making

the move, you have a brief window to refresh your drinks and pick up a few more of Matilda's amazing appetizers."

Dixon shifted toward Rachel. "What can I get you?"

"Nothing right now." Rachel shook her head. "I'm completely content."

He considered grabbing a beer, but decided he was too comfortable right where he was on the sofa.

"Go ahead," Rachel said. "If you want to get something for yourself—"

"Like you, I'm content right where I am." He settled back, liking the feel of her hand in his. "This is my first couples shower."

"What do you think of it?"

"It's not painful."

She chuckled. "Hardly a ringing endorsement."

"Being here with you makes it nice." He squeezed her hand, his gaze drifting to her lips. "Though a little more privacy would be—"

"This is your one-minute warning," Tim called out. "Grab your food and drink and resume your seats."

"He should have been a drill sergeant." Dixon spoke in a low tone, shooting Rachel a conspiratorial smile.

Her smile warmed him, and he settled in for part two of the show.

Rachel couldn't be positive, but the questions Leo had to answer about Nell seemed more difficult because they were so general. What was her favorite leisure time activity? What one chore did she hate?

Even Rachel, who'd been friends with Nell for years, would find it difficult to know which to choose from a handful of possibilities. They were zero for two on this round when Tim read the last question to Nell.

"What did Leo answer when asked about the one thing you can't live without?"

Nell smiled at her fiancé. "I hope he got this one right, because I say it all the time."

"And the answer is…" Tim prompted when she only continued to gaze at his son with love in her eyes.

"Leo. He's the one thing I can't live without."

A hush fell over the room.

"You're absolutely correct," Tim announced.

Nell jumped to her feet at the same time as Leo. The two were in each other's arms in a heartbeat.

Rachel had to swallow past the lump forming in her throat. She'd been positive that Nell loved Leo, even before Nell admitted it to herself.

When Stan Britten had come to Hazel Green flinging trash from Nell's past, it would have been so easy for her friend to run. Instead, she'd stayed and fought for her new life.

Leo had stood by her, even when such loyalty could have cost him his political career.

Rachel avoided looking at Dixon as a thought struck her. Nell had committed crimes when she was growing up. Had Dixon done the same? Was there someone out there, his own Stanley Britten, searching for him? Wanting to bring him to justice for past misdeeds?

Her mind circled back to what Marc had said to her. Not that she wanted to give Marc any credit, but she'd discovered over the years that sometimes there was a kernel of truth even in outrageous claims.

She needed to ask Dixon to be straight with her. But she wouldn't ask him tonight. No, not tonight when he was so obviously enjoying seeing his sister so happy.

"Anyone who gave an answer of three questions correct, come

see Abby for your prize," Tim announced. "The rest of you, well, enjoy what's left of the evening."

Dixon turned to Rachel. "I'd like to stretch my legs. Would you like to take a short walk, maybe get some fresh air?"

He was looking at her lips again, Rachel realized. A thrill of anticipation shot up her spine.

Yet, when she spoke, her tone was casual. "It's a beautiful night."

"We're going to step outside for some fresh air," Rachel told Abby when she and Dixon ran into her in the foyer.

"Enjoy."

Once they were outside, Rachel turned to Dixon. "Did Abby wink at us?"

"I think she had something in her eye."

"Oh," Rachel said, then frowned when Dixon laughed.

"She winked at us."

"Why?"

"Because, my little innocent, she knows exactly why we're out here." As if he couldn't wait a second longer, Dixon tugged her into his arms and covered her mouth with his.

Rachel felt herself melt, simply going boneless as she clung to him, waves of sensation washing over her. She'd wanted him to kiss her again, but hadn't realized quite how much until this very moment.

Now she didn't want him to stop…ever.

She plastered herself against him, discovering that where she was soft, he was hard.

Her heart hitched, and she had to force herself to breathe when they came up for air. She might have been kissed before, but not like this. No one had ever made her feel the way Dixon did.

"When I was twenty, I had sex with this boy I met in a math class I was taking." She slid her fingers into Dixon's thick dark hair.

"Did you?" he said with no more expression than if she'd told him she'd picked up an avocado at the market today.

"We were both virgins, and we fumbled our way through the experience."

He nuzzled her hair, but said nothing.

"Several years later, I tried it again with another fellow student." She met Dixon's gaze. "I don't know if I told you that I got my degree mostly by taking night and online classes."

He smiled.

Seeing no judgment in his eyes, she continued. "The second time was a little better, but—"

"Still not great."

She shook her head, then rested it against his broad chest. "It was then that I decided to wait."

Dixon was the first to break the lengthening silence. "Wait for what?"

"Until I was married." She planted a kiss on his neck. "Which is why I didn't have sex with Marc. I told him I was waiting until I was married."

"I'm glad."

She looked up, met his gaze with a questioning one of her own.

"He didn't deserve you."

Rachel's brows drew together. "I let him think I was a virgin. I think I knew if I told him I wasn't, the pressure would have been unbearable. As it was, he still tried to get me to change my mind."

"You were never tempted?"

Rachel thought for a long moment, shook her head. "I wonder if on some level I realized that having sex with him would have given him more power over me."

"Why are you telling me this?" His voice, soft and low, comforted and reassured.

"I-I thought you should know."

"Sex, making love, doesn't have to be a part of our relationship."

"Is that what we have…a relationship?"

He stroked her hair gently with one hand. "That's what I'd call it."

She expelled a breath, inhaling the clean fresh scent of him. "That's what I'd call it, too."

After a long moment, Rachel continued, completely sure of the course she was about to take. "I didn't tell you about my past, ah, sexual experiences because I want you to keep your distance. In fact, quite the opposite."

With hands on her shoulders, he held her away from him, his gray eyes searching hers. "Just spit it out."

"I want you." Rachel felt her lips tremble as she smiled. "I want to make love with you. Like I said, I don't have much experience, so I don't want you to get your hopes up that this will be the best ever. I'm not sure if I'd be able to satisfy you—"

His mouth melded with hers. There was no other word for it. They kissed until her blood ran hot through her veins.

This time, when their lips parted, he brought her hand to his chest. Through his shirt, she felt a rapid *thump*, *thump*, *thump*.

"This," he said, "is what simply being close to you does to me."

Rachel hesitated for only a second. Sometimes, she thought, you had to go with instinct. "Come home with me?"

His gaze searched hers. "Are you positive that's what you want?"

She linked her fingers with his and kissed him gently on the lips. "I've never been more sure of anything in my life."

CHAPTER FOURTEEN

Dixon's presence had Rachel's bedroom feeling small and closing in fast.

With hands shoved into his pockets, he glanced around. "You know this is a new experience for me."

Rachel cocked her head. She couldn't stop the tiny smile from forming at the corners of her lips. "Please don't tell me you're as much a neophyte at this as I am."

Dixon only chuckled, a pleasant rumbling sound, and began to unbutton his shirt.

"Your hands are trembling."

"I know, it's crazy." The easy smile on his lips faded as he took a step closer and slid his hands through her hair. "Crazy is just how you make me feel."

Impulsively, she lifted up on her tiptoes and kissed the underside of his jaw. "How crazy?"

"Turned inside out." He cleared his throat as she planted kisses down the side of his neck. "I've never wanted a woman as badly as I want you."

Rachel had seen that desire in his eyes. She understood, because she felt the same way about him. While there were many facets of him left to explore, she believed at the core he was a decent and honorable man.

One she could trust with her heart…and her body.

"I want you," she said simply.

Now it was her fingers that shook when she raised them to his face. Tonight, he would kiss her, touch her, make love to her and—

She stilled as a thought struck her.

His mouth had just lowered to take hers when she stepped back.

Those gray eyes, dark and stormy with need and desire, searched her face. "Second thoughts?"

"Do you have protection?" The question slipped out on a rush. "I'm not on the Pill. It screws with my system."

That had been one more reason to embrace the celibate lifestyle.

"I've got condoms."

While Rachel was happy their night together wouldn't get derailed, something about him being prepared didn't sit well. Which made absolutely no sense.

Dixon's hand cupped her cheek. "I thought we might get to this point someday. That's why, when I was in Chicago earlier in the week, I picked some up."

She smiled, pleased he'd felt the heat building the same way she had…

"You have them with you?"

"Yes, ma'am." With his free hand, he patted a pants pocket.

"Put them on the nightstand." She gestured with one hand.

"Is that how it's going to be tonight?" A gleam of mischief, one that made him look almost boyish, danced in his gray depths. "You ordering me around?"

"No, I just—" She paused, noticed his teasing smile and changed tacks. "Actually, yes. Take off your clothes."

A look of pure enchantment blanketed his face. "You, Rachel Grabinski, are a surprise and a delight."

When he removed his shirt and she saw the wide breadth of his muscular chest, Rachel's heart gave an excited leap.

With sure, confident movements, Dixon unbuckled his belt. When he reached for the button on his pants, she sat on the bed, not sure her suddenly shaky knees could hold her.

Heat rose up her neck as he let the trousers drop, then stepped out of them. A smattering of dark hair disappeared into the waistband of his boxer briefs.

His eyes locked on hers, and his fingers curved around the waistband.

"Wait." She surged to her feet, heart pounding.

He inclined his head, a question in his eyes.

"Let me." As Rachel moved to him, she found herself enveloped by the heat of his body.

When his head lowered so he could nuzzle her neck, she shivered.

"A surprise and a delight," he repeated as her fingers curved around the waistband and tugged.

Dixon awoke the next morning to the aroma of brewing coffee. It took him a second to remember that he was in Rachel's bed.

The sweet scent of her perfume, or soap, shampoo, whatever it was, was as perfect as she was. He smiled, thinking back to how the evening had ended.

She'd asked him to come home with her. He hadn't pressured her; he would never do that. The fact that she trusted him enough to let him get this close humbled and terrified him.

He was falling in love with Rachel. Heck, he was already there. Which was a puzzle. Because of his past, he carried a lot of baggage and had become an expert at keeping everyone at arm's length. It had never seemed fair to bring anyone into the mess that was his life.

Somehow, sweet Rachel had slipped past his defenses. First, by simply being his friend. Then, by showing herself to be someone he could trust, someone he could admire, someone with whom he could be himself.

The love, well, that had just come. It had flooded over him.

He understood better Nell's comment that she hadn't meant to fall in love with Leo, it had just happened.

Now, Dixon would deal with the morning after, never his favorite part of an overnight stay. In the bright light of day, would Rachel regret the choices she'd made last night?

Dixon hopped out of bed and headed for the shower, hoping that wouldn't be the case.

For him, last night had been magical. There was no other word for it. He only hoped it had been the same for her.

Rachel stood at the stove and glanced down at the pair of cotton pants and simple shirt she'd pulled on this morning. Normally, she went super casual on the weekend. These drawstring pants and shirt with tiny penguins were typical weekend attire.

She heard the shower turn off, and her heart stopped.

After behaving like a sex-crazed woman for the better part of the night, how could she face him this morning? Not that he'd seemed to mind her initiative. In fact, he'd encouraged her over and over again to venture outside of her comfort zone.

It hadn't taken much encouragement. She'd wanted, no, needed, to show him exactly how she felt about him.

"Hey."

Before she could swivel, Dixon stood behind her. His arms slipped around her waist as his lips brushed the side of her neck.

"Good morning." His husky voice stirred her blood. "Something smells awfully good."

"Strawberry-rhubarb stuffed French toast." She kept her voice steady even as his nearness had shivers coursing up her spine. "Strawberries and rhubarb from my garden."

"Sounds amazing." He sniffed her hair. "But I was actually speaking of how good you smell."

"Shampoo from the dollar store," she said with a laugh.

"Buy a whole case," he told her.

She turned in his arms. "The coffee should be ready. How 'bout you pour us each a cup while I get the food on the table?"

"Still ordering me around." He kissed her nose when she began to sputter. "And I'm still liking it."

It wasn't until they faced each other in the sunny nook, with warm syrup and butter sliding over the top of the French toast, that an awkward silence descended.

Dixon was the first to break it by reaching across the small dinette table to curl his fingers around hers. "Last night was magical."

When she only stared, he cleared his throat. "I realize that may seem like an odd word choice, but, ah, that's how it was for me."

Abruptly, he pulled his hand back and reached for the coffee mug he'd filled only moments before.

He seemed embarrassed that he'd let so much emotion show.

Touched by his openness, Rachel shoved aside her own discomfort and spoke her truth. "It was magical for me as well."

His gray eyes, framed by dark lashes and oh-so-mysterious, searched hers. A ghost of a smile touched his lips.

"You released the wild woman in me." Rachel's cheeks suddenly burned. She still couldn't believe she'd done—

The touch of his hand against her fingers had her refocusing on his handsome face.

"You are a passionate, amazing woman."

When she started to brush away the compliment with a shake of her head, he tightened his fingers on hers.

"I'm serious. You know how to care and to show your feelings. Being open and honest is a gift." His eyes darkened. "That you shared that gift with me is not something I take lightly."

She gave a jerky nod.

"I'm more myself with you than I've ever been with anyone. Do you know why that is?"

"Why?"

"Because I trust you. I don't have to be anything but who I am with you." Dixon remembered how it had been growing up. The unmeetable expectations and the rage when the ridiculous expectations weren't met. Always the push to do more, be more...

Dixon blew out a breath. "I hope you know that you can be completely yourself with me. I don't care if your hair is black, white or purple. I don't care if you're wearing evening finery or a wide-brimmed hat and garden gloves. When I look at you, I see you. A smart, sexy, caring woman."

When Rachel finally found her voice, it came out thick with emotion. "Thank you for that, Dixon. I don't know that I've ever received a more lovely compliment."

He picked up his mug, and she impulsively picked up hers.

"To new beginnings." She held out her mug, and he clanked his against hers.

"To new beginnings," he said, and his smile warmed her all the way to her toes.

It was unbelievable, Dixon thought, how one night changed everything. At one time, he'd seriously considered continuing on with his life, hoping the past would never catch up with him. Hoping was no longer good enough.

Dixon longed to build a strong relationship with Rachel and

hopefully, eventually, a life with her. But how could he do that knowing the hammer could fall at any second?

Which was why, first thing the following Monday, he reached out to Eddie Haskins, an attorney in Bakersfield. Eddie didn't seem to care where his client Kyler Lamphere was living, only that he paid him for his services upfront and in cash.

Dixon didn't trust Eddie, but for now he served a purpose. Since Eddie didn't know where he lived or under what name he was living, that made it impossible for the attorney to give out any information about him, either deliberately or inadvertently.

If Assistant District Attorney Ellyn Cole would give him immunity for his role in the Bakersfield incident, he would give the ADA the details needed to bury Gloria.

Eddie promised to make the contact and get back to him once he got a response. In the meantime, Dixon planned to keep busy.

He dressed with care for his meeting with Lilian, though on the surface the extra effort hardly seemed necessary. He'd been "courting" the woman's investment business for the past six months. They saw each other at social occasions. At this point, if she chose to work with him, it wouldn't be because he'd worn his best navy suit or leather Ferragamos polished to a high shine.

Still, Dixon considered dressing professionally a sign of respect. In his mind, it said that he valued her business.

Dixon grabbed his briefcase and was nearly to his car when a text from Lilian popped up. She asked if they could meet at the Engine House instead of at her home.

The former firehouse-turned-café was a favorite among tourists and locals. It was a lucky day when you got a table in the small outdoor seating area.

As he strode up, Lilian gave him a smile and waved from one of the outside tables. When he opened the gate and strode up, he noticed she wasn't alone. Mathis rose to his feet.

"Don't rush off on my account," Dixon told Matt.

Matt flashed a smile. "Just keeping your seat warmed and

Lilian occupied while she waited."

Dixon resisted the urge to glance at his watch. He was certain he wasn't late. He always made it a point to arrive early. Dixon never wanted to keep a client, even a potential one, waiting.

"You're not late," Lilian added, as if she could read his thoughts. "I asked Matt to meet me for coffee. We got here early, which is why I was able to snag this fabulous table."

She gestured wide with one hand toward the outdoor dining area bordered by an ornate wrought-iron fence. The decorative concrete had been poured around a tall tree with leafy branches. The café had surrounded the base with pots filled with brightly colored flowers.

"It's a great spot." Dixon smiled at Matt. He liked Leo's brother, who seemed to always have a friendly word for everyone. "Thanks for saving my space."

"Anytime." Matt shook his hand, then turned to Lilian. "I'll get some figures together. We'll talk again."

Lilian opened her mouth as if to say something more. Instead, she merely wiggled her fingers in a goodbye gesture.

Dixon gestured to the chair Matt had just vacated. "May I?"

"Please."

Once he was seated and discovered Lilian had waited to have breakfast with him, Dixon ordered the special while Lilian chose the steel-cut oats.

The waitress, a pretty blonde with a tendency to hover, brought him his coffee and refilled Lilian's cup.

Dixon took a sip. Unlike some of his counterparts, he didn't push. Either someone wanted his help with their investments, or they didn't. Over the years, he'd seen far too many of those in his profession turn potential investors off with strong-arm tactics.

Besides, he liked Lilian.

The fact that his sister liked and respected the woman only solidified his impression of her.

By the time the waitress, Brittany—she'd made sure to

mention her name several times already—returned with their food, he and Lilian were still chatting about relatively inconsequential things, like his sister's honeymoon plans.

"I can't believe Nell has no idea where they're going." Though Lilian shook her head as she drank more coffee, a soft look filled her eyes.

"Nell told Leo that she wanted him to surprise her." Dixon smiled. "That takes trust."

"They've got that in spades." Lilian set down her cup. "When Leo and the entire Pomeroy family stood beside her when she took on that horrible man from DC, she knew."

Dixon knew that *that horrible man* was Stan Britten. Dixon remembered telling Nell, way back when, that the little weasel would be trouble. Even when, at the time, the nerdy high school junior had idolized his pretty and popular high school senior sister.

Nell's friendship with Stan had been orchestrated, part of one of their mother's schemes. Just like the Bakersfield incident. Only, Dixon had been an adult when he'd helped Gloria—twenty-one and old enough to know better.

"Dixon."

Horrified he'd let himself become distracted, Dixon flashed a smile. "Yes, Lilian."

"You've been seeing Rachel."

Though it was a statement, not a question, Dixon nodded. "We're dating."

"Rachel is a lovely young woman."

"She is." Keeping a smile on his lips, Dixon asked, "Where are you going with this, Lilian?"

"I spent some time with Marc yesterday." For a second, Lilian's always-confident façade faltered. "He's very concerned about your intentions."

Dixon seized his spiking temper with both hands. His first impulse was to make it clear to Lilian that his relationship with

Rachel was not any of her business. It certainly wasn't any of Marc's.

After a moment, he released his death grip on the cup of coffee. In all the time he'd known Lilian, he'd found her to be a kind woman. Not someone who meddled in other people's business.

"What did Marc tell you?"

Lilian shifted her gaze. Instead of immediately answering, she motioned to Brittany that she'd like more coffee.

It was a stall, pure and simple.

Dixon didn't have an issue with waiting.

When Brittany returned with the coffeepot, he took the check and noticed she'd written her phone number on the ticket along with a smiley face.

"Marc is concerned you may be turning Rachel's head." Lilian met his gaze. "He told me he's in love with her and feels that by flooding her with attention, you're coming between them."

"Coming between them?" Dixon repeated the words in a cool tone, giving himself time to settle.

Don't shoot the messenger, he reminded himself. Lilian was merely repeating what Marc had told her. And the amount of time Rachel had spent with Marc was proof the man could be persuasive.

"Did Marc happen to mention how he gripped the arm of this woman he supposedly loves so tightly he left bruises?" With great effort, Dixon kept his tone matter-of-fact. "Or how he recently arrived at her home uninvited, belligerent and stinking of alcohol? That when he grabbed her, she was forced to knee him in the groin in order to get away?"

Lilian's ivory complexion paled. "These are facts?"

Dixon gave a curt nod.

"There's more, but those are Rachel's stories to tell." Dixon met Lilian's shocked gaze with a steady one of his own. "I care about Rachel. I would never hurt her."

He didn't tell Lilian that he was in love with Rachel. That was *his* story to tell. And Rachel needed to be the first to hear the words.

Before he took that step, there were several other steps that needed to come first. Dixon wanted to tell Rachel about his childhood. Having some of that information would hopefully help her understand just how important it was for Gloria to be put away for a good long time.

Rachel had likely heard from Nell some of what had gone on in Gloria's household, but his take on things would be slightly different.

Not worse or better. Just different.

Dixon knew the way he looked at life was different because of spending so many years alone with Gloria. Once Nell had left, he'd been the only one privy to their mother's crazy schemes. Sometimes, he'd gotten sucked into them. Sometimes, he'd found himself actually enjoying aspects of the cons they perpetrated.

Thankfully, he'd seen the light. Once he'd gotten out, he forged his own path. He'd embraced a new identity and made a life for himself. A life where cheating, lying and stealing weren't everyday occurrences.

Though successful in his business life, he'd been lonely.

Then Rachel had come into his world. With her sunny smile and soft, soothing touch, she'd filled the empty places in his heart he hadn't known were there.

He couldn't lose her.

Trust was important to Rachel. Marc had betrayed that trust by cheating on her, by abusing her. Which was why Dixon knew he couldn't let there be any secrets between them when he confessed his love.

He thought of the legal charge hanging over him. Just one more obstacle, he told himself. Once that matter was settled, he would be free to have a future with Rachel.

CHAPTER FIFTEEN

Rachel resisted the urge to hum as she helped Liz and her son, nine-year-old Sawyer, erect the food bank display in the Green. She told herself it was the beautiful sunny day that had her so chipper, but she knew the real reason.

Dixon. The night they'd spent together had been earth-shattering. She felt loose, relaxed and incredibly happy.

"I like this." Sawyer, tall for his age and with a thick mop of brown hair, patted the metal sculpture shaped like a whale. "If I had a can, I'd feed him."

As donations had been down this past month, Rachel hoped a lot of people in Hazel Green would feel the same way as Sawyer did. For those who preferred to give a coin donation, there was the baby pool doubling as a wishing well.

Even now, Nevaeh and Lenox stacked cans of beans around the perimeter of the wishing well pool, while Liz and Rachel finished up the information board on the food bank.

"The whale was a fabulous idea, Rachel." Liz turned back from the board. "How did you think of it?"

"I saw a YouTube video about something similar on a beach where people were encouraged to put plastics in the mouth of a whale. It was a way to not only clean up the beach but make the point about too much plastic ending up in the ocean." Rachel shrugged, not wanting to make a big deal out of it. Although she had to admit, finding a metal whale had been difficult. "I located an artist who was happy to donate this big guy for the weekend, as long as we advertised it as his work."

She pointed to the sign, prominently displayed, that thanked Lin Koolaard for his generosity.

"Mom."

Liz shifted her gaze to her son.

"Is it okay if I go over there?" Sawyer gestured with his head toward the small playground where several moms watched a handful of children on the equipment.

"I suppose that'd be okay." Her voice held a warning note. "If you decide to leave the play area, you are to come straight back here. Understand?"

He nodded and took off running.

"Sawyer is such a nice boy." Rachel remembered her brothers when they were his age. Always messing up the house with their collections of twigs and rocks and various other treasures. Her lips tipped up in a fond smile. "I hope when I get married, if I do ever get married, I have a son just like him."

Most people who didn't know her well thought she'd be tired of raising children. But caring for her siblings after they'd lost their parents had been a joy, not a chore…most days anyway.

"You and Dixon seemed pretty chummy at the party." Liz's expression might convey only casual interest, but the sharp look in her eyes said otherwise.

"We're dating." Rachel stopped herself from saying more, but couldn't stop the smile from blossoming on her lips.

Liz's hands froze on the stack of brochures she'd been arranging. "Is that right?"

"Dixon is a great guy." A warmth spread through Rachel like syrup on a stack of hot French toast. "I really like him."

Setting down the brochures, Liz turned to face Rachel, resting her back against the display table. "You were just with Marc."

"I never felt about him the way I feel about Dixon."

"You dated Marc for nearly a year."

"The connection wasn't there."

"It seemed to be."

"Why are you sticking up for Marc?" Despite her best efforts to control it, Rachel's voice rose, then cracked. "You never liked him. None of you did."

Liz didn't attempt to deny it. How could she? Though Rachel had to admit that after she'd dismissed her friends' concerns, they'd still been supportive.

Embarrassment had heat rising up Rachel's neck. She should have listened, been more open to her friends' worries. Instead, she'd dug in her heels and insisted she knew best.

"I'm not sticking up for Marc." Liz spoke in a soft, soothing voice as she stepped to Rachel. "I just don't want to see you rush into anything with…someone else."

When Rachel said nothing, Liz tried a lighter tone. "You know what they say about rebound relationships."

"Dixon, he—" Rachel paused, searched for the words that would convey the light that Dixon had brought into her world. "He makes me feel good about myself."

She was still trying to find the words, better words, when Liz took her hand.

"You know that Dixon and I went out a couple of times."

Rachel's heart gave a solid thump against her chest wall. "Early in the summer. I remember."

"He's very smooth." Liz's lips curved. "And so very handsome with that thick dark hair and gray eyes."

Rachel nodded, but knew there was so much more to Dixon than his outward appearance.

"Why did you two quit dating?" Rachel asked when the silence lengthened.

"We never spoke of anything of substance." Liz gave a little laugh as a gust of wind caught the brochures and sent them flying. "Hold that thought."

Before Rachel could react, Liz scooped up the brightly colored pieces of paper and set them under a heavier stack of promotional material.

"Okay." Liz heaved out a breath. "Where were we?"

Rachel cleared her throat. "You were saying that you and Dixon never spoke of anything of substance."

Liz chewed on her lower lip. "He's just so…so smooth on the surface. You know what I mean?"

Rachel gave a nod, because she'd seen him act that way around other people, both men and women. He wasn't that way around her. A couple of times, he'd seemed downright awkward.

"Is that why you ended it?" Rachel inclined her head. "Because he was too smooth?"

"Actually, after a couple dates he quit calling." Liz shrugged. "I wasn't really looking for anything permanent, so it wasn't as if I was heartbroken or anything."

Rachel nodded. "I wasn't heartbroken when I ended things with Marc. I was hurt he cheated on me, but once I got over the shock, I was relieved."

"Would you ever consider getting back together with him?"

"No. Never."

"Because of Dixon?"

"Because Marc isn't who I thought he was. He's mean, and he's a cheater. He takes no responsibility for his actions. I'm happy not to be with him anymore."

"I'm sorry he ended up to be such a disappointment." Liz hesitated and appeared to carefully choose her next words. "But I'm glad you found out what he was like before you, well, married him."

"I don't think I'd have married him." Rachel pulled her brows together. "Something held me back. I'm extremely glad I never slept with him."

Liz's eyes popped wide. "You didn't?"

"Nope." It was at this moment that Rachel realized just how far her friends had gone to not bring up Marc. And how much she'd kept all aspects of her relationship with him to herself. "I'd had a couple of sexual relationships in my college days. They, and I know this sounds cliched, but those encounters left me feeling unfulfilled and sad. I told Marc I wanted to wait until I was married to make love."

Liz snorted back a laugh, then raised a hand when Rachel stared.

"I say good for you, but I can only imagine how he took that news."

"Not well." Rachel couldn't help but recall the accusations he'd flung at her, blaming her for him seeking sex elsewhere.

"Dixon will probably be the same."

Rachel inclined her head.

"When he finds out you won't sleep with him." Liz waved a hand in the air. "I'm just making assumptions here, because he and I, well, we didn't even kiss."

A tight little ball in Rachel's chest released. While she'd tried to tell herself it didn't matter if Dixon had kissed Liz, or even slept with Liz, she realized it did matter.

She wondered if it mattered to him that she hadn't slept with Marc.

"I don't think not sleeping with Dixon is going to be a problem," Rachel began. "We—"

"This setup is incredible." Nell strolled the last few feet to them. "Really impressive."

As Nell wasn't one for effusive praise, Rachel basked in the warmth of the words.

"We're nearly ready for tonight." Rachel smiled. "Liz and

Sawyer—who's taking a well-deserved break on the playground —have been wonderful helpers."

"What are you doing out and about?" Liz asked Nell.

Between Nell's busy law practice and her upcoming wedding, sightings of Nell, either as herself or in her role as Hazel Green, had been few and far between.

"I'm on my way to Abby's for some last-minute wedding planning. Will it ever end?" Nell gave a little laugh, but her blue eyes sparkled.

Rachel marveled at the change in the bride-to-be. In the past month, Nell had become more open, more relaxed and definitely happier.

Is that what being in love does to a woman?

"I believe your conversation sounds a whole lot more interesting than the one I'll be having with Abby." Nell's expectant gaze shifted from Liz to Rachel.

Liz cocked her head, clearly not following.

Rachel knew immediately where this was going. She closed her eyes briefly, wishing with all her heart that Nell wasn't Dixon's sister.

"Oh." Liz had apparently remembered what she and Rachel had been discussing when Nell strolled up. "Rachel and I were just talking about her breakup with Marc and her and Dixon hooking up."

Nell's brow lifted. "Hooking up?"

Before Rachel could respond, Liz answered. "Sorry, poor choice of words. As a journalist, I know better." Liz shot Rachel an apologetic look before turning to Nell. "Rachel was just telling me that she'd made it clear to Marc when they were dating that sex was off the table."

"Is that right?" Nell studied Rachel, her eyes clear and very blue.

Rachel flushed. Even in the bright light of day, there was something a bit, well, unsettling about discussing her sex life.

She cast a quick glance to where other booths were in the process of being erected. Thankfully, none of those people were close enough to overhear.

"Yes." Once again, Liz answered. "He wasn't happy about it. I told her that Dixon probably wasn't going to take that news well."

"I heard you say that wasn't going to be a problem." Nell studied Rachel, her gaze sharp and assessing. "You're not attracted to my brother? Or is it that he sees you only as a friend?"

"Why would you think that?" Rachel asked, confused.

"Those are the only reasons I could see it not being an issue," Nell said.

"Exactly my thought." Liz nodded decisively. "Dixon is too much of a virile man to go without sex."

"That isn't at all what I meant," Nell said. "For it to not matter, either Rachel or Dixon, or maybe both, don't look at each other in a romantic way." Nell turned to Liz. "Even if he felt differently, my brother would respect Rachel's wishes."

"He would," Rachel agreed. "The thing is…"

She hesitated for a second and flushed as two sets of curious eyes focused on her.

"The thing is," Rachel repeated, "I wanted him as much as he wanted me. Which is why we already slept together."

"Send her up," Dixon told Anthony when the concierge advised him that his sister had arrived. Then Dixon refocused on the email attachment displayed on his iPad.

Eddie had surprised him with a quick response. The ADA would very much like to discuss the case with him and maybe offer immunity.

"Not yet," Dixon murmured, his gaze focused on the letter Eddie had attached. While it sounded as if she was eager to discuss a deal, he wasn't ready to give up his identity or his location on a *maybe*.

He didn't trust her.

And, he realized, he didn't trust Eddie's skill in brokering a deal.

The knock on his door had him glancing up at the clock. As he wasn't getting together with Rachel until six when her shift at the food bank booth ended, he had time to speak with his sister.

He strolled to the door and opened it before Nell knocked again. Dixon swept out one arm. "Welcome."

"How are you?" she asked in lieu of a greeting.

After pretending to run his hands over his body to check for aches and pains, he smiled. "I'm good."

"Is that because you're sleeping with one of my friends?" Nell arched a brow. "Is that why you're 'good'?"

Her air quotes made him smile. His sister wasn't one for air quotes. She'd thought they were silly. Or she had when they were popular.

"Oof." He took a step back, rubbed his side. "Why did you elbow me?"

"Why did you sleep with Rachel?"

He stilled and offered his sister a confused look. "Who said I did?"

"Rachel." Nell blew out a breath and plopped down on the sofa. "What were you thinking, Ky?"

Dropping into a nearby chair, Dixon studied his sister for a long moment. From the flush to her cheeks and that sharp elbow jab, the news that he and Rachel were sexually involved had clearly upset her.

"When you were having a sex-only relationship with Leo, did I ask what you were thinking?" He continued without giving her a chance to respond. "I did not. That was your private business. What's between me and Rachel is private and, frankly, none of your business."

"She's my friend." Nell's blue eyes met his, and the intensity of the emotion there told him she was in full-on mama bear mode. "Rachel means a lot to me."

"She means a lot to me, too." He scrubbed a hand across his face. "I'm in love with her."

Nell opened her mouth, then shut it. Her eyes narrowed, and he saw the suspicion. "Are you serious?"

He nodded, then chuckled. "Kind of funny, isn't it? Both of us finding someone at the worst possible time in our lives."

"Not the worst," Nell said with a sardonic smile. "Worst would be if Gloria was in town stirring things up."

"She might not be within the city limits, but she's got a long reach."

Nell leaned forward. "Forget about Gloria for a moment. I'm here to talk about Rachel. I don't want her hurt."

"You think that's what I want?" Dixon surged to his feet. "I love her, Nell. That's why I have to get this Bakersfield thing resolved."

"What have you told Rachel?"

He began to pace the room. "Not much. The time hasn't been right."

"It's difficult to find the right time for that kind of discussion. Trust me." A self-deprecating smile lifted Nell's hot-pink lips. "Yet, if I had told Leo about my past before it all came crashing down around us, I could have saved myself—and him—a whole lot of grief."

"I plan to tell her."

"Make it soon." Her eyes were serious when she reached out and squeezed his hand. "Rachel is someone you can trust."

"I heard from my contact. The ADA seems interested in the information I have about the crime." Dixon rubbed the bridge of his nose. "They have enough evidence to charge her, but convicting her will be a different story."

"Is the ADA offering you immunity if you testify?"

"Sounds that way."

"Use and derivative use immunity or transactional immunity?"

Dixon rubbed his chin. "I don't know the difference."

"You want the transactional, or blanket, immunity." Nell stood and held out her hand. "Show me what you received."

"It's on the counter." Before he could reach for the iPad, Nell scooped it up.

He watched her scan the document once, then her gaze returned to the top, and she read it again.

"She doesn't come right out and say it," Dixon said, "but, reading between the lines, it sounds as if she's interested in making a deal with me." Dixon spoke slowly, cautiously, not sure if his own bald hope had caused him to read more into the letter than was actually there.

"That's my impression as well." Nell rested her back against the counter. She studied him for several long seconds. "What are you going to do?"

"Before I do anything, I want this blanket immunity." He went to the sink, filled a glass with water and took a long drink. "If they give me that, I'll happily give them more."

"What if she refuses?"

"Then all communication ceases." He absently took another drink. "I go back to living my life here and hoping no one ever tracks me down."

"You don't want to do that." Nell's brows furrowed. "That isn't any way to live, not long term."

"If she won't deal, I won't have a choice, Nell." Dixon stared at the glass in his hand, turning the cut crystal as if seeing it for the first time. "They'll go with Gloria's account of what happened in Bakersfield, and you know she'll put everything on me."

"That's the worst-case scenario," Nell insisted. "They'll want all the dirt on her. We could clear up a lot of cases."

He shook his head. "Not we, me. You're out of this. You were still a minor when you left home."

"I remember details. If it could help you—"

"Nell. No." He spoke firmly, though he wondered why he bothered. That kind of male forcefulness had never had any impact on his sister. "You need to stay out of this. This is my battle to fight, not yours."

"I want to help." She grasped his hand and met his gaze. "We can start by getting you the right attorney. This man, Eddie, has served his purpose. Now you need a shark. My friend Tish is a seasoned criminal lawyer who spent six years in the LA County District Attorney's Office. "

"What makes you think she'll want to help?"

"She and I were college roommates. She'll want to help." Nell smiled. "Best of all, though she's recently relocated to practice law in Chicago, she can still practice in California. Tish graduated at the top of our law school class. If I wanted someone to represent me in a criminal proceeding, I'd go with her."

It was high praise, Dixon knew, as well as a ringing endorsement.

"How can I reach her?"

"I'll call her first, if that's okay. Feel her out. She may be too busy getting started in this new practice, but I think if I ask, she'll agree."

"Thanks."

"You'd do the same for me."

"I'd do anything for you." He turned away, the rapid rise of emotion taking him by surprise.

"Tish will know what the prosecuting attorneys in Bakersfield will need from you in order to grant you immunity. While we wait for that information, we can go over your list of Gloria's past crimes and make sure all relevant details have been included."

"We can do that," he agreed. "But not now. Leo's parents are in town for the wedding. They, and your upcoming wedding, take priority."

"But—"

He stood and ushered her toward the door. "Reviewing the list can wait. Although I must admit I'm looking forward to making sure it's a comprehensive list of all of Gloria's sins. Especially if the documentation helps send her to prison."

Nell inclined her head. "Why are you so eager to get rid of me?"

"You're not the only one with plans for the evening." He grinned. "I have a festival to attend."

CHAPTER SIXTEEN

Rachel resisted the urge to pull out her phone and glance at the time. There was no need. When her replacement at the food bank booth arrived, she'd know it was time for Dixon to make an appearance.

In the meantime, she'd continue to smile at those who walked by and chat up the food bank with those who paused to grab a brochure, drop some coins into the pool or put a food item or two into the whale.

Both the whale and the pool, er, wishing well, were a hit. The number of families stopping by had kept her busy, but she was ready to be off.

Rachel was more than ready to walk with Dixon through the maze of booths. Maybe go crazy and get her face painted or her fortune told. Grab a turkey leg—the delicious aroma had been taunting her for the past hour—or enjoy the sweet taste of the rainbow cotton candy being spun nearby.

For sure she hoped to wander over to the bandstand, where a different group of musicians took the stage every ninety minutes.

"You look festive."

Rachel flushed with pleasure at the sound of Dixon's voice,

then glanced down at her khaki capris and the cherry-red tee with its "Fighting to Feed the Hungry" logo. "We're selling the tees in all sizes and colors."

To her surprise, he took out his wallet and handed her a hundred-dollar bill.

"What colors do you want?"

He flashed a smile. "Not for me. Buy however many this will cover and do a giveaway. Or simply give them away to random people who wander by."

Such a good man, Rachel thought.

She turned to Nevaeh, who'd strolled up and was watching them with interest. "Hear that, Nev?"

The teen didn't bother to pretend she hadn't been listening. "I did. How would you like me to distribute the shirts?" she asked Rachel.

"You decide."

Surprise skittered across the young girl's face. "You're leaving it up to me?"

"I am." Rachel linked her arm with Dixon's. "If you run into any issues, my cell is on and I'm available. Thanks again for volunteering today."

"Can I…" Nev hesitated. "I mean, would it be okay if I give one to my sister? She thinks the shirts are cool, but my dad isn't working right now and—"

"Absolutely give one to her."

"The food bank is lucky to have you." Dixon didn't even bother to keep his voice low. "I've never managed volunteers, but it seems as if it'd be difficult to hit the right balance."

She lifted her face to him, struck once again by his classic beauty. "I'm not sure I follow."

"Well, you're there to make sure they do their job. But they aren't getting paid, and if helping out becomes too much of a hassle, they'll quit. You have to walk that fine line between being the boss and showing appreciation."

"It isn't that difficult," Rachel protested. "I really do appreciate everything they do."

He nudged her arm down until his fingers locked with hers. "You'll make a good mother."

"Why, Mr. Carlyle, I believe that's the nicest thing anyone has said to me."

Surprise flickered across his face. "Really?"

She nodded. "My mother set the bar high. She was a wonderful person, so kind and loving, but not a pushover. I wish you could have met her."

"I'm sure I'd have liked her."

"What about yours?"

The fingers wrapped around hers tightened. He gestured with his head toward the stand they were about to pass. "How about some cotton candy and a walk to the duck pond for some quiet?"

"I'd love some." Rachel reached into her pocket for money, but by the time she'd extracted a rumpled bill, Dixon had paid.

When he handed her the cone of rainbow-colored, spun sugar, she handed him the money. Or rather, attempted to hand it to him.

With a look of puzzlement on his face, he pushed her hand back. "My treat."

"You don't have to pay for me. Marc and I always paid for our own."

He looked at her then, the soft look in his eyes nearly undoing her. "I'm not Marc."

"Thank God for that," she said and made him laugh.

It wasn't until they'd reached the bridge that Rachel realized she'd been chattering practically nonstop since he arrived.

"Enough about me." She pulled a tuft of spun sugar from the cone and popped it into her mouth. "How was your morning?"

"My sister came to see me."

Something in the way he said the words put Rachel on high

alert. She lowered the cone and swallowed the sugar. "I, ah, told her we slept together."

He nodded. "She was pissed."

Rachel braced herself and started to apologize. "I shouldn't have—"

She stopped herself. What did she have to apologize for? Telling her friends that she and Dixon were together? Unless, and this thought was a knife to the heart, he didn't want anyone to know.

But that didn't make sense. If he didn't want anyone to know they were involved, then why would he be holding her hand and putting his arm around her? Not to mention the occasional kisses when—

"You're thinking too hard."

She looked at him then, saw the look in his eyes.

"I'm glad we're together, and I don't care if everyone knows. In fact, I'd like everyone to know."

"I never thought Nell might be upset." Rachel's brows drew together. "She wasn't when I told her, or she didn't appear to be. I certainly never thought she'd come down on you."

"It isn't what you think." Instead of facing her, Dixon moved to stand beside her, his back, like hers, resting against the wooden rail of the bridge. "I come with a lot of baggage. Nell wanted to make sure I shared my past with you."

When she cast him a quizzical glance, he flashed a grin.

"My dear sister cares about you. And me," he admitted. "She wants you to be absolutely sure you know what you're getting into by consorting with the likes of myself."

"I don't care—"

"Hold that thought." Dixon waved over a teenage girl carrying a huge garbage bag and a pickup stick.

"May we give you these?"

The girl's smile was nearly as bright as her freckles. "That's what I'm here for."

Her Respect Nature shirt popped. For a second, Rachel studied the eye-catching color scheme and wondered if the food bank could do something similar.

"Are you finished with yours?" Dixon asked as he dropped the rest of his cotton candy into the sack.

Rachel blinked. "Yes. It's a lot of sugar."

The girl grinned. "That's what makes it so delish. Have a good afternoon."

"Where were we?" Rachel asked when the girl sauntered off.

"I was about to give you all the reasons you should think twice about getting involved with me."

"Too late." She laughed. "I'm already a goner." Her laugh faded at the look in his eyes. "I mean, I'm already fond of—"

He took her hand and brought it to his lips. "I'm already gone, gone, gone for you."

Her heart swelled, becoming a sweet mass in her chest.

"Let's walk, and I'll tell you a little about my childhood." Instead of heading in the direction of the festival, they went the way that took them to the area of town where Abby and Jonah lived.

Here, large Victorian homes sat far back from cobblestone streets. Immense front yards reminded Rachel of plush green carpets adorned with huge leafy trees and punctuated by brightly colored flowers and bushes.

Most of the homeowners had added hanging baskets of flowers and ferns to their front porches. On a few, decorative flags flew, a mixture of summer designs with a few autumn ones tossed in every so often.

Despite the fact that the area wasn't far from the Green, separated only by the bridge, it was remarkably quiet.

Rachel inhaled the scent of freshly mown grass while birds sang from trees and dogs barked. Forgetting all about the music in the Green and the turkey legs, she found herself content to simply stroll down the sidewalk with the man she loved.

Could you really fall in love with someone that quickly? Recalling Liz's warning about rebound affairs had her frowning.

"It's not anything really bad—" Dixon began, then stopped himself. "Well, actually, it is."

For a second, she wasn't sure what he was saying, then she realized he'd misinterpreted her frown. "I was—"

Rachel clamped her mouth shut. Seriously, it wasn't as if she could tell him that instead of being concerned about his childhood, she was worried she'd fallen in love on the rebound.

"What?"

"Nothing." She waved an airy hand, admiring for a moment the way the light caught the colored beads on the bracelet Becca had given her for her last birthday.

"I hope you know," he said, his expression suddenly serious, "that if you decide for whatever reason that you'd rather not be with me, I'll understand."

"You're acting as if you killed somebody." Rachel gave a nervous laugh, sensing the weight of this moment, but not understanding its origins. "I mean, it's not like you're a criminal or anything. You're a good guy."

For a long moment, he didn't say anything. "I'll tell you about it, and you can be the judge."

Dixon swallowed with difficulty, realizing his throat had gone bone-dry. Feeling so tense, so…nervous was ridiculous. While he didn't like to talk about his past, he retained control over just how much to tell Rachel.

"I stole for the first time at eight…under my mother's direction." Dixon spoke in the same tone one might use to announce when one had learned to ride a bike. "Gloria liked it that I was small for my age back then."

"Gloria?"

"My mother. Nell and I were told to call her Gloria. I prefer to use her name even now. She was never a mother."

Rachel cocked her head. "What about your father?"

"Never knew him or his name. He was never a part of my life."

"Okay. Sorry to interrupt." Rachel took his hand as they walked.

The simple gesture touched him more than any words could have.

"Gloria, as Nell may have mentioned, is what I would call a charismatic sociopath. She's beautiful, intelligent and can be extremely charming. Men and women are sucked in by her larger-than-life persona. They don't realize, at least not until it's too late, that the only person Gloria cares about is herself. I believe she'd push me in front of her to take a bullet if it meant saving herself."

The increased pressure on his hand told Dixon that Rachel was listening.

"Gloria's whole life has been a series of cons. Once I was deemed old enough, I acted as a decoy."

Rachel shot him a questioning look.

"I distracted others from what she was doing." He thought back to an early incident. "One time, Gloria was inside a house down the block, picking up some jewelry and art that she'd seen during a housewarming. A party, I might add, that she attended without an invitation."

His lips quirked. "The couple were supposed to be out for the evening, but they got back early. Gloria was still inside."

Rachel stopped, turned to him, her eyes wide. "Where were you?"

"Riding my bike up and down the sidewalk. When I saw their car coming down the street, I waited until they were close, then wiped out on their driveway and started screaming that I broke my arm."

Rachel gasped.

"The couple couldn't get into the driveway, not with me sprawled there. Gloria heard the noise and left out the back door."

"What happened?"

"They were kind. The woman was an emergency room physician. She checked out my arm. It wasn't broken, only badly scraped. She tended to me."

"Was your mother pleased…?"

"No." No need, Dixon thought, to tell her how Gloria had grabbed his injured arm, nearly breaking it herself. "She felt I should have given her more warning."

"I can't imagine how difficult it was for you to grow up with such a person."

"As I grew older, I developed a skill with computers. I used those skills to help her."

"Did you ever tell anyone about her?"

"She would have killed me."

"I'm sure she'd have been angry—"

"She'd have killed me," he repeated as his lips lifted in a humorless smile. "She told me that's what would happen if I ever crossed her. Based on her propensity for violence, I believe she'd have done just that."

"Nell's older, right? Did she help you get away?"

"My sister left home at seventeen. She wanted to take me with her, but I was only thirteen. We wouldn't have gotten far together." Watching his sister slip out the window that night had been brutal. As had been the beatings he'd endured until Gloria finally believed he didn't know where his sister went. "I encouraged Nell to leave and not look back."

"When did you finally get away from Gloria?"

It appeared Rachel wasn't going to delve too deep or ask questions about other things he'd done, the crimes he'd committed. Dixon wasn't sure if he was relieved or disappointed.

Still, he'd given her an honest picture of life with Gloria.

"I left when I was twenty-one." Dixon stared, unseeing, at the beautiful homes. "I should have gotten away sooner, but that crazy, dysfunctional life with her was all I knew."

"What made you finally make the decision to go?"

"Gloria was getting more out of control. She was always reckless, but things always worked out for her. But after Nell left, she took even more chances." Dixon paused. "I noticed she was setting things up so that if anything went south, it would be my head on the chopping block."

"Oh, Dixon. Do you really think she'd do that?"

He nodded, wishing he could tell Rachel that Gloria was contemplating doing that right now.

Lost in his thoughts, Dixon jolted when Rachel wrapped her arms around him.

"I'm so sorry," she murmured as she held him tight. "You didn't deserve a mother like that. No one does."

Which was true, but she seemed to have missed the point.

"I lied and cheated and stole."

"You were a child." She leaned back in his arms, her hands still encircling his neck. "Once you had the chance, you turned your life around. I know how difficult that can be."

He shot her a quizzical look.

"Not me." She gave a little laugh. "I never strayed far from the straight and narrow. I was referring to my brother Ben. Our parents' deaths hit him hard. He's almost two years younger than me, and we all thought he'd end up going to college on an athletic scholarship. Instead, he started drinking and doing drugs his senior year. He was picked up a couple of times for disorderly conduct and barely made it through high school. The day he graduated, he took off."

"Where is he now?"

"I got a text from him last fall. He was working on some ranch in Wyoming." Her lips curved, but there was a bleakness in his eyes. "He sounded happy."

She did understand, Dixon thought. Not completely, but at least it wasn't as if she'd never experienced life's difficulties. In fact, she'd had her own share of tragedies with the loss of her parents and her brother running off barely a year later.

"Why did you tell me about your childhood, Dixon?" She paused as if a thought had just struck her. "Is that your real name?"

Everything inside him went cold. He should have anticipated the question. Nell's past, which had come to light in only the past couple of months, wasn't widely known except among her circle of close friends.

They knew that his sister had changed her name from Susannah Lamphere to Cornelia Ambrose. If any of the three women had given the matter any thought, they'd have wondered about him.

No one had asked. Until now.

"I trust you, Rachel." Dixon leaned his head down until their foreheads touched. "Other than my sister, there isn't anyone I trust more."

"Don't tell me if you don't want to," she said.

He was tempted. Oh, how he was tempted to take her up on her offer.

In his mind, divulging his real name was big. Even bigger than the criminal charge. Just saying his name would be stripping himself bare.

No pretense. No artifice. The boy, the young man who'd made so many mistakes. Mistakes that, as much as he'd like to, he couldn't all blame on his mother.

"Kyler Lamphere."

"Kyler." Rachel rolled the name around on her tongue as if tasting it. "Did you go by Kyler? Or—"

"Ky. That's what S—" He stopped, then said, "That's what Nell called me."

"I can call you Ky. If you want. When we're alone."

"Thank you for the offer, but I'm Dixon now." He slid his fingers into the silky strands of her hair and realized they weren't gray anymore. "You changed your color back."

"Leeza worked her magic in reverse." She smiled. "I guess being stylish just doesn't work for me."

"I liked your hair that way, but I like it this way, too." He twirled a strand around his finger. "You're perfect however you are."

She laughed and pressed the back of her hand against his forehead. "Are you sure you're feeling all right?"

"Standing here, being with you, I couldn't feel any better."

"You're good for me." Her gaze searched his face. "I hope you know you can tell me anything."

Guilt stabbed like a freshly honed knife. *Just a couple of days*, he promised himself. As soon as he got his immunity, he'd tell Rachel everything.

"Can I tell you that I wish we were at your house right now?" He brushed a kiss across her forehead. "Can I tell you that I want to kiss you, but I know that once I begin, I won't want to stop?"

"I've an idea." An impish gleam filled the dark depths of her eyes.

"What is it?"

"Let's go to your place because it's closer."

"And…?" he prompted, unable to stop the grin.

"We'll start with kissing." She winked. "And take it from there."

CHAPTER SEVENTEEN

"Your friend Tish is convinced that if I can deliver the information I promised about this case, the prosecutor will give me a
deal." On Monday morning, Dixon leaned back in the chair in
Nell's office, giving the appearance of a man confident and in
control. The truth was, he was feeling anything but self-assured.
His entire future rested on the outcome of the negotiations. "Tish
offered to come to Hazel Green on Wednesday to meet with us. If
that works for you."

Dixon was willing to meet with his new attorney alone, but
Nell had made it clear she wanted to be there when the meeting
took place.

Nell picked up her phone, scrolled to her calendar. "What
time?"

"She suggested ten. At your office."

"I can make that work." Nell's brows pulled together. "Why is
she coming to Hazel Green? We could take the train into Chicago
and meet her at her office."

"I offered. She said something about representing me outside
of her new practice. I got the feeling she doesn't want to mix the

two. She also alluded to the wedding and how busy you must be. I didn't realize she was invited to the wedding."

"I told you we were roommates in college. Tish is one of the few friends I've kept over the years."

"I'm glad you did. She appears to know her stuff."

"Like I told you, Tish is a seasoned criminal lawyer. Her years as a prosecutor in LA will serve you well." Nell tapped a pen idly against the shiny surface of her desk.

With her wedding on tap for the weekend, Dixon knew his sister was running short on time. But then, so was he. Gloria's lawyers were giving the prosecutors fits. The evidence against her was murky enough that she could go free if Dixon didn't testify.

"I don't just want to see Gloria convicted for this crime," Dixon said. "I want her to go down for Bobby John's murder."

"Every time Bobby John looked at me, my skin crawled." Nell's eyes turned to blue ice. "But he didn't deserve to die. If they do charge Gloria with his murder, the case would be much stronger if we both testified."

Dixon shook his head. "You've got too much to lose."

Nell arched a brow. "You don't?"

"I'm only a financial planner. As an attorney, you could be disbarred." Dixon fixed his gaze on her. "I'm also not married to someone with political aspirations."

"Thanks to Stan Britten tracking me down, Leo and his family know everything about my past." Nell lifted her chin. "Leo will support me whatever I decide to do."

While Dixon knew that was true, he held out hope that his testimony would be sufficient. "Don't make any decisions now. Don't even give her another thought."

Without warning, Nell reached across the desk and covered his hand with hers. "After you testify, Ky, she'll be out of our lives for good. No more looking over our shoulders. No more wondering if she'll show up one day on our doorstep."

Dixon nodded. The hope of having Gloria in jail for decades was why he was willing to take this step, instead of waiting and wondering. He wanted to embrace his new life in Hazel Green. He wanted to build a life with Rachel.

His sister was right. Once Gloria was behind bars, they'd both be free.

~

Latisha Doogan was a tall, busty redhead with a hearty laugh and a firm handshake. Dixon bet a lot of attorneys and clients underestimated the woman. The second he'd shaken her hand and gazed into her sharp hazel eyes, Dixon felt lucky she was on his side.

After the normal pleasantries, she'd taken her time studying the information he'd compiled. Names, dates, crimes and every scrap of information about the incidents that would tie Gloria to the crimes.

"You've done well." Tish's gaze slid from Dixon to Nell. "There's a lot to check out here. Prosecutors will be happy if they can convict her on even half of these."

"What about the murder?" Nell asked.

Tish expelled a breath, her brow pulling together. "I know detectives working this case would welcome new information. Especially if, as you say, there was considerable doubt at the time about Bobby John's death being a suicide."

"But…" Nell prompted.

"From a prosecutorial standpoint, it's been nearly two decades since the death." Tish lifted her hands, let them drop. "We have Dixon's testimony, but he was a child at the time."

"I was twelve," he said when the attorney glanced at him.

"Little more than a child."

"I was sixteen. No, I'd just turned seventeen," Nell said. "Bobby John's murder happened just as Dixon described."

"You were your mother's alibi." Tish's brusque tone cut through the air. "You lied to the officers who interviewed you."

Nell's gaze never wavered. "She'd have killed me if I'd said any different."

"I realize she's—"

"Tish, listen to me. She murdered Bobby John without the slightest bit of remorse." Nell's blue eyes went stormy. "She never cared about Dixon or me. She beat us for minor infractions. We knew that if we didn't go along, if we didn't say exactly *what* she wanted us to say, it was over for us. First, she'd discredit us. Then, not long down the road, some sort of tragic accident would occur."

Tish studied Nell for a long moment. "Okay."

"I want her behind bars for life." Dixon glanced at Nell, then at Tish. "I'll blow up my entire life if it means she won't ever come around and cause trouble for Nell."

Nell reached over, took his hand and squeezed hard. "We're in this together, Ky."

After a long moment, Dixon nodded. He met Tish's gaze with a steady one of his own. "You know our goals. Tell us what we need to do to reach them."

Dixon planned to have lunch with his sister and Tish before the attorney returned to Chicago. But a last-minute crisis with a client had Nell unable to join them.

Before Dixon and the attorney left Nell's office, Tish's gaze turned stern. "We won't speak of anything related to this case in any public area. I realize you know this, Nell, but, Dixon, it's essential that all of these negotiations remain confidential. When we're at lunch, we're simply two people enjoying a meal. Attorney-client privilege does not extend to overheard conversations."

Dixon nodded. "Understood."

Tish narrowed her gaze. "Nell mentioned you have a new girlfriend."

Dixon shot a glance in his sister's direction.

Nell simply shrugged.

"How much does she know?" Tish demanded.

"Rachel knows I have a crazy mother. That's it."

"Keep it that way."

Dixon frowned. "Pardon?"

"I don't want you to say anything to this woman about the charges against your mother, your involvement in the Bakersfield incident or that I'm your attorney. At this time, there is no reason for her to know we're working on getting you immunity."

"If I ask Rachel to keep this confidential, she will."

Tish shook her head. "The fewer people who know about this, the better. Until we have a deal, anything related to this case is between us."

Dixon turned to Nell. "I assume Leo knows."

"I've told him what's going on." Nell's tone remained easy. "I wanted him to be prepared in case my testimony is necessary."

Tish pressed her lips together, then expelled a breath. "We can't do anything about that now. I assume he knows not to speak of this to anyone else."

A startled look crossed Nell's face. "Leo would never break a confidence."

Neither would Rachel, but Tish appeared stuck on the confidentiality thing, so when her gaze shifted back to Dixon, he nodded. "My lips are sealed. For now."

"Keep them that way." Tish stood and smiled at Dixon. "Tell me where we're going for lunch. I'm starved."

Thirty minutes later, Dixon realized that taking Tish to lunch, especially alone, had been a bad idea. At the time that he'd agreed to lunch, it was going to be the three of them. Then, when Nell's conflict had her bowing out, that left just him and Tish.

No problem. Or so he'd foolishly thought. He had lunch with clients all the time. Before they'd left Nell's office, that was the story they'd settled on. Tish was an old college friend of Nell's and a potential client of his.

For so many years, lies had been his business. They'd slipped off his tongue like butter off a hot knife. Since leaving home, he'd done his best to speak the truth whenever possible. Now he was being asked to bend the truth, okay, lie, but for the greater good.

It didn't make lying to those he cared about any easier.

Lilian was the first to stop by their outdoor table at the Green Gateau.

"Dixon. I thought that was you." The older woman's curious gaze slid to Tish. "Hello."

Dixon stood. "It's good to see you."

After only a momentary hesitation, he made the introductions, adding that Tish was Nell's college roommate.

Lilian smiled brightly. "Old friends really are the best. Will I see you at the wedding this weekend?"

"I wouldn't miss it." Tish lifted her cup of cappuccino to her lips.

"Well, I'll see you there." Catching sight of the group of women she apparently was meeting for lunch, Lilian waved. "Henrietta hates waiting, so I best skedaddle. See you both Saturday."

"She seems like a lovely woman." Tish studied him over the rim of her cup. "Very protective."

"Protective," Dixon scoffed. "Of what?"

"Of you." Tish sipped her drink, then set down the cup. "I assume she's acquainted with your girlfriend."

"She knows Rachel."

"You should have told her you were working with me on my portfolio."

"The opportunity didn't present itself." And, Dixon thought again, he hated to lie.

"She clearly wondered if this lunch was of a more personal nature." Tish's gaze turned serious. "I don't want to cause any trouble. Our relationship is strictly professional."

"Yes, it is." Because he sensed other interested eyes, and likely ears, focused on their table, Dixon waved a careless hand. "The assets in your portfolio are the only assets that interest me."

Tish laughed, a full-bodied laugh that had her hazel eyes sparkling. "You remind me so much of Nell."

"This is a surprise," Liz said.

Dixon slowly turned to find Liz and Abby staring at him and Tish. He forced an easy smile. "I'm beginning to think everyone I know is eating lunch at the Green Gateau today."

"Oh?" Liz raised a brow.

He wasn't fooled. Right now, the reporter was playing it cool, but it wouldn't be long before the direct questions would start.

"You, for instance," Dixon said. "I thought you'd be working today."

He turned to Tish. "Liz used to be a reporter at the *Sun-Times*. Now she's with—"

"I work for the *Trib*." Liz cocked her head. While her smile was friendly, the look in her eyes was sharp and assessing.

"I'm Abby Rollins." Never one to sit on the sidelines, Abby extended her hand. "I own the Inn at Hazel Green. I don't believe we've met."

Tish shook Abby's hand. "Tish Doogan. Nell and I were college roommates. She, Dixon and I were planning to have lunch together when there was some kind of court snafu, and she had to cancel. Dixon is helping me with my portfolio, so lunch has given us a chance to discuss some financial questions I have."

Relief swept across Abby's face. "Well, we'll let you two get back to business."

"Sorry for interrupting," Liz said.

As they walked away, Dixon heard Abby tell Liz in a hushed tone, "I told you it had to be a business lunch."

Tish tried to hide a smile, but couldn't quite manage it.

"Why are you smiling?"

"Like I said, it's easy to be overheard."

Or, Dixon thought, for simple things to be misunderstood. Which was why he was going to do everything in his power to push this deal along.

He didn't want to have to lie to Rachel any longer than absolutely necessary.

CHAPTER EIGHTEEN

The Friday night rehearsal dinner at Matilda's was a relaxed affair, complete with excellent food and drink and funny stories about the bride and groom.

Leo's brother Mathis brought the most laughs with his story about his younger brother's first date.

"Leo had been crushing on Sidney Donovan for months, and she'd finally taken pity on the poor sap and agreed to go out with him." Matt paused to take a drink of his IPA. "I remember Leo telling me that his stomach was jumpy, but we both thought it was just because he was stressed that a hot girl had given him the time of day."

Matt glanced at his brother.

Leo held up a hand. "Go on. You know I've never been able to stop you."

"Well, he actually ended up tossing his cookies all over the front of her new outfit." Matt shrugged. "The stomach flu effectively ended his first romance."

Matt shifted his gaze to Nell. "I'm really glad he didn't throw up all over you."

"That makes two of us," Nell said with aplomb.

"And I'm glad he waited for you." Matt's expression turned serious. "I believe you're the one who was meant to travel down the road of life with my brother. I even think, heck, I know, he could puke all over you and you wouldn't walk away."

Matt paused and waited for the laughter to die down. "I'm lifting this glass in toast to my almost sister-in-law. I believe I speak for everyone when I say welcome to the family."

Applause broke out, and Leo bent to kiss Nell, then shook his brother's hand.

Beside Rachel, Dixon rose. Though he'd laughed and spoken with everyone seated near them, he seemed distracted. Rachel had tried to get him to talk to her about whatever was bothering him, but he'd insisted he was just tired.

She could tell he was lying, the same way she'd been able to tell when one of her siblings was skirting the truth when they were kids. Of course, her siblings had stumbled over their lies, avoided looking her in the eye and had generally done a bunch of fidgeting.

Dixon displayed none of those signs. Still, she knew in her heart that he wasn't being truthful.

"When Nell and I were growing up, we used to talk about how we wished our life could be." He smiled at his sister. "To say we didn't have the best childhood would be an understatement. Looking toward the future gave us hope. Hope that when we were all grown up, life would be different. We promised ourselves that we would make it happen."

Dixon settled his gaze on Leo. "You love my sister, and she loves you. You've gone through some tough times already, things that would likely have destroyed a weaker relationship. But you stood together and came out of that difficult time stronger and more committed."

Now, Dixon widened his gaze to include Nell. "I'm happy those long-ago dreams have come true. I couldn't have picked a better brother-in-law."

"Thank you," Nell mouthed to Dixon as Leo tugged her close and kissed her temple.

"Let's suspend the speeches for a bit," Abby said, taking her duties as matron of honor seriously. "Matilda has signaled me that the baked Alaska will be coming out in less than five minutes."

A tall woman and a young man made their way around the table with silver carafes of coffee.

"That was a lovely speech," Rachel told Dixon when he sat down. "I think Nell—"

"Hold on just a minute." Dixon pulled his phone from his pocket.

Only then did she hear the buzz and realize he must have had it on vibrate.

"Who—"

He lifted a hand. She wasn't sure if it was deliberate or not, but he tipped the phone in such a way that she couldn't see the readout.

His expression remained inscrutable as he read the message.

"I'm sorry." He turned to her then, giving her hand a squeeze and offering an apologetic smile. "Something has come up. I need to go."

When he started to rise, Rachel grabbed his arm. "What is it? Can I help?"

He opened his mouth, then shut it. The emotion in his eyes was one she couldn't decipher. He brushed a strand of hair back from her face, then leaned down and kissed her before straightening.

"Will you be back?"

He hesitated. "I don't think so. There's a matter I need to attend to."

As he made his way to the door, Rachel watched Nell move to him. He spoke to his sister in quick, hushed tones.

When Leo rose, Nell waved him back down and continued to

focus on her brother. The slight frown told Rachel she wasn't pleased he was leaving.

What he said must have convinced her, because she gave him a hug before he turned toward the door.

Jackie, the wedding soloist, gestured toward him with the wineglass that hadn't been empty since she'd arrived. "Hey, Dixon, don't tell me you're leaving your little lady here so you can hook up with the redhead."

But Dixon was already at the door, too far away to hear her. Rachel heard, though. Along with everyone else in the room.

"Jackie." Jonah's sharp rebuke of his twin sister only made her giggle.

Nell stepped to Jackie, her eyes flashing a cold blue fire. Whatever Nell said to her had Jackie glancing in Rachel's direction, a sloppy-drunk smile on her lips. "I was just kidding. You knew that, right?"

"No worries." Rachel had heard all about Dixon's lunch earlier in the week with the gorgeous redhead.

He'd assured her, when she'd asked, that Tish was a client. The words came easily, and the explanation made sense—a friend of his sister, recently moved to the area, successful attorney with money to invest.

Yet, Rachel had been left with an uneasy feeling.

She hated this suspicious part of herself. Until Marc, she'd trusted. But that wasn't fair to Dixon. Just because Marc had cheated on her didn't mean that Dixon would.

Keeping that thought firmly in mind, Rachel made an effort to enjoy the rest of the evening.

Exhausted, Dixon gratefully accepted the coffee Nell offered him early the next morning. He took a big gulp, hoping the caffeine would work its magic.

"I'm sorry about last night." Dixon kept his fingers wrapped around the mug. "When Tish texted that we had a deal, but she wanted to meet to discuss the particulars, I had to leave."

Nell leaned back in her chair, the morning light just beginning to stream through the kitchen window. "I appreciate you sending me the information. I'd have been there if I could."

"I know." Dixon took another gulp of coffee, savoring the strong blend.

"I reviewed the deal. It's good, Dixon. It gives you blanket immunity on this incident, the only case where the statute of limitations still applies. But—"

"But I have to go to California and testify. Which means Gloria will know I've been living in Hazel Green as Dixon Carlyle. If she gets out—"

Dixon went cold all over again at the thought of what Gloria might do in retribution. She wouldn't necessarily target him first. The people he cared about would be in her cross hairs. His sister. And Rachel.

"We'll have to make sure that doesn't happen." Nell's jaw hardened. "You and I will give the prosecutors enough information to bury her."

"You're talking about Bobby John."

She nodded. "There's others. Oh, she may not have killed anyone else, that we know of, but between you and me, we gave Tish details on a number of crimes."

Dixon shifted his gaze out the window.

"Hey, you should be happy. This won't be hanging over your head anymore."

"She'll know where I am. Because of that, it won't be hard for her to discover you're here." He shook his head. "I should have kept my distance."

"Gloria is going to know where I am, because I'm going to testify against her when prosecutors bring charges against her."

Nell grabbed his arm, forcing him to look at her. "Don't give her any additional power over you."

"She could hurt you. Or Rachel."

"We're breaking her power. This is our chance to take her down, to take control, to do what we've wanted to do since we were kids."

The way Nell said the words, with such conviction and fervor, he nearly believed it was possible.

"Was Rachel very upset that I left?"

Nell hesitated. "Let's just say it didn't help that Jackie, who I'd never seen drunk before, blurted something about you leaving to meet your new redheaded girlfriend."

Dixon winced.

"Rachel laughed it off." Nell's brows drew together. "But she was quiet the rest of the evening."

"Tish and I leave tomorrow for Bakersfield."

"So soon?"

"The trial is scheduled to start next week. The prosecutor wants to meet with me. Get me ready to testify."

Nell rubbed her temples. "Any other time, I'd be there with you."

"Tish will be there. You trust her. You said so yourself. I'll be fine." He smiled. "This is your wedding. Enjoy every minute."

"But—"

"No buts," he said firmly. "You better not even think about me during your honeymoon. That's your time. And Leo's. I'll be fine. Once you're back, we can hit the ground running on the other charges."

"Did Tish say when you can tell Rachel?"

"She said once I testify, I can tell her. As soon as I return from California, I'll give Rachel all the details." Dixon blew out a breath. "If she's still speaking to me."

"It will turn out okay."

But Nell didn't sound so sure, and Dixon realized he wasn't the only one with doubts.

≈

The room in the church where the bridesmaids gathered had full-length mirrors and tables littered with a plethora of makeup and hair accessories. The fresh flowers in the room added another festive touch.

During the past week, whenever Rachel thought ahead to Nell's wedding, it had been with anticipation. There would be dancing at the reception, under the big tent that had been erected in Leo's backyard.

Once the eating, drinking and dancing concluded, she and Dixon would go home and make love.

Last night, she'd been left wondering.

She hadn't heard from Dixon until this morning. When he called, he acted as if leaving his sister's special dinner last night had been no big deal. The explanation he'd given her for why he'd left—a meeting with a client in financial crisis—had been vague and unsatisfying.

"You look amazing." Abby let her gaze linger on Rachel's A-line pale pink satin dress and the single strand of pearls around her neck.

"The dresses are very flattering." Rachel smoothed her hand along the smooth, shiny fabric. She liked that Abby's dress, as matron of honor, was the same style as hers, just a shade darker.

"This is going to be so much fun." Liz strolled over.

"I'm glad you think so." Nell stepped into the room. "Because that's the way a wedding should be."

Abby crossed the room to take her friend's hands. "I have never seen a more beautiful bride."

"Well, I'm not sure that's accurate, but thank you."

"It's true." Rachel studied Nell. "You're gorgeous."

Like her bridal party, Nell had gone with a tea-length dress, only hers was white lace over the palest of pink tulle. Simple and elegant, just like the woman.

"The picture of a happy woman in love," Abby agreed.

"Well, that's certainly true." Nell laughed, a joyous sound. Then she glanced at Rachel. "Do you have a minute? There's something I need to ask you."

"Ah, sure." Rachel touched the gentle waves of her hair. "You said we could do our hair any way we liked. I know the style is rather simple, but I thought it looked good with the flowers in my hair."

"This doesn't have anything to do with hair. Yours looks fabulous, by the way." Nell motioned for Rachel to follow her to the far side of the large room. When they reached the windows, she stopped, leaving her back to the others.

"Did I do something wrong?" Rachel asked.

"No. No." Nell touched her arm. "I just wanted to apologize again for Jackie's behavior last night."

"You didn't have anything—"

"My dinner. She was my guest." Nell's eyes went dark. "Her comment was uncalled for."

Was this, Rachel wondered, because Jackie's comment had maligned Nell's brother? Possibly. Probably.

"She has a right to say and think whatever she likes."

"We'll have to disagree on that point." Nell's gaze bored into Rachel's. For a second, she felt as if she were on trial. "Do you trust my brother?"

"I want to trust him," Rachel answered honestly. "I'm just scared of not seeing the signs, like I did with Marc. With Dixon, everything has moved so fast. I fell in love so—"

Rachel flushed, then repeated, "Everything has moved so fast."

Nell nodded. "Dixon isn't a cheat. He wouldn't do that to you. He's an honorable man. Give him a little more time. Trust him, even when your instincts are making you wonder if you can. As soon as he can explain everything, he will."

"But—"

"Take your places, ladies," Matilda called out. "It's show time."

"I'm ready, Mommy." Eva Grace, adorable in the same color of dress as her mother's, held a basket of rose petals.

Jonah's mother had arrived early to help with Eva Grace, freeing Abby to focus on her matron-of-honor duties.

"We're all ready," Matilda said, motioning for them to line up.

Liz and Wells were the first to walk down the aisle, followed by Rachel and Mathis.

"You're gorgeous," Matt whispered as they started to walk.

Rachel felt beautiful.

The look in Dixon's eyes when he'd seen her had lightened her heart. She'd been foolish to worry.

She reached the front and got to watch him stroll down the aisle with Abby. Just before he reached the front and turned, Dixon shot her a smile and a wink.

Eva Grace tossed out flowers, reveling in the attention of the guests.

Then the organ swelled, and Nell and Tim appeared.

Because of Nell's independent nature, Rachel had been surprised her friend chose to have Leo's father escort her down the aisle. She'd assumed Nell would walk alone.

When she'd asked Nell about it, her friend told her that Tim was the father she never had, but had always wanted. She was grateful he'd agreed to be such an integral part of her and Leo's special day.

Rachel's heart pounded as she listened to the vows and to the amazing love songs sung by Jackie. The woman really did have a beautiful voice.

When the service ended and Rachel strolled back down the aisle with Mathis, she almost felt as if everything would be okay.

Then she spotted an unfamiliar redhead seated on the aisle.

Though the woman could be anyone, Rachel somehow knew this was the beautiful friend of Nell's whom Jackie had mentioned. The one Dixon had taken to lunch.

The question was, was she also the client who so desperately needed his help last night?

CHAPTER NINETEEN

Dixon knew Tish had been invited to Nell's wedding and reception. He'd hoped that, at the last minute, she'd decide not to come. After all, between his case and settling into her new job and apartment, she was one busy woman.

He didn't want to diss her, but this was his night to spend with Rachel. He decided he'd be polite, but not spend any more time than necessary in Tish's company. The last thing he wanted was Jackie Rollins, or anyone else for that matter, commenting on his *relationship* with Nell's redheaded friend.

Wells and Mathis didn't have dates. Perhaps he could encourage one of them to keep her company. The intervention likely wouldn't be needed. Tish was a gorgeous woman who'd undoubtedly have the men flocking to her.

Instead of a head table, Nell and Leo had encouraged the wedding party to mingle with the other guests. That was just fine with Dixon.

Once they'd made it through the introductions of the wedding party, he and Rachel stood on the edge of the wooden dance floor, watching Nell and Leo dance, then Leo danced with his mother while Tim showed off some fancy moves with Nell.

When Tim returned Nell to her new husband's arms, the love on Nell's face was nearly palpable. The same emotion he saw in Nell was reflected in Leo's eyes.

"Seeing her so happy…" Dixon stopped to clear his throat.

Rachel squeezed his sleeve. "I understand."

"Would you like to dance?" he asked Rachel when the band launched into a slow set. "I promise not to step on your toes…not too much anyway."

She laughed. "I'd love to dance."

They'd stepped onto the dance floor when Tish approached.

"Tish, I'm happy you could make the wedding and reception." He smiled politely. "Having you here means a lot to Nell."

"I'm glad I could be here." Tish glanced curiously at Rachel, but when she opened her mouth, Dixon took charge.

"I'd like to introduce you to one of Nell's close friends, Rachel Grabinski." The second the words left his mouth, Dixon wished he could call them back. Nell's close friend? While it was true, it didn't say a thing about *his* feelings toward her. "Rachel, this is Tish Doogan, Nell's college roommate."

"It's a pleasure to meet you." Tish extended a hand, giving Rachel no choice but to take it.

"You're the one who had lunch with Dixon at the Green Gateau," Rachel said, her friendly smile never wavering.

Tish gave a good-natured laugh. "I think you're the third person to mention that lunch to me this evening."

Mention that Nell was supposed to be there. Dixon willed her to say the words. When she didn't, he added, "Nell was supposed to be there, but had a last-minute conflict."

"Speaking of last minute…" Tish glanced at Rachel. "Would you mind terribly if I borrow your dance partner for a minute? There's something I need to ask him."

Rachel's smile froze. "Of course not."

"I'm sure this will only take—"

Wiggling her fingers in a gesture of goodbye, Rachel strolled off. "I'll catch up with you both later."

"This better be good." Dixon turned to Tish. "What—"

"Not here." She slipped her fingers around his arm. "Somewhere private."

Dixon turned back, scanned the crowd, frowned when he couldn't spot Rachel. "Okay, but make it quick."

If Tish needed privacy for this, Dixon knew just the place. A bench near a small pond close to the house. They were nearly there when Marc stepped into their path.

"Isn't this a nice surprise?" Marc flashed his fake smile at Dixon, then turned to Tish. "Marc Koenig."

"Tish Doogan."

"Did you just move to Hazel Green?" Marc asked before Dixon could grab Tish's arm and pull her along.

"I live in Chicago."

"What—"

"'What' is a good start to the question I have for you," Dixon interrupted. "What are you doing here?"

"I was invited."

Dixon narrowed his gaze.

"You want to see my invitation?" Marc reached inside his suit jacket and pulled it out. "You kids have fun out here in the dark. Me, I'm going to check out the dancing."

Marc strolled off, whistling.

Dixon gritted his teeth. The night was on a downward trajectory that he seemed powerless to stop. "What's this about?" he asked Tish.

"The trial has been postponed. Your mother's attorney had a death in his immediate family." Tish sighed. "We don't need to leave for California tomorrow after all."

～

Rachel danced with Matt, who made her laugh, and Wells, who looked like he'd rather be anywhere than on a dance floor. The band had just announced a brief break when Marc strolled over.

"What are you doing here?" Rachel frowned. "Nell and Leo don't want you here."

"They sent me an invitation."

"That was back when you and I were together," she reminded him.

"Perhaps that was the only reason. Perhaps not." He offered a conciliatory smile. "I want to say I'm sorry for all that's happened between us. We both have to live in this town, and I hope we can move forward without any lingering animosity."

Rachel hesitated, not sure how to respond. She didn't want it to be awkward when they ran across each other at various events. But she certainly didn't want him to think she'd forgiven him.

"You were really dancing up a storm." He offered her a boyish, engaging smile. "I thought you might be thirsty."

He held out a glass filled with clear liquid and topped with a lime.

"What is it?" she asked suspiciously.

He chuckled. "Your favorite. Club soda with a lime."

As her throat was dry, she took the drink from him. "Thank you."

"You're very welcome." He glanced admiringly at her dress. "That's a perfect color for you."

Marc gestured with the hand holding his own drink. "Looks like quite the turnout."

Rachel let her gaze skim the crowd. Dixon should be back by now.

"If you're looking for your new boyfriend, I ran into him and Tish back by the pond."

Rachel frowned. "What pond?"

"You know, the one up by the house, just outside the French doors."

She knew the spot, but the house was off-limits tonight, and that area would be dark.

"It was dark and very private," Marc said, almost as if he'd read her thoughts. "I was surprised to see them huddled there together."

"Huddled?" Her brows slammed together. "You're telling me they were embracing."

"Whoa. No." Marc held up his hands. "I'm not saying anything of the sort. They were talking when I came up."

"About?"

"I don't listen to other people's conversations." He chuckled. "Okay, sometimes if they're talking really loudly, I can't help myself. Remember when we went to the movies in Chicago, and those kids in front of us were talking about how they'd meet up with their vampire friends and drink each other's blood?"

Rachel chuckled. "The boys in the trench coats."

"Then the girls joined them, and when one asked what they were talking about, they told her."

This time, Rachel laughed aloud. "She said something like, 'Cool, invite me along sometime.'"

Rachel was still laughing when she felt a hand on her shoulder.

She turned, and there was Dixon.

He bent and brushed a kiss across her cheek. "Sorry I kept you waiting. That took longer than I anticipated."

His gaze settled on Marc.

Marc smiled. "I was just keeping Rachel entertained while you were…having your meeting."

"Was he bothering you?" Dixon asked as they watched Marc skirt the dance floor, then disappear into the crowd.

"He brought me a club soda." She lifted the glass.

Dixon inclined his head.

"It's a favorite." Rachel expelled a breath. "He also said he hoped things could be cordial between us going forward."

"You believe him?"

Rachel shrugged and slipped her arm around Dixon's sleeve. "How did your meeting go?"

"Fine."

Rachel waited for him to elaborate, perhaps tell her what was so important that the woman had practically dragged him off the dance floor. Maybe give her a clue why it took so long.

When he said nothing more, merely took the drink from her hand and set it on a table before pulling her into his arms and out onto the shiny hardwood, a part of Rachel's heart closed.

She'd been a fool once before because she ignored signs.

She wouldn't make that mistake again.

Dixon sensed the change in Rachel even as she rested her head against his chest. Damn Gloria. Damn the legal system.

Nell had told Leo. Why shouldn't he tell Rachel?

Then he thought of how he'd seen her laughing with Marc. Though Dixon was in love with her, she'd just gotten out of a serious relationship. He couldn't imagine her going back to Marc, not after how the man had treated her.

Then again, hadn't he stayed with his mother long after he should have left? Despite repeated episodes of emotional and physical abuse, hadn't he let her charm her way back into his good graces again and again?

Staying with her hadn't been simply a fear of what would happen if he left and she found him. It had gone much deeper. Gloria had never apologized for the abuse, but she had bought him video games and other things he wanted, and she had constantly told him that she loved him more than anyone else.

Gloria had scoffed at the notion of therapists, bragged there wasn't a psychologist or psychiatrist alive she couldn't manipulate.

Dixon wasn't too proud to admit that after he left her, he'd struggled with his feelings. With his guilt. With his anger. At Nell, for leaving him alone with Gloria, even though he'd urged her to go. At Gloria, for the abuse she'd heaped on him. At himself, for going along with her schemes.

He'd seen abuse victims villainized in the media, their decisions questioned as if they were blame. Why didn't they tell someone? Why didn't they leave? How could they stay year after year and let themselves be abused?

No one could fully know what he and Nell had endured. He'd bet his last dollar that most had never met anyone as evil or as charismatic as Gloria. Dixon knew without a single doubt that no one would have believed him, and he'd have paid the price for telling tales outside of the family.

The therapist he'd sought out after leaving Gloria had told him that…

"You're very quiet this evening." Rachel's voice broke through his thoughts, flinging him back into the present.

Dixon pushed back the emotion that those old memories still held. "There is nowhere I'd rather be than right where I am at this moment."

He tightened his arms around her, as if to reassure himself that she was still there.

"You know, don't you, that you can talk to me about whatever is troubling you."

Tell her, a part of him urged, even as the cautious side that had guided his steps and actions since he'd left Gloria told him to wait. Just wait a little while longer.

"I know." He kissed the top of her head. "When I first saw you in the church, I couldn't breathe. You are so lovely."

She laughed, lifting a hand from his arm to flutter it in a dismissive wave. "That's over the top, even for you."

The comment stung. "Even for me?"

"You're very generous with your compliments. The fact is there are any number of women in this room far prettier than me."

"You do that a lot."

She jerked her head back. "Pardon?"

"You wave away compliments, put down your appearance. Why is that?" He kept his tone easy, but the words had her eyes blazing hot.

"I don't do that."

"I went to a therapist for a while. Did I ever tell you that?"

Confusion replaced the anger in her eyes. "You did?"

"It wasn't easy walking into that first session." He tugged her closer, finding it worked better to tell her something so personal when he wasn't looking into her eyes. "I equated therapy with not being able to handle things on my own."

She was silent for several long seconds. "What made you go?"

"I told you about my crummy childhood."

He felt her nod.

"I wasn't able to move past my feelings, or old patterns of behavior, as easily as I'd hoped. Gloria was a perfect example of what not to do, but she was my only role model."

Her hand tightened on his. "Did you find the therapy beneficial?"

"I did. My therapist told me that the worst things that happen to us can play a part in making us a better version of ourselves." Dixon blew out a breath. "It took some hard work, but I began to see myself in a different light and to believe that I could be the person I wanted to be."

"I'm glad."

Though she didn't say so, Dixon sensed her confusion about why he was telling her this while they danced at his sister's wedding. "One thing I learned is to accept compliments. More so, to actually believe they are true. I was smart. I was accomplished.

I knew a lot about stocks and bonds. Though I never brushed aside compliments like you do, I didn't believe them."

She was silent for such a long time that Dixon wondered if he'd made another mistake. There was so much going on in both of their lives. Was this really the time for such a discussion?

"My sister Becca was, is, the pretty one in the family. Me, I'm the steady, dependable one. I was good ol' Rachel who could be counted on to get things done." Rachel leaned back in his arms and gazed into his eyes. "Handsome men like you aren't attracted to women like me. That's been my experience. I know I'm pretty enough, but in the looks category, you're a ten. Tens go for other tens, not a seven."

Dixon wasn't quite sure how to respond to this numbers game. "All I can tell you is I'm being honest when I say that, to me, you are the loveliest woman in this room, in this town, hands down."

"What about Tish?"

Dixon blinked. "What about her?"

"She has all the men buzzing about her."

Was this what was at the root of Rachel's insecurity tonight? Did she think he preferred Tish?

Marc.

Yes, the man had undoubtedly fanned those flames.

"I'm not attracted to Tish." He fought for the right words, ones that would reassure Rachel that she didn't have to worry about Tish. "She's Nell's old roommate. She's a nice person. But you're the only one I want."

He lifted a hand to her face.

When she leaned into his palm and expelled a soft sigh, Dixon did what he'd been wanting to do all evening. He lowered his head and kissed her.

CHAPTER TWENTY

Rachel didn't have time to ponder Dixon's words before Mathis cut in. By the time the evening was nearly over, she'd tossed her silver sandals to the side, and her feet practically wept in gratitude.

She was back with Dixon when the musicians returned from a short break.

Matt stepped onto the raised platform with the band and shot the leader a thumbs-up as the musicians performed a snippet of the Chicken Dance.

"Get out there with your bride, Leo," Matt said, confiscating the microphone. "The Chicken Dance and the Macarena were our two favorite wedding dances when we were kids."

Leo let out a good-natured groan as he and Nell were motioned to the center of the room.

"They're not doing this by themselves." Matt indicated everyone should join the couple on the dance floor.

Rachel had always loved the Chicken Dance and the Macarena. She and Marc had gone to a wedding in the spring, but he'd pronounced both songs "ridiculous," and they'd stayed on the sidelines for them.

Dixon grabbed her hand. "This will be fun."

Startled, she only stared.

He stopped tugging. "We can sit this one out if you'd like."

She laughed. "Not on your life."

Her back was to Dixon for the start of the song, and she saw Wells speaking with Marc and pointing toward the exit. Her gaze locked with Marc's for only a second.

When he smiled at her, she looked away.

Her heart was pounding hard, and by the time the Chicken Dance ended, she was laughing.

Eva Grace clapped loudly when it was over. The child had partnered up with Wells's daughter.

Lilian danced with an older man whom Rachel didn't recognize.

"A wedding reception wouldn't be complete without the Macarena." Matt pointed to Wells, who stood on the sidelines. "You're not getting out of this one. We'll wait for you to get on the dance floor."

Wells smiled, but something in the look he shot his brother told Rachel that Matt would be paying for this tomorrow.

Feeling young and carefree, Rachel moved her hips in time to the music and saw Dixon's eyes darken. She wasn't surprised that he knew all the moves.

A laughing Nell stopped to kiss her husband, and Rachel's heart melted. Only then did she realize everyone in her line had shifted in the other direction. Grinning, she joined them.

She wondered what was next, but Matt had left the stage, and the songs turned slower until they were down to the last one.

"I hope no one cuts in." While it had been fun to dance with so many different men, right now there was only one man Rachel wanted to hold her.

Rachel hadn't realized she'd spoken aloud until she felt the low rumble of Dixon's chuckle. "I couldn't have said it better myself."

When a guy she recognized as a distant cousin of Leo tapped Dixon on his shoulder, he shook his head. "Sorry, buddy. Not this time."

The man merely shrugged good-naturedly and stepped away.

"I feel bad we said no."

"It's the last dance." Dixon pulled her even closer. "Anyone can see we're together. He should have known better than to ask."

She nodded and laid her head against Dixon's broad chest, his words circling in her head.

Anyone can see we're together.

It was true, she realized. Other than those few minutes when he'd stepped away to speak with Tish, Dixon had been at her side. They'd eaten hors d'oeuvres and drunk champagne. They'd danced and chatted with friends, his arm slung over her shoulders or her fingers laced through his.

Why was she so afraid of trusting her feelings for him? He'd spoken with a woman for five minutes, and suddenly they were having a secret affair.

Tish had been at the reception the entire time, and Dixon hadn't given her a second glance. On the other hand, she'd watched Marc sidle up to the gorgeous redhead several times over the course of the evening before Wells had asked him to leave.

Was Dixon right? Rachel wondered. Was she insecure about her own looks? Her own appeal?

She thought about Dixon's earlier comments. While Rachel was sure her parents hadn't meant to do any harm, each of their children had been given a label. She'd been *dependable*. Becca had been *pretty*.

"You're thinking so loud I can practically hear you." Dixon brushed his lips against her hair.

"I hope not." She lowered her voice until it was barely above a whisper. "Because I'm thinking what I'd like to do to you once we leave here."

He stopped for a second. Just stopped in the middle of the dance floor. When his gaze locked with hers, his gray eyes swarmed with emotion. "You do trust me."

Shoving aside the tiniest, barest hint of doubt, Rachel nodded.

"Let's leave now." His voice took on a hushed urgency. "Your place or mine? You pick."

"We can't leave before Nell and Leo."

Dixon glanced over to where his sister and her husband slow-danced.

"They couldn't get much closer if they were fused." He narrowed his gaze, then smiled. "It's obvious they're ready for this part of the evening to end. We won't have to wait much longer."

"Dixon." She spoke his name, then paused, not sure what she wanted to say.

"What, sweetheart?"

"Do you really think I'm beautiful?"

That night, in her bed, Dixon showed her how he felt, how much he cared. If he hadn't put all her fears to rest, he hoped he'd hit most of them.

For the next week, Dixon stayed close. They had lunch together nearly every day. According to Tish, Gloria was pushing to get the trial started so she could be cleared and the right person put behind bars.

As she had so many times in the past, Gloria had gotten the victim, Leon Janik, on her side. He'd taken his former lover's case to the local media, insisting that Glo was incapable of pulling off such a crime, casually mentioning that her son, a computer guru, had been opposed to his sweet mother having a relationship with any other man from the beginning.

"Find the son," Janik said, "and you'll find the true perpetrator of this crime." A crime, the man asserted, that had damaged both his and Glo's reputations.

Watching the interview online had Dixon seething and insisting to Tish that they needed to act now. Why the delay? Didn't Tish realize he was being crucified in the press? That now, when he testified, it would appear that he was guilty and they should let Gloria go?

The problem, Dixon knew, without Tish even mentioning it, was that he *was* guilty. Though Gloria wasn't the innocent she claimed to be, he had used his computer skills to help his mother perpetrate the crime.

At the end of his rope, he shut himself up in his condo and told Rachel he wasn't feeling well. When she offered to bring him soup, or simply come and tend to him, he told her no.

Nell was on her honeymoon, and he couldn't talk to Rachel. Never had Dixon felt so alone.

Sitting at the kitchen table, Dixon dropped his head into his hands. His attempt to shut the door to his past had turned into one big cluster—

The sound of the intercom had him jerking up his head. "Yes, Anthony?"

"Miss Latisha Doogan is here to see you."

Dixon frowned. Tish hadn't said anything about getting together. If she had, he'd have suggested they meet in Chicago.

An uneasy feeling crawled up his spine.

Whatever reason had brought Tish to Hazel Green, it couldn't be good.

Rachel glanced up at the sky, happy to see that the clouds that had dogged the sky all morning had disappeared. The Stuff the Bus for the Hungry event would have been a difficult one to reschedule.

Though she'd worn a jacket that morning, she shed it by noon. At least all her volunteers had shown up, and things were running smoothly. The location of the bus, directly in front of the Hazel Green Market, was prime.

There were volunteers inside and out. Once a sack was filled, the volunteer would be given another empty one, while a runner would deliver the full bag to be added to the contents of the bus.

The volunteers standing by the bus helped people who drove up to drop off nonperishable food items.

"Nevaeh, have you taken your break?" The girl, her auburn hair pulled back in a serviceable tail, nodded. "I was the last one, except for you."

"I've got a granola—"

"I've got a turkey on rye," a familiar voice said. "And it's got your name on it."

Rachel turned slowly to see Marc holding up a bag from the deli they'd frequented when they were dating.

He flashed a smile. "I also have a check for a hundred dollars made out to the food bank."

"It's okay, Rachel," Nev told her. "I can handle things here. Besides, the picnic table is just over there."

The table that Nev referred to was a temporary one on the far side of the bus, specifically brought in for the volunteers' breaks.

"Oh, and I forgot." Marc lifted his other hand. "A club soda."

They'd be in full view of everyone, she told herself. Considering they'd both likely be living in this town for the rest of their lives, there was no reason not to be civil.

Still, she hesitated.

If he had pushed, she would have said no. No reason. No excuses. Just no.

He didn't push. Just stood there with the bag of food in one hand—a peace offering?—and the drink in the other.

"Okay," she said finally. "I only have fifteen minutes."

Eating the sandwich and drinking half of the club soda took

ten of those fifteen minutes. During that time, Marc kept the conversation general, alluding to several new building projects in town as well as rumors of a possible renovation of an historic structure.

"I've heard Lilian might be involved in that," he said. "But she changed the subject when I asked her about it."

"Thanks for the lunch and the donation." Rachel wadded up the paper napkin that had come with the sandwich and tossed it into the sack. "I need—"

"I have to tell you something, Rachel." He raked a hand through his thinning hair. "I—"

"Let's leave the past in the past." Rachel blew out a breath. "We can be civil, but it's best if you don't come around again."

A swath of angry red sliced Marc's cheeks, but his voice remained calm when he spoke. "I assume this is because of your new boyfriend?"

"It's because I don't trust you."

"Yet, you trust Dixon Carlyle." Marc sneered the name.

"I do."

Marc made a tsking sound. "I don't think you will once I tell you what I know."

Rachel gritted her teeth. "I'm not interested in anything you have to say."

"Did your new boyfriend tell you he's a criminal? That he's under investigation in California, and word is he'll soon be arrested and charged?"

Rachel inhaled sharply.

"I didn't think so." Marc's lips curved as if the thought of being the bearer of such happy news gave him much pleasure. "Which means he probably didn't mention that Tish Doogan is a prominent criminal attorney."

Rachel fought for composure. She would not, *would not*, give Marc the satisfaction of seeing how much he'd rattled her.

It was clearly apparent, if it hadn't been before, that Marc didn't care about her. It was all about him. Even tossing out these revelations wasn't for her benefit, but rather his way of getting back at Dixon.

"I need to get back to work."

He reached out for her as she pushed back, but her icy glare had his arm dropping to his side.

As she passed by the trash can, she dropped the sack into the dark depths, wishing she could do the same with Marc.

CHAPTER TWENTY-ONE

Dixon sat at the table across from Tish. Only years of practice allowed him to keep all emotion from his face.

"You're saying that even though I've been given blanket immunity for this incident, it won't extend to any other crimes I tell them about."

"That's always been true." Tish inclined her head. "I didn't see it as an issue, because the others occurred when you were a minor. I just want to reiterate that because your mother—"

"Please," Dixon interrupted, "refer to her as Gloria."

Tish nodded. This morning, she was in full lawyer mode in a navy suit, her mass of red hair pulled back in a clip. "Gloria, along with her ex-lover, are eager to place the blame on you. They're building quite a case against you in the press."

Dixon stared over Tish's shoulder at the view of green topped by blue skies. A sight that normally soothed and steadied him. Not today. When he refocused on Tish, he kept his voice flat. "I have to testify in this case. I have immunity, so they can't charge me."

"Correct. But—"

He held up a hand, needing to work this out in his own head.

"But if I bring up other incidents, and I have any culpability, I could be charged."

She nodded.

"If she's convicted, this will be her first conviction, and the so-called 'victim' is on her side. Not only that, she has a top-notch attorney and—"

"You're familiar with his record?"

"Gloria only hires the best." Dixon drummed his fingers on the table. "If I don't bring up her other criminal activity, and she doesn't face those charges, she could be out on parole in a few years."

Tish nodded again.

"And out for revenge," he added.

"You don't know—"

"I know." His firm tone brooked no argument. He pushed back his chair and stood. "I'm between a rock and a hard place. I want her in jail for as long as possible, but in my zeal, I could be putting my freedom at risk."

"Yes, but we'll be going through these additional cases to see if you're at risk before we bring them up to the prosecution. Your sister can also review them."

Dixon understood, but he didn't trust the system. Hadn't he seen plenty of people take the fall for Gloria while she walked away laughing?

He thought of Nell and how happy she'd been at her reception. She was fully convinced she could weather any storms wrought by Gloria. But at what cost?

"I need to get back." Tish rose, her hazel eyes searching his. "Take your time and think about it. You don't need to make a decision this minute. We'll fly to California next week. If you like, we can take this one step at a time. Get your testimony in this case out of the way, then decide what direction you prefer to go."

"I'm going to tell Rachel what's going on," Dixon announced as he walked Tish to the door.

Tish whirled. "I thought we agreed you'd wait until after your testimony."

"I'm not going to lie to her anymore about this, about who you are and why we're talking." Just saying the words had a weight lifting off Dixon's chest.

He realized that keeping all this a secret from Rachel had taken a toll, far more than he'd let himself believe.

"I don't think—"

"One step at a time," Dixon said, repeating her words. "First step, I'll tell Rachel. Next, you and I will meet with Nell tomorrow about these new developments. She and Leo will be back tonight, but they'll need time to get settled. Then I'll testify."

What would it be like, he wondered, to see Gloria again? Though it had been a number of years, he had no doubt she would be as beautiful—and as canny—as ever. How would it feel to sit in the witness chair and see her behind the defense table?

Dixon knew going to California and being in the same room with her again would be difficult. But, for him, removing the threat of arrest from charges stemming from this incident would make the trip—and seeing her again—worthwhile.

"We'll talk tomorrow." Tish might not be happy about his decision, but he was the client.

Dixon watched her push the elevator button before shutting the door.

How would Rachel react to the news? he wondered. Unlike Nell, he hadn't been a child when he'd helped his mother in Bakersfield. He should have known better, *had* known better, but had done it anyway.

The therapist had helped him work through most of his guilt and anger—at himself, at Gloria, even at Nell for leaving him alone with their mother when he was only thirteen—but some still remained.

Would Rachel find him lacking in character? How could he blame her if she did? She deserved the best, and he fell far short of that mark. But he loved her, would do anything for her, and shouldn't that count for something?

Dixon had just opened a bottle of beer when a knock sounded at the door. He let his gaze do a quick sweep of the room, wondering if Tish had forgotten something.

Setting down the beer, Dixon strode to the door and flung it open. "Did you—?"

He stopped when he saw Rachel in the doorway.

She pushed past him. "Tish held the elevator for me. I told Anthony you were expecting me."

During his years with Gloria, Dixon had become an expert at reading body language. Even without that experience, he'd have seen that Rachel was fuming.

"What's wrong?" Concern had him reaching out a hand, which she promptly batted away.

"Don't touch me." Though her jaw was set in a hard line, her voice shook with emotion, and her eyes shimmered with unshed tears.

He gestured vaguely in the direction of the sofa and chairs. "Would you like to sit down?"

She strode to the window, then whirled. "You lied to me. Lied to my face. How could you do that?"

"Tell me what you're talking about." He lifted his hands. "I'm sure I can explain."

"Don't you mean so you can come up with a convincing lie?" She flung out the words like a warrior tossing down a gauntlet.

Dixon felt his temper flare. "What happened to innocent until proven guilty? It appears you've already tried and condemned me when I don't even know the charges."

The situation in Bakersfield was much the same. He'd been found guilty in the court of public opinion based on the spewing of a woman who wouldn't know the truth if it bit her in the butt.

When Rachel only clenched her hands into fists at her sides, his mind raced. Dixon could think of only one person in Hazel

Green who'd want to create trouble between him and Rachel. Marc.

That Marc would say or do something to manipulate Rachel didn't surprise Dixon. What did surprise him was that Rachel believed a man who'd already shown her he couldn't be trusted.

"What did Marc do?" He kept his tone cool.

Rachel lifted her chin. "What makes you think he has anything to do with this?"

"I've never been stupid." Suddenly exhausted, Dixon dropped down into the chair Rachel had ignored. "Did he tell you something?"

Dixon didn't even look in her direction. He couldn't bear to see the anger and reproach he'd seen when she'd barreled her way into his condo.

To his surprise, she crossed the room and sat on the sofa. She still wore her food bank shirt, which told him she'd come from her stint at Stuff the Bus.

He knew he was right about Marc. She'd have been a captive audience because she was working. But if she'd wanted to get rid of him, it wouldn't have been a problem. Not with so many supporters around.

Which meant she'd willingly listened to Marc's trash talk.

The knowledge was a sharp blow to the heart.

"He told me you're a criminal. That you're wanted on charges in California. That you'll soon be headed there to face those charges. Oh, and that Tish is your lawyer." Rachel's face remained stony as she finished the laundry list of his failings. "You never said one word to me about any of this."

Dixon experienced a momentary surge of hope. It sounded as if the fact that he hadn't told her bothered her more than the fact that he might have done something criminal.

"Would it bother you if it was true?"

"What kind of question is that?" She surged to her feet. "Of course it would bother me to know you're a wanted criminal."

The shell that Dixon had kept around his heart, the one that had opened for Rachel, snapped shut. Though it pained him to admit it, Gloria had been right about one thing.

The only person you could trust was yourself.

No one really cared, and you were a fool if you believed they did.

He'd been a fool.

"Marc said—"

Simply hearing the man's name on Rachel's lips was a jagged piece of glass dragged slowly across his skin.

"Now you're quoting your abuser?" Dixon offered a humorless laugh. "It's funny how you can forgive him for everything he did to you, but you judge me without even getting the facts first."

"You lied to me." Her chin jutted up. "Lies of omission are still lies."

"Is that what you told your siblings when they were growing up?" A sneer filled his voice. "Did you offer those words of wisdom in that same prim, sanctimonious tone?"

She inhaled sharply. An instant later, two bright swaths of red colored her cheeks. "What tone I use doesn't change the fact that it's true. Lies of omission are still lies."

"It's also true that there should be trust between people who love each other." Dixon didn't give her a chance to respond. He rolled on, while he saw whatever tenderness she'd felt for him die. "Oh, wait, we just had sex. Love never came up. Well, I'm sorry you broke your sexual fast to have sex with a criminal. Better luck next time."

When she only pressed her lips together, he felt blood pour from his body where the glass had scored his skin. He'd said too much, hurt her too much, and that made him hate himself all the more.

Gloria was right. He was just like her. Why had he tried so hard to deny that fact?

It didn't matter that he hadn't intended to hurt Rachel when he lashed out. It mattered only that he'd hurt her. And if he didn't get her out of his apartment very soon, he'd do something that would hurt her even more.

He'd tell her he loved her and beg her to stand by him.

He moved quickly to the door and held it open.

She stood for a long moment and studied him. Then she walked out of his life.

The tears Rachel held inside started to fall the instant Dixon's door slammed behind her. He'd been so cold, his usually warm gray eyes hard as steel when he'd accused her of—of what?

Of being concerned about his criminal past? Of being upset that he hadn't said one word about any of this to her? He had, of course, mentioned his mother, but that wasn't the same as telling her *he* was in trouble with the law.

Swiping furiously at her eyes, Rachel punched the elevator button. Where did he get off with all that talk about trust? She'd trusted him. Where had that gotten her?

She took some deep, steadying breaths on the ride down to the opulent lobby, replaying their conversation in her head. How could he accuse her of forgiving Marc but not him?

Trying to turn the tables on her, she thought. Well, she hadn't let him, had she?

It struck her as the door slid soundlessly open that he still hadn't explained. Would she have given him that chance if he hadn't gone off on her first?

She was still pondering that question when Anthony sprang up to open the exterior door for her. When she reached her car, she found Marc standing beside it.

"You look upset." Marc's attempt at a sympathetic look fell flat. "I'm sorry, but you were smart to get rid of him now before he dragged you down with him."

"Why are you here?" she demanded.

"Something told me you might be coming here. I knew you were upset." There was that faux smile again. "I thought perhaps you'd need a friend, someone to comfort and console you."

"You're not my friend."

Anger flashed in his eyes, but he somehow managed to hold on to the smile. "I know we've gone through a rough patch, but—"

"Go away, Marc. I don't want to see you or speak with you again." She blew out a breath, squared her shoulders and felt herself steady. "Whatever we had is over."

"But you and Dixon aren't together."

"The status of my relationship with Dixon—or any other man —is none of your concern."

A muscle in Marc's jaw jumped. "I went out of my way to find out just what kind of scum you were screwing…and this is the thanks I get?"

His menacing step forward hit a brick wall in the form of Anthony.

"You need to get off this property, sir."

"Or you'll do what?" Marc sneered.

"Call the police." Anthony offered a pleasant smile. "Have you charged with trespassing. This is private property."

Marc's gaze shifted from Rachel to Tony, then back to her. "Maybe you can screw him, too. You seem to gravitate toward the low-life type."

This was one of those times that Rachel wished she was more like Becca, the comeback queen. As it was, Rachel knew she'd probably think of the perfect pithy retort tonight just before she drifted off to sleep.

She told herself to simply be grateful Marc was walking away.

"Thank you, Anthony. For being here. I'm sure you have other things to do."

"As chief of building security, the safety of the residents and their guests is my number one concern." His smile was professional, but Rachel swore she saw sympathy in his blue eyes. "Mr. Carlyle would not want anyone accosting you in the parking lot. He cares for you."

Startled, Rachel glanced at Anthony, then only nodded. While he might be correct that *Mr. Carlyle* wouldn't like someone accosting her, the concierge was wrong about one thing.

While Dixon might have cared what happened to her once, that was no longer the case.

CHAPTER TWENTY-TWO

By Monday, the news from Bakersfield had become *the* topic of conversation in Hazel Green. Hank Beaumont, though a friend of Nell and Leo's family, was first and foremost a newsman. When he'd received word, and Dixon would bet money that the *tip* had come from Marc, he couldn't ignore it.

News was, after all, news.

To Hank's credit, he reached out to Dixon for an interview, which Dixon declined. His request for a statement to run with the newspaper article also received a "no comment."

Dixon wanted nothing more than to remain in his apartment, but forced himself to be visible. Nothing made a man look more guilty than refusing to show his face.

He'd spoken with Nell yesterday about the changes that had occurred since she and Leo had left for Bali. While he hadn't wanted to put a damper on her honeymoon afterglow—and seriously doubted anything short of death would do that—he did want her prepared.

Which was why they'd agreed to strategize tomorrow night immediately after Nell gave her speech as Hazel Green to the annual meeting of the Green Machine organization.

Dixon had spent the past seventy-two hours going over the document he and Nell had put together detailing Gloria's criminal activities. While he refined it, he found himself becoming lost in the memories.

As troubling as they were, they beat thinking about the present and Rachel. He hadn't heard from her, not that he really expected to…but still, in a small corner of his heart, he'd hoped.

Dixon met Tish in the lobby of his building, but instead of taking her upstairs, he asked if they could simply take a walk.

"Her rhetoric is heating up," Tish told him as they took one of the footpaths through the Green. "Your moth—" She stopped and tried again. "Ah, Gloria's attorney insists none of it is coming from her, but we both know she's doing a stellar job of convicting you in the court of public opinion."

"What about the prosecutors?" Dixon finally asked the question that had been troubling him since all this came out. "Are they concerned about making this deal with me?"

"No." Tish slanted a glance in his direction. "They already had enough evidence against Gloria to bring her to trial. Plus, she has the motive. But the evidence—while there—isn't as strong as they'd like. Which is why they were willing to make the deal with you in the first place."

Dixon nodded.

"Have you made a decision about sharing additional information on other crimes?"

"I'm going to do it."

Surprise flickered across Tish's face.

Dixon smiled. "You thought I'd change my mind."

"It's a risk."

"Not much of one. I don't believe there is a way even the best attorneys can link me to any of these crimes. I may have been traveling with her back then, but I wasn't directly involved in any of these activities."

Tish remained silent. She didn't need to say anything for him to know exactly what she was thinking.

"While I realize there are plenty of innocent people in prison," he said, "I have to take the chance that this once, good will triumph over evil." He met Tish's gaze. "I don't want Gloria coming around in three or four years to make trouble for Nell. I want her locked up for a long time. If that puts my own future in jeopardy, then I'll take that chance."

They continued to walk, enjoying the afternoon sunshine and the warmth of a late summer day. Some of the people they passed were known to him, but you'd never have thought that by their response. Either they looked away or gave him a scowl.

"Have you and Rachel…?"

"That relationship is over and done. I'd prefer you don't bring up her name again."

"I feel to blame for the trouble between the two of you." Tish expelled a breath. "I was the one who told you we needed to keep information about the immunity quiet."

"That's because that was what the prosecution recommended."

"Yes, but—"

"What went wrong between me and Rachel isn't your fault. It's on her and it's on me. Bottom line, I didn't trust her enough to tell her. Once she found out, she didn't trust that I had good reasons for keeping the information from her." His lips curved up in a humorless smile. "I'd say a busted relationship is just what we both deserve."

That evening, Dixon ignored the sidelong glances and took a seat at the end of an empty row toward the back of the Pavilion in Gingerbread Village.

The open-sided building in the heart of the brightly colored and unique homes that made up Gingerbread Village, had been the site of several early-twentieth-century Chautauqua performances. Which made it the perfect venue for tonight's annual meeting.

By skipping the cocktail hour, Dixon timed it so he arrived as everyone was taking their seats. Nell was in full Hazel mode tonight, wearing an auburn wig, makeup that changed the shape of her pretty face and a fashionable early-twentieth-century gown that brought to mind a single word: *torture*.

Even so, he saw the happiness in her eyes. In that moment, Dixon knew he'd made the right decision. He would protect his sister's new life at all costs, even if that meant sacrificing his own freedom.

Nell caught his eye over the rows of seats and offered him a bright smile. While Tish was her friend, she was Dixon's attorney, and he'd forbidden her to discuss with Nell her concerns about the risk he was taking.

Near the front of the room, he spotted Rachel seated beside Liz and Jocelyn Valentine, the milliner. With Rachel's gaze facing forward, Dixon doubted she even knew he was here.

For the best, he told himself.

The row he sat in stayed empty until he felt a tap on his shoulder. "May I sit with you?"

He looked up, and there was Lilian.

Dixon glanced down the empty row. "I believe there's room for one more."

She gave a delighted little laugh, sat down and patted his knee. "I'm pleased to see you haven't lost your sense of humor."

There wasn't a chance to say more, because Leo took the stage.

"It's my pleasure to introduce our speaker tonight, as well as thank you all for coming to the annual meeting." Leo's gaze scanned the crowd, more as a way to connect than to search for anyone. "I think of the Green Machine as an organization that keeps our community vibrant and strong. Within this powerful machine, there are many committees and outreach programs. I know if I tried to thank you all, I'd miss some. So I'll just say thank you for all you've done, continue to do and will do in the upcoming year. Now, it's my pleasure to introduce Hazel Green."

Applause broke out as Nell rose and waved to the crowd with one gloved hand before moving to the microphone on the dais.

"I was telling Mayor Pomeroy how excited I am to speak to my friends in the Green Machine on a day that is so special to me."

Dixon considered the date and realized he had no clue about its significance. Not surprising, because his sister was the one who was the town expert on everything Hazel Green. But from the reaction of the crowd, whatever auspicious occasion Nell, er, Hazel, referred to wasn't well known.

"As many of you know, the 1920s was an especially prosperous time. Most people didn't fear debt because the market was so stable. My husband, Richard, an astute financier, believed the period of prosperity wouldn't last. He took our money out of the markets that summer and encouraged everyone he knew, including Mayor Pomeroy's relative—Jasper Pomeroy—to do the same.

"When the Dow peaked in September of 1929, many began to doubt Richard's business acumen. I never doubted him. When things looked good, I was there for him. And when others turned from him or tried to convince me that my husband was a fool, we stood together."

Hazel smiled. "You're probably wondering what this story has to do with celebrating another successful year of the Green Machine. It's because that incident from the past reminded me of the importance of standing together. Whether it's standing up for a friend or family member or standing with fellow business leaders, the thing we must keep in mind is that we're not only in this together, we're stronger together."

Like Leo had, Hazel gazed out over the crowd. "I wish you all another year of continued success and prosperity."

She finished to thunderous applause, then stepped from the dais. Dixon could see her headed his way before she was waylaid by several business types.

Dixon wanted to speak with his sister, but now was not the time or place. He turned to Lilian. "A pleasure, as always."

Her fingers on his sleeve detained him for a second.

"I've decided to invest some of the money I received after the sale of that commercial property last year." Lilian met his gaze. "Let's set up a time to get it into those funds we've been discussing."

Dixon couldn't hide his surprise. She'd kept from investing all these months, and now she had chosen to trust him with her money. "Are you saying you want me to handle your investments?"

She smiled. "I don't know a better man."

Rachel had just finished congratulating Nell on her speech as Hazel when Lilian stepped up to join them.

"A timely topic," Lilian told Nell. "In today's times, so many are quick to judge."

"Sometimes, judging is simply being smart," Rachel heard herself say. "There's no benefit to putting your head in the sand, or seeing only what you want to see."

Lilian turned then and surprised Rachel by wrapping her arms around her, squeezing tight. The older woman wore the sweet, floral scent that Rachel's mother had favored. For a second, Rachel closed her eyes and let herself draw comfort from the embrace.

Opening her eyes, Rachel blinked rapidly. Listening to Nell's speech, she'd wondered if it was directed at her. Then she'd told herself she was being ridiculous. Nell had just returned from her honeymoon. The speech had to have been prepared before she'd even gotten married.

Still, Rachel had to admit the thought of Hazel standing by her husband touched her. Of course, standing by a man's business decision was not the same as standing by a man accused of a crime he'd likely committed.

Nell's gaze settled on Rachel. "When Dixon and I were children, we dreamed of a different kind of life."

Rachel wasn't sure what surprised her more—that Nell was breaking character from her act as Hazel Green, something that *never* happened, or that she'd brought up Dixon in such a public area.

"We made mistakes growing up. One of mine was leaving him alone with that monster when he was only thirteen." Nell glanced at Leo, who now stood beside her.

Rachel saw he wanted to say something. As if he sensed Nell needed to get the words out, he only took Nell's gloved hand and gave it a supportive squeeze.

"The one thing both Dixon and I needed was to know someone had our back. That this person saw who we were at the core and would stand by us when times were tough." Nell slanted a glance at Leo. "At the darkest point in my life, Leo risked everything to support me. He did that despite the fact that I'd let him down by not confiding in him. But he knew the woman I was deep down, and he believed in that woman."

Nell made it sound so easy.

Rachel's temper spiked. Did no one understand how it felt to be betrayed in such quick succession by two men she'd trusted? "I trusted Marc. Look where that got me."

The warmth in Nell's eyes cooled. "We're not talking about Marc."

Rachel turned away. She couldn't listen to any more advice, *wouldn't* listen. For every Nell and Lilian encouraging her to forgive and forget, there were a dozen others in Hazel Green telling her she was lucky she'd found out about Dixon's sordid past before it was too late.

The walk home was a cold one, but Rachel welcomed the brisk wind that carried sharp droplets of rain. She wrapped her arms around herself and kept her gaze focused straight ahead.

Her house came into view far too quickly. She didn't need warmth and comfort. She needed…oh heck, she didn't know what she needed.

After stripping out of her damp clothes, she rummaged through a drawer and pulled out her favorite flannel pajamas, covered in hot-pink penguins. Even with a low of forty-five forecast for tonight, they would probably be too warm. But the soft fabric against her skin soothed and comforted.

As did the fire she started in the hearth. If a couple of tears slid down her cheeks as she opened the bottle of wine she'd bought weeks ago for her and Dixon to share, she felt entitled.

Though television held no appeal, sitting in silence had her mind going in a hundred different directions, all of them centered around Dixon.

The tears continued as she topped off her wineglass for the third time and continued to stroke Violet's soft fur.

When the jarring ring of the phone split the silence, she was tempted to ignore it. Until she remembered that the orientation for new volunteers was coming up, and one of them might be trying to reach her.

The unfamiliar number with an out-of-state area code should have had her hitting the decline button. Instead, feeling reckless, she answered. "Hello. Who is this?"

"Rachel."

She set down her wineglass with fingers that trembled. "Ben?"

The last time she'd heard from her brother had been nearly a year ago. He'd been in Wyoming then, but she'd sensed he'd be moving on. "Where are you?"

"I'm in the ER at NorthShore hospital in Evanston." Her brother spoke quickly as if he feared she'd hang up. "I spilled my bike and got banged up. But I'm okay. Or I'll be okay. Can you come get me?"

Rachel wanted to ask if he was clean and sober, but swallowed the words. "I'll be there."

"Thanks." There was a long pause and she heard him clear his throat before he repeated, "Thanks."

The pajamas came off, replaced by yoga pants and a long-sleeved tee. Rachel's keys were in her hand when she noticed her empty wineglass. How many glasses had she downed this evening? Two? Three?

She didn't feel the slightest bit buzzed, but hadn't that been what the driver whose car had fatally struck her parents car said? He'd thought he was okay to drive.

Even as Rachel opened the front door, keys in hand, she knew she couldn't get into her car. She would have to find someone to take her to Evanston. If that failed, she'd call an Uber.

Her phone was in her hand when she noticed a tall figure striding up her sidewalk.

Dixon.

His gaze slid to the keys in her hand. "Going somewhere?"

"I was, but I've had too much to drink." Rachel hesitated for only a second. He was here and she was desperate. "My brother has been in an accident. Can you take me to NorthShore hospital in Evanston to pick him up?"

CHAPTER TWENTY-THREE

Sensing she was in a hurry, Dixon waited until they were in his car and headed toward Evanston before asking her any questions.

"What happened?"

"I don't really know." Her hands remained clenched into tight little balls in her lap. "Ben called and said he'd been in an accident with his motorcycle and that he was at the ER. He asked me to come get him."

Dixon nodded.

"Why were you at my house?"

Did he really want to get into all that now, while she was worried about her brother? The truth was, while he knew the speech Nell gave tonight had been composed weeks ago, it might have appeared to Rachel as a not-so-subtle rebuke of her inability to trust him.

The truth was, he wouldn't blame her. He'd made so many mistakes, not only before arriving in Hazel Green, but since he'd met her.

Their relationship was new and shiny, and she'd just come off of a bad breakup. Instead of coming clean with her when she'd confronted him, he'd attacked. He owed her better.

That's why he'd come to set the record straight. Dixon didn't have any hopes that his confession would patch things up, but he didn't want her going through the rest of her life thinking all men were scum.

"I should never have drunk all those glasses of wine." She heaved a heavy sigh.

The fact that she hadn't noticed he'd yet to answer her question told him she was smart not to be driving.

"You drank more than usual?" Dixon somehow managed to keep the surprise out of his voice. With her parents dying in an accident caused by a drunk driver, one drink had always been her max.

"I was feeling kind of low." She kept her gaze focused out the passenger-side window. Then she abruptly turned back to him. "I wouldn't have driven. I was thinking of who I could call when you walked up."

He nodded. There was so much he needed, wanted, to say, but with her brother injured, this hardly seemed the time.

"Why did you stop by?" she asked as if for the first time.

"I wanted to explain." Dixon blew out a breath. "I realized that I reacted badly when we spoke about this the other day. You deserve the whole truth."

"It won't change anything."

The quiver in her voice might have given another man hope, but Dixon was too much of a realist. "I know. But I think it will help with closure."

"Tell me now."

He understood. Getting this out during the ride would ensure that it was over between them, and nothing more would need to be said once he dropped off her and her brother at her home.

Getting it over quickly, like pulling off a Band-Aid, was what he wanted, what he'd expected to do, so Dixon wasn't sure why he hesitated. Probably because once he was done, it'd truly be over between them.

All the hopes and dreams he'd built around her would be dust.

"This is confidential," he told her. "Until after I testify."

"What are you talking about?"

"I was involved in the crime Gloria is currently facing charges on. It was the last job we did together." He cleared his throat. "My role involved hacking into her ex-boyfriend's work account and siphoning off money."

"You stole money."

He heard the condemnation loud and clear.

"I helped her steal the money. I didn't take any of it." It was a small distinction, but seemed important that she knew. "Gloria could have probably gotten away with the money, but she couldn't stop there. She tried to frame the guy for embezzlement. It was a sloppy frame, and it didn't take the police long to make her their number one suspect. I left shortly after that and never looked back."

"Now you'll face theft charges." Rachel said the words as if it was a done deal.

"I've been granted immunity to testify against Gloria. They've built a good case against her, but her attorneys are top-notch."

"The news articles didn't mention anything about immunity." Puzzlement laced Rachel's words.

"That was something my attorney and the team for the prosecution wanted to keep under wraps." Dixon tightened his fingers on the steering wheel. "I'll testify this week."

"If you hadn't gotten immunity, you'd be on trial."

"You're right. I'm guilty."

"Was this your only crime?"

"It's the only one I need to worry about. I hope anyway."

"So there are others?"

He wasn't sure how to answer. "I plan to give the prosecution a list of crimes I know Gloria committed, along with as many details as I recall. Once that happens, she'll try to drag me into the middle, even though I had no involvement in them."

"Why would she do that?"

"For sport. Because she can. Payback for testifying against her. Any and all three."

"If you're innocent, you won't have anything to worry about."

"Innocent people go to jail all the time."

"Then why do it? Why do it if you know it'll set her off?"

"She deserves to pay. And because in order for Nell to have the life she deserves, in order for me to have any kind of life, Gloria needs to be behind bars for more than a handful of years." He smiled grimly. "If I have anything to say about it, a long prison sentence is in her future."

Dixon helped Ben into Rachel's house before driving away. In addition to a number of fairly nasty scrapes and some bumps that were already turning to bruises, Ben had a swollen knee that made walking difficult.

Other than the beard in need of a good trim and hair that went past his collar, Ben hadn't changed much since Rachel had last seen him.

From the time he could walk and talk, he'd been the "athletic one." After their parents died, he'd become the "rebellious one." Losing them both so young, then having his future so unsettled until Rachel had been awarded custody, had taken its toll.

Their aunt, who hadn't a clue how to parent, had given him too much freedom. Ben's wild streak had blossomed like a dandelion gone to seed.

The day he'd turned eighteen, he was gone, leaving Rachel bereft and feeling like a failure.

"I won't stay long," he assured her.

"This is your home, too, Ben." Rachel took a seat beside him on the sofa where Dixon had deposited him.

"Is that guy your boyfriend?"

"He's a friend." Based on how things had been between them, even that was a stretch. But it was the simplest explanation.

"He's no-bullshit."

"I'm not sure I understand."

"The guy's got sharp eyes. He's nobody's fool."

Rachel thought about what he'd said about Gloria and what she would do once he testified against her. Dixon knew the score. He was going into this with his eyes wide open.

She hadn't thought, or had a chance, to ask if he expected Gloria to sway public opinion against him in those future cases. It seemed likely, as his mother going on the attack in this case hadn't surprised him.

What had surprised him, Rachel knew, was *her* finding out.

Before he could tell me.

Dixon would have told her. Now that the anger had cooled, Rachel saw more clearly. Given time, he'd have shared it all. Thanks to Marc's snooping, he hadn't had time.

All would have been okay if she hadn't reacted and labeled him a liar without giving him a chance to explain.

"I was scared," she murmured.

"I told you it was no big thing." Ben's chin lifted in that familiar defiant tilt. "You didn't have to come. I have buddies I could have called. Guys who wouldn't hassle me. Or make me feel guilty."

Rachel clenched her jaw shut to keep from snapping back. In the past, that was just what she'd have done, and the battle would have been on. "I'm happy you called. I've missed you."

The storm in his eyes calmed. "Well, you were the first one who came to mind."

If that was his way of saying he'd missed her, too, she'd take it. "I'd love for you to stay in Hazel Green."

How many times had she said that to Ben over the years? Dozens? Hundreds? All she knew was, each time he'd snapped back with some derisive remark about his hometown.

She paused, waiting, but the negative response didn't come.

"Maybe," he said finally. "Is it okay if I sack out here on the sofa?"

She smiled. "I seem to remember it being a favorite spot of yours."

His lips curved. "You're different. Not so uptight."

The retort that would turn this conversation into a sibling bickering match sprang to her lips. When she swallowed it, she realized Ben was spot-on. She had changed.

Not in time to make a difference with Dixon.

But maybe in time to make a difference in her relationship with her brother.

Dixon stared at the phone in his hand. This indecision wasn't like him. He'd always considered his options, decided on a course, then acted.

An exception was when he'd gone along with Tish's directive not to tell Rachel about his plans to testify.

Look how well that turned out, Dixon thought with a derisive snort.

He would simply call and ask Rachel how her brother was doing, see if there was anything he could do to help. She could hang up on him. But somehow, he didn't think she would.

"Hello."

Perspiration dampened his palms. "Rachel. It's me."

"I'm glad you called."

"You are?"

"It was so chaotic trying to get Ben into the house, I never thanked you for driving me to the hospital and…everything."

"I was happy to help."

"Still, thank you."

"Rachel—"

"Dixon—"

He laughed as they spoke at once. "You go first."

"I've been thinking. I reacted…badly when I learned about the court case. I never even listened to your side." She sighed. "If you ask my brother, he'd tell you that I've never been a good listener."

"I blindsided you. I should have told you what was going on from the very beginning." He cleared his throat. "I screwed it up between us."

"Nothing that we can't get past, if we both want to get past it."

"Do you?" he asked. "Want to get past it?"

There was a long pause. "I do. I've missed you so much."

"Not half as much as I've missed you. I'm sorry, Rachel."

"Me, too. I'm really, really sorry."

"May I come over?"

"I'd be disappointed if you didn't." She thought of her brother, hopefully asleep by now on the sofa. "Ben is sleeping in the living room. I'll be waiting for you out front."

Rachel stood on the porch, waiting, her heart hammering. Though he'd taken responsibility for their breakup, she knew it was on her. Which meant it was up to her to literally take the first step back to him.

His car pulled into the driveway, and she was there before he could even open the door. The second he stepped out, she was in his arms.

"You're the only one for me," she told him, planting kisses all over his face. "The only one."

He laughed and pulled her tight. "I feel the same."

Then he kissed her, long and slow and sweet. When they

came up for air, she rested her head against his shirtfront. "I'm never going to let you go."

He stiffened for a second.

She lifted her head. "What's the matter?"

"Gloria and her attorneys will bring trouble of biblical proportions raining down on my head when the other charges are filed against her and she realizes I'm the one feeding the information to the police."

"Let her try." Rachel linked her fingers with his. "We'll be a united front."

He rested his forehead against hers. "There's every chance this could spill back on me."

"Whatever happens, I'll be there."

"Worst-case scenario, I could end up in prison."

"That's not going to happen, but if it does, I'll wait. As long as it takes. Because you're not just the one for me." She lifted a hand and cupped his cheek. "You're the only one for me."

EPILOGUE

Rachel held the wedding bouquet tightly in her hands. The past nine months had been a roller coaster. Finally, blessedly, just this week—and thanks to Dixon's testimony—Gloria had been sentenced on several additional charges.

She would be in prison for a good long time, leaving Dixon and Nell free to live their new lives.

Today, Rachel and Dixon would truly be a united front. She was ready, had been ready, but had agreed to wait until all the trial stuff was behind them.

Although she'd enjoyed Nell and Leo's large wedding and reception, she and Dixon had decided to go with something small and intimate.

This summer, they would throw a backyard barbecue and invite all their friends and family. Today, it would be just her and Dixon and a dozen or so of those closest to them.

His sister, Nell, and Rachel's brother Ben would serve as their only attendants. The two waited, along with Dixon, under the pretty arbor in Abby's backyard. They stood with a friend of Rachel's who had recently completed the certification to perform marriages.

Rachel took a shaky breath.

When Dixon spotted her in her simple, gauzy white dress with the ring of flowers in her hair, the bright flash of his smile steadied her.

Somehow, she made it across the lawn without tripping. Dixon held out his hand to her when she reached him. The slight tremble in his fingers was somehow reassuring.

The ceremony went by in a blur. Until the vows.

She and Dixon faced the other as instructed, hands clasped.

They'd decided to write their own vows. This was their chance to say whatever they wanted to say to their future spouse.

"Rachel, my love." Dixon's fingers tightened on hers. "The past year with you has transformed my life. By example, you've taught me that love can be patient and kind and giving. Every day, you show me that trust and honesty are essential for a relationship to grow and flourish. Thank you for being the wonderful woman you are. I promise to not only tell, but also show you every day how much I love you. I promise to put you and our relationship before all others. Most of all, I promise in front of the friends and family gathered here that I want you—and only you—to be my wife, my partner on life's journey. I love you, Rachel, and I always will."

By the time Dixon finished speaking, tears filled Rachel's eyes. She blinked rapidly and saw him clearly despite the haze of tears. "I love you, Dixon. Finding true love was the furthest thing from my mind when I ran into you at Palmer House. What I'd considered the worst day of my life actually ended up being the best, because for the first time I saw you, the caring man behind the handsome face.

"I know when women see you, the first thing they think is 'hot guy.' You are handsome, there's no argument there, but your looks are just a bonus. What drew me to you is your sweet and kind heart.

"You're a good man. My rock. I know you'll always be there

for me, through good times and bad. I also know that whatever rocky times we hit won't be half as bad, because we'll be walking through those, hand in hand.

"You know my faults and my weaknesses, but you love me without reservations. Your unconditional love and support make me strive to be a better person, to be worthy of that amazing love you offer.

"I promise to love you, to be there for you, to support you through the good times and the bad. I promise to love you, to honor you, to cherish you above all others for as long as I live.

"I cannot imagine my future without you at my side. I want you to be my husband from this day forward, on this wonderful life's journey."

By the time she finished speaking, she was out of breath, and her eyes weren't the only ones holding a sheen.

When it came time for the kiss—to seal the deal, as Dixon often joked at other weddings they'd attended—Rachel's heart overflowed with happiness.

"I love you," he whispered as his lips closed over hers.

"Only you," she murmured. "Forever."

I'm so glad you came along with Dixon and Rachel on their heartwarming journey to love of the lasting kind. I think we can agree that this couple is perfect for each other.

You'll see more of Dixon and Rachel, and the rest of the Pomeroy clan, in the next book in the series, NO ONE LIKE HER. This story brings together Wells Pomeroy and Dani's best friend from childhood, Erika. I have to admit that Wells had fascinated me from the time I first mentioned him in One Fine Day. His deep love for Dani and his daughter said so much about the man with the rather stuffy exterior.

NO ONE LIKE HER is an engaging story about two lost souls

find love in a most unexpected way. Get your copy today OR read on for a sneak peek:

SNEAK PEEK OF NO ONE LIKE HER

Chapter One

Tears filled Erika Eads's eyes as she stared at her laptop screen. She'd briefly considered not opening the attachment. After all, when you were thirty-eight and having irregular periods and hot flashes, good news was not sure to follow.

She'd hoped the reason was simply stress. She and Paul, her partner for over a year, had called it quits six months ago. Though if Erika was being honest, their relationship had been on the skids for nearly half that time.

Working closely at the same architectural firm had kept them together longer than necessary. Toward the end she realized Paul's first love, his only love, was his career.

Erika glanced at the letter on the screen again. The doctor, after reviewing her test results, had diagnosed her with primary ovarian failure and told her she was going through premature menopause.

It appeared now, not only a sperm donor but an egg donor would be needed to make her dream of a baby a reality.

The emotion welling inside her proved too much. Erika let the tears stinging the backs of her lids slip down her cheeks. She wasn't one to cry. Ask Paul. When they'd ended things, she hadn't shed a single tear.

This news, well, this flattened her. She swiped at her cheeks and finished off the glass of wine in one gulp. Her life was definitely not turning out as she'd planned.

She wished Dani were here. Dani, who'd been her bestie since grade school. She knew what Dani would do if she was in the room with her now. After wrapping her arms around her and giving her a big hug that would last a full minute, she would tell Erika it was time to get out of this hotel room.

Which, would be Dani's gentle way of telling her to quit feeling sorry for herself.

The thought of Dani's smiling face had tears falling even harder. God, how she missed her friend.

Erika gave into her grief. When she was all cried out, she steadied herself. The time on the bedside clock caught her eye.

Eight o'clock on a Thursday night. Past time to get out of this room before the four walls closed in and crushed her.

With too much pride to go anywhere without making herself presentable, Erika sat in front of the vanity mirror. It took some work to hide the evidence of her tears, but she had an experienced hand.

The bright lights over the mirror were harsh and critical. Still, when Erika studied herself, she gave a satisfied nod. Her dark hair hung like a thick, luxurious cloud around her angular, but pretty face. Her eyes, a deep emerald green, were her best feature. Well, that and her breasts.

Menopause? Puh-leeze. The image reflected back at her didn't look at all ready for hot flashes. She saw a young, attractive professional woman ready for a night on the town. The white summer dress with a gold belt emphasized her slim waist and the heels she slipped on accentuated her long legs.

There wouldn't be any flirting or dancing or revelry. Emotionally, Erika wasn't ready for that. But the Cubs were playing tonight. The game should be on one of the televisions in the bars on the main floor.

She'd get a beer. Beer and a ball game. As American as apple pie.

Paul had never liked baseball. Thankfully, she didn't need to be concerned about his likes anymore. Tonight was about what she wanted and needed.

What she wanted was a ball game, a bottle of beer and eventually, a comfortable bed.

+

Wells Pomeroy needed a break. From his position with WLM, the real estate development company he owned with his brothers, from the frustration over seeing a woman he loved like a mother blow her money on a renovation project doomed to fail, and from his own loneliness.

Not even thoughts of the funny text sent by his sweet daughter could bring him comfort this evening.

This weekend marked eight-years since his wife and sister had perished in a helicopter crash.

Even when he wasn't consciously paying attention to the date, inwardly he knew when that time drew near. Waves of sadness washed over him and it took everything he had to keep from going under.

That's why he was in Chicago this evening instead of at home in Hazel Green. When his daughter, Sophie, had been invited to spend the night with a friend, Wells's plans changed direction.

Instead of staying home and working, he caught a train into the city and rented a downtown hotel room. After a solitary dinner at Maggiano's, a restaurant his wife loved, he walked Michigan Avenue.

When the sight of all the happy couples strolling down the glittery sidewalks holding hands became too much to bear, Wells returned to the hotel.

The Cubs were playing at Wrigley tonight. He could have

gotten tickets--he had connections--but sitting in a stadium surrounded by rabid fans held little appeal.

Sitting alone in a bar watching a game on a screen should have seemed equally pathetic, but for some reason it didn't. Maybe it was because he'd once traveled frequently for business. Being alone in a hotel felt, well, normal.

He briefly considered which bar on the main floor of the hotel to choose. Likely both would have the game on. As he walked by one with a decided sports vibe and heard the roars from the patrons, he kept walking.

The other bar, the one with dark, cherrywood paneling and a hushed atmosphere got the nod.

After taking at a table near the doorway, Wells let his gaze slide around the room. The impressive bar, in a rich cherrywood curved, its polished wood gleaming in the soft lighting. Behind it, a mirror with beveled edges and rows of bottles drew the eye.

The television near the bar showed the game with closed captions. Three other screens scattered around the room displayed news stations, also with closed captions.

Nothing to disturb the hushed elegance, Wells thought with a smile. In this room, only quiet conversations and soft, piped-in music disturbed the silence. Most of the tables held either couples or single men. Only one table held women, obviously friends, if their animated gestures and occasional bursts of laughter were any indication.

Wells ordered a beer and the server quickly brought it, along with a basket of bar mix.

As Wells munched, he kept his eyes on the screen. Yes, he thought, coming here tonight had been the right move. Just getting out of the house, a home that held so many memories, helped.

Out of the corner of his eye Wells noticed a guy, who'd been sitting alone, sidle up to the brunette at the bar. She was seated at such an angle that he couldn't see her face in the mirror. But if that mass of hair falling like a dark cloud to her shoulders and those gold heels were any indication, she was a stunner.

Whatever the man said must not have impressed, or maybe she was waiting for someone, because the guy quickly returned to his table.

The next guy, mid-forties with a receding hairline and sporting a wedding ring, didn't fare any better.

Wells found it pathetic that the interaction between strangers captured his attention more than the game on the screen.

He forced his attention back to the ballgame.

"I said no."

Wells swiveled his gaze back to the bar just in time to see the brunette jerk her arm away from a short man with a Van Dyke beard and the beady eyes of a rat.

"Touch me again and I'm calling security."

Wells wasn't paying any attention to Mr. Van Dyke now. His gaze was firmly fixed on the woman.

He knew her, Wells realized. Though it had been years since he'd seen Erika Eads, he was certain it was her.

Her voice, one which commanded rather than asked and those now flashing green eyes were unforgettable.

Wells had never been attracted to her, still wasn't attracted to her, he assured himself. It wasn't her beauty that had him considering whether to approach her, but her red-rimmed eyes and the sadness in the green depths.

Another man might not have noticed, but Wells had become something of an expert at seeing the sadness others tried so hard to hide. Perhaps because he'd spent the past eight years hiding those same emotions from the world.

Let her be, he told himself, recalling the last time they'd spoken.

It had been at Dani's funeral. He'd been a wreak that day and had taken out of his grief on Erika.

Though he'd seen the quick flash of anger in her eyes, she

hadn't snapped back. When he'd later texted an apology, after unsuccessfully trying to reach her by phone, her response was gracious; something to the effect that it had been a difficult day for both of them.

There was no reason for him to approach her, no reason at all. *She's my friend, Wells. My best friend. She's sad.*

As he had so many times, Wells heard Dani's voice in his head. His wife had the softest heart of anyone he knew. Dani never held grudges or walked away from a friend in need.

The fact that Erika had been Dani's closest friend since childhood had Wells picking up his barely touched bottle of beer and sitting down beside her at the bar.

She whirled. "Listen, why can't you guys—"

Erika stopped as recognition dawned. "Wells. What are you doing here?"

He smiled, took a swig of beer. "I could ask you the same thing."

The years had been good to her. Erika was as pretty at thirty-eight as she'd been at eighteen. The only difference tonight was the sadness in her eyes.

Other than at Dani's funeral, Wells couldn't recall ever seeing Erika without a devilish spark in her eyes.

"I'm relocating to Chicago. I have the opportunity to join a firm here." She lifted her bottle but didn't take a drink. "I haven't yet found a find a place to live."

Lifting his bottle, he clanked it against hers. "Congrats on the new job."

"Thank you." She set her beer down without taking a drink.

Wells inclined his head. "You're not staying with Lilian while you look?"

Lilian De Burgh, Erika's aunt, lived in Hazel Green. With the town being the last stop on Chicago's Metra Rail line, the commute would be an easy one.

Though Lilian wasn't part of the Pomeroy family, she might

as well have been. Wells wasn't sure how he would have gotten through the months after Dani's death without Lilian's support.

"—with her."

Wells realized with a jolt that while his mind had been wandering, she'd answered his question. He supposed he could have asked for clarification, but it wasn't important enough for him to pursue the topic.

"What about you?" she asked. "Did you have a meeting in Chicago?"

Polite interest showed on her face, just like it probably did on his.

"I didn't." Wells expelled a breath then took a long pull on his beer. "This weekend is the anniversary of the accident."

There was no need to elaborate on that point. They both knew he referred to the crash in the Grand Canyon.

"I know." She absently trailed a finger down the bottle in front of her. "Every year around this time I start to feel sad. Sometimes I can't pinpoint why I feel so low…then I remember."

Wells nodded, the unexpected lump in his throat making speaking difficult. As the years went by, he rarely mentioned Dani and the anniversary of her death.

His parents didn't need the reminder. They'd lost a daughter and a daughter-in-law that day.

"I think of Kit, too." Erika's slight smile quickly vanished. "Your sister was a force of nature."

Erika shook her head and chuckled, seeming not to notice Wells's lack of response. "I still remember the time I told her I wanted to try out for the softball team. She must have thrown that ball to me a thousand times before I finally got the hang of it. When I made the team, she cheered the loudest."

Wells had forgotten that Erika and his older sister were friendly. Not surprising since they'd both grown up in Hazel Green.

Only two years older than him and Erika, his smart, funny and extremely athletic sister had perished that day, too.

"Nobody talks about Kit anymore," Wells said almost to himself.

Erika inclined her head. "Not even Mathis or Leo?"

Wells thought of the conversations with his brothers. "Occasionally one of them will do the 'remember when' and bring up something."

"You wonder if it's too painful for them. Or is that they think talking about her, or about Dani, is too painful for you?"

Startled, Wells blinked. It wasn't the response he expected. He thought she'd say something about as the years passed how easy it was to forget someone.

Which was silly, since he sure hadn't forgotten either of them. Though, lately, he worried Dani was becoming a distant memory to Sophie.

"How's Sophie doing?" Erika asked, as if reading his mind.

"She, ah, appreciates the letters you send on her birthday."

It wasn't simply a letter that arrived every year, but a card and a gift. Though he knew Erika longed to be a bigger part of Sophie's life, he knew she'd stayed away because of him and the things he'd said to her at the funeral.

Each time he looked at Erika he was reminded of the tears on Dani's face the night before they'd left for Tucson. His wife never did tell him what she and Erika fought about, but it still made him angry to know that Erika had been the cause of Dani's sadness.

"I'm glad." Erika shifted her gaze to the screen, effectively dismissing him.

Wells cleared his throat. "Are you okay?"

The genuine concern in his voice must have gotten through. She gave a little laugh and didn't meet his gaze. "Bad day times ten."

"I'm sorry about the funeral."

Her puzzled gaze shot to him.

"I should never have yelled at you at Dani's funeral. I was way out of line." That day was such a horrible blur. Wells only knew he'd turned his anger and grief on her.

Instead of lashing back, she'd absorbed the verbal punches that held more power than a fist.

"You already apologized for that." Her voice, soft with understanding soothed the still raw place in his heart.

"In a text." He shook his head, knowing he should have continued to try to reach out to her. "I really am sorry."

"You're forgiven." Her expression softened. She reached over and placed her hand on his in a gesture of comfort. It was the first time Wells could recall her touching him. "I understand the grief. I felt it, too. Like you, I have my own regrets."

He inclined his head.

"I should have checked more on you and Sophie."

"After how I acted," he offered a humorless chuckle, "I'm surprised you're even talking to me."

"Life is too short for so many regrets."

Wells studied her for a long moment. "That's one of the things Dani always loved about you. You were always so forgiving."

Erika laughed. "I don't know about that."

"Think about the Halloween party our senior year." Wells took another pull of beer. "Your committee spent all afternoon putting up decorations and the janitor took them down."

"The guy was new. He thought the party had been the previous night." Erika lifted her shoulders in a slight shrug as a smile played at the corners of her mouth. "We rallied and put them up again."

"Dani said it was you who made that happen."

"It was a group effort."

Wells didn't often look back on those high school years, but he found himself enjoying talking with Erika. They knew so many of the same people and that time in his life had been, for wont of a better word, idyllic.

Still, despite the joking and the laughter, Wells continued to sense a sadness in Erika. "Are you sure that you're okay?"

"I got some bad news today."

Wells pulled his brows together. "Anything I can help with?"

She waved a dismissive hand. "I don't really want to talk about it."

"Is that why you decided to drown your sorrows in the hotel bar?" He kept his tone light, but worried he'd gone too far when she frowned.

"Other than a glass of wine in my room, this is my first drink."

"Sorry." He lifted both hands, palms out. "Making a joke that fell flat."

After a moment, Erika chuckled. "You never were good with telling jokes. I remember how you used to give too many details and we were all, hey, just get to the punch line. We don't have all day."

Wells smiled and shrugged.

"Yeah, this will be better." A male, in his early twenties, motioned a large group of friends into the bar.

"That other place was packed," a dark-haired man who reminded Wells of his brother Mathis, told his friends. "This way we can sit and get some food while we watch the game."

"Hey," the one said to the bartender. "Can you turn on the sound?"

The bartender, a portly man in his forties, glanced at Wells and Erika.

"Fine with me," Erika told him.

Wells nodded. "Seriously, Erika, if there's anything—"

His sentence was cut short by a fielder flashing the leather. A series of loud cheers erupted from the group behind them.

Again, Wells heard Dani's voice in his head. *You're never going to be able to talk to her with all this noise. I'm surprised you can even hear me.*

He gently nudged Erika's beer with his own to get her attention. "How would you feel about moving someplace where it's easier to talk? The other bar is out, but I got upgraded to a suite. There's space to sit there and catch up. It's been too long."

He didn't have a clue whether she would agree or not, but hoped she'd say yes. For the first time since he'd arrived at the hotel, the tension gripping his shoulder eased.

Not sure what came over him, he reached over and took her hand. "Please say yes."

Put your feet up and be prepared to lose your heart to Wells, Erika and Sophie in this touching novel that is sure to tug at your heartstrings but leave you with a smile on your face. No One Like Her

ALSO BY CINDY KIRK

Good Hope Series

The Good Hope series is a must-read for those who love stories that uplift and bring a smile to your face.

Check out the entire Good Hope series here

Hazel Green Series

Readers say "Much like the author's series of Good Hope books, the reader learns about a town, its people, places and stories that enrich the overall experience. It's a journey worth taking."

Check out the entire Hazel Green series here

Holly Pointe Series

Readers say "If you are looking for a festive, romantic read this Christmas, these are the books for you."

Check out the entire Holly Pointe series here

Jackson Hole Series

Heartwarming and uplifting stories set in beautiful Jackson Hole, Wyoming.

Check out the entire Jackson Hole series here

Silver Creek Series

Engaging and heartfelt romances centered around two powerful families whose fortunes were forged in the Colorado silver mines.

Check out the entire Silver Creek series here

Made in the USA
Monee, IL
18 March 2023

30133533R00146